D0590224

House
of
Green Dragons

House
of
Green Dragons

ROSA HILL

St. Martin's Press
New York

Library of Congress Cataloging in Publication Data

Hill, Rosa.
    House of Green Dragons.

    I. Title.
PR6058.I449H6   1983   823'.914   83-2930
ISBN 0-312-39261-3

First U.S. Edition
10 9 8 7 6 5 4 3 2 1

Published in Great Britain by Methuen London Ltd.

To my dear friend Laura Jago,
in gratitude for many happy hours
spent in her company.

CHAPTER ONE

Cross was an isolated village among the flat lands of the fen. At one time its link with the world outside was the old coach road, ten miles to the west, but now there was a branch railway line only five miles off. Cross seemed as unchanged as ever. Life there still moved at the pace of the heavy gleaming farm horses and the revolving seasons. Spring had brought to the village its benison of renewed life and was slowly turning into summer.

'What'll you do now, Rebecca?'

Rebecca Redfearn looked over the table at Annie Bell's thin pointed little face, with its bright blue eyes alight with curiosity. Then she looked past Annie, through the open door. The brick path, which led through borders of gillyflowers to the gate, was glowing in the sun.

'I don't know,' she answered slowly. But the decision had already been made. It was in the bottom of her mind, curled up like some little animal in its winter sleep. It had been made four days ago and in time would emerge as a conscious thing, which would take her far from hearth and home.

'You can't stay here, can you?' asked Annie. There was sadness, as well as curiosity, in her voice. All her life she had lived near to Becky. The thought that the cottage would no longer be Redfearns' seemed to Annie like the end of the world; an event so unimaginable that it might be followed by who knew what – by the moon riding backwards in the sky or apples ripening in June. But she knew and Becky knew that Becky could not stay on in

Redfearns' cottage. Why, the rent was one and six a week, and Becky had no more money than Annie herself. Annie looked across the table and enjoyed what she saw, though she could not have put it into words, unless she had said, 'Ee, she's a bonny looking woman, is Becky Redfearn.' She had always loved looking at Becky's rich brown hair, in its thick coils, and had sighed many a time, peering into the little cracked bit of glass propped on her bedroom windowsill, to think that her own was so mousy and thin. And then, Becky had such a grand way with her, somehow.

Rebecca got up, and stretched her arms above her head.

'I'm fair arrered,' she said, and Annie took it as a signal that she was to go. All the pots were washed and sided away on to the dresser. All the leftover food had been cleared. Only their two cups and saucers, where Becky had given her a cup of tea for helping, were soiled, in all the spotless kitchen.

They'd put him away decently, after all, though the parish had had to pay for it. All the neighbours had given Becky something towards the funeral meats, so that she could have them back afterwards, as was proper. Mrs Bell, Annie's mother, had stood accepting a piece of cake from Rebecca as though she hadn't baked it with her own hands not three hours before. Yes, Jim Redfearn was gone, and his daughter, alone now in Redfearns' cottage, knew that this, the only home she had ever known, would be her home no longer.

There was something else, though, which had shaken her life as an earthquake could have shaken the brick walls and the tiled roof. Something Jim Redfearn had told her, just four days before. His death she was prepared for; it had been long expected. People with weak lungs should not become millers, they said; but how was anyone to know if they had weak lungs before they tried the trade? Rebecca had wondered that many a time, sitting by her father's bedside as he slowly drifted from life; and she wondered how much longer she could manage on the two shillings a week from the parish.

He had been grateful for the way she looked after him. That had seemed to her the most pathetic thing of all, that the big, strong, saintly man, who had loved and cared for her the whole of her life, should be grateful because at last she had been able to do something for him, so little!

The whole cottage seemed to her to be alive with his presence, even though she knew that they had buried him that day in the churchyard. His pipe lay on the mantel, and she could almost see him sitting in his chair by the fire and reaching for it. Almost see him digging in the garden and bringing the potatoes and greens for dinner, or easing off his boots at the end of the day.

She didn't need to go upstairs to feel his hand on hers as it had been four days ago, and hear his voice, saying, 'You've been a good girl to me, Becky, and there's something I must tell you before I go.' How could you! she thought in rebellion for a moment. Why not let me go on believing what I have always believed, content – no, proud, – to be Rebecca Redfearn! Proud to live in this cottage where Redfearns have lived dear knows how long, where Grandmother and Grandfather Redfearn minded me when you were out at work after Mother died, where together you and I, father and daughter, had been so happy in our quiet life. Even approaching death had united and not divided us!

She was divided now, and knew it, as she went upstairs into her own room and stood by the window looking out over the green of the fen. Nothing to do until bedtime, except think; and maybe become conscious of that decision which had been made without her knowing it, four days ago.

'You're not my daughter, Becky,' he had said. 'Your mother was expecting you, when I met her again. We'd known each other as children, she and I. When I was working away I met her in her trouble. We were married, and when we came back here no one knew you weren't mine.'

9

When he knocked the foundations from under her life, she had not spoken. This meant that she had no right to the name she bore, the home she had lived in, the grandparents she had loved so dearly and this man himself, her dear, dear father. He was no relation at all except that in his love he had been the best of fathers to her . . .

'You're not upset, Becky?' Calm-eyed, she had looked at him and said that she was not upset. 'I had to tell you.' He went on to tell her what he knew of the man who was, in nature, her father and of the circumstances of her conception. She could have screamed, held her hands over her ears and cried out, 'Don't tell me! I don't want to know! You are my father, you, no one but only you!' But his soft failing voice was remorseless and in her duty, bred in her through the years, and in her reverence for him, she had not been able to speak, to stop him. She had not shown any emotion. Her firm, full lips had been as steady, her fine fair skin as pale, her deep blue eyes as rich and true in their gaze, as though he had told her that the hares were dancing in the meadow and the brown hen was laying away again.

Except that on hearing those things she would have lit up in glad response to the glory of life, and as he told her of her parentage she showed no more emotion than a rock when the sea throws its weight against the black basalt.

He had lain anxiously looking at her, and then she had stroked his hand gently.

'I had to tell you,' he said again, and, bending her head, she had murmured, 'Yes.' He had been content then. If he had wondered at her imperviousness it had been a mere cloud shadow on a mind which could now approach tranquillity.

'You can't stay here, can you?' Annie had said, and she couldn't; not because of the one and six a week rent, impossible though it seemed to raise it and keep herself on any work she would be able to find in the village, but because as from four days ago she felt she had no right to.

She started, as though from a trance, and moved from

10

the window, round the bed, and went into his room. There, in the bed where he had lain, she had been born, Rebecca Redfearn. Going over to the window and standing on a box, she took down the curtains, thin with many summers' washing. Folding them, she laid them on the bed. This would be her first night ever alone in the house. Last night and the night before Annie had come round to sleep with her, for Mrs Bell had not liked to think of Becky alone with the dead man. She had not wanted Annie's company. Acquiescent as ever when people around her acted as they thought for her good, she had put up with Annie's bony elbows and incessant chatter, when all she longed for was to keep vigil beside him, herself, alone. To have quiet to realize her loss, to think of that earthquake he had inflicted on her and try somehow to come to terms with it.

The landlord had come up to her at the funeral and spoken gently and sympathetically.

'You'll be going, I expect, Becky, but don't you hurry, lass. Redfearns have been in that cottage long as I remember and it isn't for me to hurry them out of it. Bide your time, lass. We won't talk about rent for this week or next.' She had bowed her head and tried to smile in response to his concern, knowing that she was stiff, unyielding, a pillar of salt; knowing also that he had put it down to grief, and forgiven her.

The decision, made without her knowing it, had come to life in her mind and was working its way up into her consciousness. She was now for the first time aware of a resolve to leave.

While Jim Redfearn had been ill she had been determined to stay on, whatever happened. Here she had walked her first steps, learnt her first prayer, wound her first wool, learned to do the washing by helping Grandmother Redfearn at the dolly tub. As she took Jim Redfearn's clothes down from their nails, she relived in her thoughts all the happy years. As she folded and sorted, she dwelt on every little incident, hearing again voices and laughter.

11

Before the sun had gone down she had taken his clothes and personal possessions and given them to his friends. They had been pleased to have them, saying again and again, so that she could hardly bear it, 'A good man, your father, Becky; you'll never meet a better.' Quietly she had endured being thanked . . .

Taking from the mantelshelf the last things – his pipe and tin for tobacco – she suddenly could not bear to part with them. Putting them into the corner of the old trunk, she at last gave way, bowing her head in tears on the hard, unyielding lid. There was no more done that night.

Morning found her just as resolute, even if her eyes were burning and heavy. She walked the five miles to the bigger village of Mere Drove and went to the auctioneer's, where she had to wait patiently before being seen. Then she explained that she wanted to sell up and everything was arranged for a sale on the following Friday.

Normally she walked quickly, with the gait of the countrywoman who walks in order to get somewhere, unaccustomed to dawdling. There was now no hurry to go anywhere, or do anything. Returning, she paused often at stiles, gazed over the flat meadows, and breathed in scents of leaves and flowers. The ladysmocks were in bloom in swathes, looking like linen put out to bleach, in the way which had given them their name. Passing through the winding lanes, she touched the may blossom on the hedgerows with wondering fingers, revelling in its beauty and wishing Jim Redfearn was there to share it with her.

As she walked back into the village of Cross, her mind was numb, but her resolve was unbending. He who had gone had taught her to be true in all things, and she no longer had the right to live in Redfearns' cottage for by blood she was not one of them.

'Come in for your dinner, Becky,' Mrs Bell called out to her from Bell's front doorstep, between the two holly trees.

'Thanks, Mrs Bell, but I've a lot to do. There's enough left from yesterday for my dinner.'

12

'Do you want any help? I'll send Annie.'

'No! No – thanks; you need her, and you've spared her enough to me already. I can manage.' A weak, watery sort of smile, meant to show confidence, stopped Mrs Bell insisting.

'Well – there's enough ironing to keep her busy, and that's a fact,' said Mrs Bell, who had a family of eight and some of them earning. Annie was kept at home like a maid of all work, happier, if not less hard worked, than she would have been in some little household with enough pretensions to keep a maid but not enough means to feed one. 'What are you going to do, then, Becky?' It was Annie all over again, even to the sharp, inquisitive blue eyes.

'I'm selling up on Friday,' and that put a stop to it.

Mrs Bell, nodding, said, 'Oh, you poor thing,' and went back into her house, busy for the rest of the day in deciding which of the Redfearn possessions she coveted and what they were likely to fetch.

Cross was a big village and Rebecca had no doubt of selling everything well, if it were a fine day. She pulled the trunk out from the wall and began to pack it with her clothes, her few books, the daguerrotype which no one but herself would treasure. While in Mere Drove, she had spoken to the carrier and he was calling for her at two on Friday, when the sale would be over. There was not so much to do.

The hens she had sold to Tom Stamper, her next-door neighbour on the other side to the Bells. There had not been a horse in the outbuilding, nor yet a pig in the sty, for many a year, and the dog had been given away to the village mole-catcher towards the end of Jim Redfearn's illness. The cat had been sitting waiting patiently for Rebecca's return from Mere Drove, and, putting a saucer outside the door, she gave it the last milk in the house.

'Now then, Becky,' said a voice on the other side of the garden hedge, and she looked up to see Tom Stamper, with the reins of his heavy carthorse in his hand.

13

'Now then, Tom,' she answered. The horse wondered why they had stopped, stamped its great feathered feet, blew down its nose and finally reached with its lips to snuffle at the collar of Tom's working smock. Tom's eyes went from Becky to the cat.

'I'll get my missus to give it a bite to eat,' he said.

'It will be all right once the next people come, unless it goes wild first,' she answered, thinking of the many cats which went to live free in the hedgerows.

'T'missus'll feed it,' said Tom again, and nodding he went off on his way.

By Thursday, there was only one thing left to do. Rebecca had been putting it off, and hiding it from herself. But it must be done. For ten minutes she stood holding in her hand a thick book in a red cover tooled with gold, looking down at it and turning over the pages, before going out of the front door and down the path between the gillyflowers, pausing just at the gate and plucking a tiny spray from the lavender bush. She held it to her cheek, then laid it between the pages, with such meaning in the gesture that anyone watching would have guessed it to be a love token. Then she went, unhurried but as usual quickly, towards the church.

The door was open to let in the sweetness of the air. Reverently, she entered, to find the curate leaning against the end of a pew, looking up at a stained-glass window in contemplation.

Rebecca loved the church, though she had never analysed the feeling, the pleasure and the reassurance she got from the long, calm lines of the stone building. It lay like a great ship at anchor among the flat land and the simple brick-built cottages. Inside, the long expanse of clerestory windows was like an exaltation, filling the interior with a light which had a different quality from everyday light. The slight musty smell did not detract from the soft atmosphere, which seemed to expand her lungs as she stepped into it, giving her a slight headiness and buoyancy. She hesitated for a moment, then moved forward towards

14

the curate, almost floating through the wash of calm light.

Simon Lloyd was young, handsome, and intelligent. He was also poor, in his first post, and honourable. At the soft sound of Rebecca's entrance he did not turn; he remained in the same position, looking up at the stained-glass window. As she halted a yard away from him, he still looked upward; it was only after half a minute that, at last, he turned his head slowly and looked at her.

He saw that her eyes were swollen and red and that her face was pale. It was only a few days before that he had read the service over Jim Redfearn, but he did not, as might have been expected, at once speak words of sympathy and comfort. Instead, turning completely to face her, he said, 'What do you think of the window?'

No one would have known, to look at the two of them, that he was having to restrain himself from striding to her and taking her in his arms, or that her heart was beating wildly at the sight of him, so that she almost feared it would leap out of her body, and wondered if she were likely to faint.

'Lady Marwood's window?' were the words she spoke, when her longing was to cry, 'I am leaving, forever, does it mean nothing to you?'

'You must have heard about it. She has given it in memory of her second son, who was killed in the Crimea, and it was fixed this morning. The dedication ceremony will take place next month.'

'I had heard something of it.' She had been so preoccupied by Jim's illness that the events of the village had of late passed her by, but she remembered hearing of the window and, standing within the calm of the church, she looked up at it critically. 'The colours are very rich and deep,' she said at last. 'I like that. It seems right, in a church, somehow. But I don't understand the figures. Who are they?'

'The figure on the left is St Margaret, the figure on the right is St Catherine, and the figure in the middle is Our Lady enthroned in glory.'

'It seems a strange memorial to a young soldier.'

15

'You haven't heard the story about it, then. You know that the church is dedicated to St Margaret?'

'Yes.' Of course I know that, she thought.

'Once, in the Middle Ages, long ago, there was a window here showing the same figures as this one; it was destroyed by the Puritans, but it is described in an old book of travels through the county. Lady Marwood thought she would like to replace that ancient window as her memorial to her son.'

'I see, now.' She looked up again at the glowing blues and reds and purples and soaked in the richness of the colour. 'But why is St Margaret killing a dragon? It was St Michael who killed a dragon.'

'And St George.'

'I had forgotten St George; but there is a window of St Michael killing a dragon in Mere Drove church.'

'Not only men kill dragons. St Margaret killed one too.' The dragon writhed in decorative coils round the feet of the saint, seeming to welcome the spear which she was wielding to slay him.

'So not only men kill dragons . . .what a beautiful green he is. Are dragons always green?' She longed to stay there for ever, talking to him of dragons, with sales, and carriers' carts, and packed trunks, far away.

'Green seems to stand for some of the evils we have to fight.' His voice was dreamy as he tried to think of an example. 'We say "green with envy".' They stood in silence for a while, looking up together at the green dragon; then, as though it had been spoken of and agreed between them, they turned and side by side walked slowly to the open door.

'I really came to return your book,' she said. 'Thank you for lending it to me. I enjoyed it very much. I have enjoyed all the books you have lent me.'

'I heard,' he said, taking the book, 'I heard that you are selling up. What are you going to do? Where are you going?' There was a note almost of desperation in his voice. Then he added, 'It is not idle curiosity. As your

16

priest, your welfare is very dear to me, and if I can give you counsel, advice, help, it is my duty to do so, as much after you leave here as during these last years.' Simon deceived himself, thinking his concern only pastoral. He would not have spoken so to some farm labourer, with beer on his breath, who was leaving the village, or to a tramp in the ditch. His light grey eyes would not have given that clear glance, nor his blood pulsed so quickly through his wrists.

'I am going to see a relative, first of all.' It was the first time she had spoken of her decision, the first time it had been put into words.

'I understood you to say that you would have no relatives when your father was dead. Did you not tell me so?'

'When I said that I did not know of the existence of this person.' Even now she could not bring herself to think of the name Jim Redfearn had told her as being that of her father. Father seemed a name sacred to himself. Yet latterly she could not bring herself to refer even to Jim as father. At the last he had repudiated his fatherhood and left her in more than one way fatherless . . . 'Before he died he told me of this person,' she concluded, fighting a longing to throw herself into Simon's arms and, in tears and sobs, burst out with the truth.

Simon Lloyd had been brought up to have a proper sense of his position as the son of a gentleman. More recently he had come to terms with all the facets of a clergyman's life. He had his way to make in the world, a career in the church to pursue. One snare of the devil which must be avoided at all costs was an entanglement with one of his parishioners. It was a snare he was very much aware of since he had begun to visit Jim Redfearn during his sickness and to take books, first for Becky to read to the sick man, but later for her to read for her own pleasure. On their first meeting he had thought her lively, but that had been quenched by months of nursing. He could not have said when he had begun to think her

17

beautiful. Yet today, if he had dared to look sideways at her, he could only have thought her beautiful with the eyes of love, for she had grown thin and pale and with her red eyes, severe black dress and work-roughened hands, few would have thought her so.

Lady Marwood, the donor of the window, had three children still living. Her son and heir was married with a young family, and she had two unmarried daughters at home. They always welcomed the young clergyman when he called and marriage with either of them would further his career. Union with a village girl, with her country accent, would be the signal for him to remain a curate for ever.

That is why Simon Lloyd walked at the side of his love, and did not declare his feelings to her; why he would stand by and see her leave the village, go into unknown dangers, and not lift a finger to stop her.

And she, the simple girl who had never spent a night outside the village – for when, before Jim's illness, she had been in service for three years, it was only at a farm not a quarter of a mile from Redfearns' cottage – she would never have made a move to attach him. To her he was as socially remote as the squire, or the vicar himself. Yet he had met her on common ground, where no other man had been her equal; expanded her mind by contact with his; spoken to her of ideas, of books, of philosophy, of the beauty around them, as no one else had ever done. In return she had given him her entire devotion. A week ago she would have fought tooth and nail to stay in her home and near to him. Now she had no right to her home, and her new knowledge had another effect. If her own mother had been unchaste – had given in to strong passions – then that trait was within her, too. Sometimes she had wondered if she had the same depths of calm that characterized the other Redfearns. Wondered from where came the passions she could feel stirring within her. Now she knew that this dark force was real and not stemming from her imagination, and she dared not linger any longer in the

18

constant society of Simon Lloyd. Still numb from her loss, she had the strength to go; and go she must.

'What is the name of this relative?' asked Simon, and his voice was stern, as though she were a miscreant.

'Boville,' she said, bringing it out at last. 'Mr Giffard Boville.'

He frowned.

'That name is familiar, somehow. Where does he live?'

'In Yorkshire.'

'A long way off!' The words burst from him, and he felt unable to say anything else. They stood at the churchyard gate, while the hunting swifts flew low about them catching the insects of the evening.

'I have something to ask you,' he said abruptly.

Her heart thumped against her breastbone.

'I have just rented the cottage next door to Mrs Wainwright's, where you know I have been living since coming to Cross. She is going to come in each day to cook and clean for me; but I need furniture. I would like to buy some of the furniture from your home, if you will allow me, at the sale. It seemed insensitive to do so without mentioning it to you. Then, in the future, who knows what may happen – you may return to the village, or you may meet someone whom – whom you wish to marry – and if you then want, for old times' sake, to have the furniture back again, I will be willing to sell it to you.'

By then, he was thinking, I will no doubt be married to one of Lady Marwood's daughters, and the simple oaken furniture will be too unfashionable for her, and will remind me too much of you . . .

For a moment she had thought that he was going to ask her something else – something quite unthinkable of course – to marry him; as soon as she heard his request she knew how ridiculous she had been in that wild moment.

'Of course. You may buy it at the auction. I would rather you had it than other people, Mr Lloyd.'

'I thank you,' he said formally. 'God go with you on your future way, Becky. I will pray for you. In difficulty,

19

you may write to me.'

'Thank you, Mr Lloyd, I will always remember how good you have been to me. But I can earn my bread. I am young and strong. There should be no need to ask for help.'

'Don't forget the green dragons!' he replied playfully. 'You may meet green dragons on the way, Becky, and need help in slaying them. No one's life is without its green dragons.'

'Then I shall need the powers of St Margaret. But I shall kill them.' He wondered from where she got the strength that sounded in her voice.

'Goodbye,' he said. 'Fare thee well.'

'Goodbye.'

The words were over; but, in spite of themselves, their eyes met, and lingered, and their glance was like the clasp of arms, or the enfolding of wings. At the corner she turned again, and he raised his hand in farewell, and over the distance of ten yards their eyes still sought each other, and clung as the eyes of lovers cling . . .

CHAPTER TWO

While the sale was going on in the garden, Rebecca sat on her trunk on the red-brick floor of the living-room. It was the end of a life. As they had carried out the furniture, the stirring life of the cottage had come to an end, until it stood an empty shell, waiting. Waiting for new tenants, a new family, for life to begin again.

'No, leave that,' Rebecca had said sharply, as one of the auctioneer's men had reached up for the cheap coloured print on the wall of Queen Victoria and Prince Albert with their children. 'It can stay here.' A gift for the next people, she thought; bringing a blessing in an image of family life as it should be, smiling, serene, ordered. The way it always had been in Redfearns'. Death took its place too, for it was natural and in the order of things, an end and a new beginning was natural. Yet she could not bear to be outside and see the dresser and the table and the dolly tub and all the inanimate things which had furnished her life sold one by one to the highest bidder. Annie Bell was in and out like an intrusive bluebottle, telling her everything that was happening, and neighbours kept coming in to say goodbye and wish her well. Simon Lloyd was at the sale and she heard of everything he bought, but she did not see him, and was glad.

Glad to think that he had the dresser and the table and the bed where she had been born and the old oak cupboard from the corner, and glad not to see him because she knew she could not endure saying goodbye to him again, and with everyone about.

All was over at last, and carts and barrows were used to

21

shift the stuff, taking it round the village and distributing it to many different households. The weather had stayed fine and when the auctioneer came in and finished his reckoning he gave her, there and then, the best part of ten pounds, far more than she had expected. The vicar had walked over from Mere Drove and paid a good price for the grandfather clock, and Simon Lloyd's bidding had pushed up the prices. It seemed like a fortune. Many a farm hand was rearing a family on a shilling a day.

Mrs Bell had offered her dinner and she was glad to eat among the rowdy, friendly family, and stay with them until the carrier drew up at the door.

'This it?' He heaved the one trunk of her possessions on to his cart.

'Goodbye, Becky,' chorused the Bell family, crowding out of their door to stand between the holly trees. Annie held on to the tail of the cart with a wistful face. Becky kissed both her and kindly Mrs Bell.

'Come on, love,' cried old Mrs Fox from down the lane who always went into Mere Drove on Fridays to see her sister. Becky climbed up into the cart and sat beside her and they set off on their slow, rumbling way. If it had not been for the trunk, Becky could have walked rather quicker.

'You're never setting off tonight!' Mrs Fox was incredulous when she heard of Becky's plan of catching the next train from the station. 'You'll do no such thing. You'll just come with me to my sister's and stay the night, Becky Redfearn. Then you can set off first thing and have all day to get to wherever you're going. Not that I believe in those new fangled trains. They're against nature, going without horses, mark what I say. But you young folks is all alike. I've been to London once, you know. In this very cloak. It was new, then. It's not every day that you sit next to a cloak that's been to London.'

Rebecca gazed with proper respect at the cloak, and agreed to stay the night with Mrs Fox's sister. There would be a chance to think. The night was what she dreaded, in a strange bed far from her home; for, right to it or not, it was her home. Would she lie, unable to sleep, listening to the buzz of an insect in the window?

'Were you going to catch the mail train?' asked Mrs Fox's sister. 'That runs through the night.'

'Oh,' said Becky, feeling very ignorant. 'I thought trains would stop at night time and the people would get off and stay somewhere.'

'Lord bless you, no; are you thinking of catching the express from Burgh, then? You'll have to catch the local to Burgh. The express goes through every day at twelve.'

'Would that be a good one?'

'I wouldn't go on it. Not the way it rushes and shakes about at forty miles an hour.'

'It sounds a bit frightening.'

'It's against nature,' put in Mrs Fox.

'There's the excursions.' Her sister was glorying in giving all this information. 'But they get real crowded, do the excursions. There's one on Monday, though. Do stay till Monday, Beck; it will be a pleasure to an old woman to have company.' Rebecca discovered after questioning that the excursion train went to Skegness and nowhere else for its special cheap rate, and she rejected it.

'It's nice at Skeggy,' remonstrated Mrs Fox's sister. 'Why don't you go to Skeggy?'

'I'm going to Yorkshire,' said Becky gently.

'But you can go to Yorkshire any time. It might be a year before there's another excursion train to Skeggy. I went last year and it was grand.' Mrs Fox, annoyed at having her own glory of having been to London overshadowed by her much travelled sister, put in a remark.

'It's not a bit of use, our Sarah, telling the lass to go to Skegness when she wants to go to Yorkshire. You might as well talk to our cat.' The old ladies turned to each other and argued fiercely, after which, as Rebecca on being appealed to still refused to go to Skegness, Mrs Fox's sister was in a slight huff, or as huffy as a kindly old lady can be to a young woman who has just been left alone in the world. By the time the clock on the church tower across the street had struck half-past nine she had come round again and she made a hot posset for them all to drink before they went to bed. It was due to that hot posset that Rebecca had fallen to sleep at once, after creeping in between the sheets of the narrow bed in Mrs Fox's sister's spare room.

When she woke at dawn she thought for a second that she was back in service at the farm, for it was not her own familiar room about her. Recollection came with gathering consciousness and with it, all the pain of the previous days. Afterwards, she marvelled at the steady determination with which she had left the village and all that she had loved. This morning, Rebecca, who had never travelled on a train, got up to prepare herself for the journey. The luxury and convenience of having a jug full of water and a bowl for washing in the bedroom pleased her. Then she put on her chemise, her long open drawers, her flannel and her linen petticoats, then squeezed herself into her eighteen-inch corset, without once wondering what she was doing, intending to catch a train to a place she had never seen, where no one knew her.

Rebecca was unaware that she had great physical beauty. The strain of nursing and grief had only eclipsed it. She stood with her head bent and her rich brown hair tumbled down her back, looking down at the curve of her creamy breast over the top of the corset, as she passed her hands over her body, smoothing out creases and folds in her underclothing. She had been a long time coming to womanhood, but when it came it was all the better, like the slow ripening of a perfect flower.

It was still early when she slipped the faded black dress over her head.

The two old ladies fussed around and saw her off with the stout lads who lived next door, aged ten and twelve, who carried her trunk between them. It still needed a quarter of an hour to seven o'clock.

On arriving at the station she looked around her shyly, dared not speak to the station-master who was wearing a frock coat, but went up to a porter. He told her where tickets could be bought but, the office not being open, helped her to use the time by labelling her trunk and putting it in the van.

'You've not been on a train before then?' he asked in a friendly way.

'No.'

'You ought to see this place when it's really busy. Since this station opened we load twenty or twenty-five wagons with strawberries in the season. The station yard gets that full of horses and wagons you'd wonder how they crammed them in.' Becky looked interested in this information, so he went on to tell her the local gossip, then warned her to try to find a seat with her back to the engine of the train and if there was an accident, to throw herself on the floor immediately.

By this time tickets were being sold, so she went to stand among the people waiting to buy one.

'Kirkby, two singles, second class,' said a bent, elderly man in front of her. Rebecca looked up, pleased to find that someone was going to the same place as herself. She had liked the sound of the voice, and she watched him leave the ticket place with interest.

'Is this where you buy tickets for trains, young man?' asked a bulky woman.

'Yes, madam.'

'Is there a train going to Fossthorpe?'

'Yes, madam, the Parliamentary, leaving in ten minutes.'

'How much is a ticket to Fossthorpe?' she asked, after thinking for a minute.

'Do you want first, second or third class, madam?' The traveller became agitated at having to make this decision, but at last decided on second class. On being told that it would cost one shilling, she pulled up her skirt to get at her pocket, bringing out as well as a sixpence, a threepence,

25

two pennies, and four farthings, a pair of scissors, and a humbug. Rebecca was growing worried and impatient behind her. Suppose the train left, with her trunk on it, before she managed to get a ticket?

'You do remind me of my cousin's boy, her that married Isaac Simpson,' remarked the stout lady to the railway clerk, putting away her pocket. 'Are you any relation?'

'I don't think so, no, madam.'

'You're not a Simpson?'

'No, my name's Wilson.'

The stout lady moved away, and Rebecca went to the counter.

'Kirkby, second class, single,' she said, imitating the smart delivery of the elderly man. She had really meant to ask for a third class ticket, but in the fuss of the minute forgot that, and echoed the man whose brisk approach to the problems of ticket buying she had admired. The little bit of card once tucked safely inside her glove, she was walking towards the train, when the sudden ringing of the bell alarmed her, and she ran forward.

'It's all right, miss!' That was the porter. 'The bell is for five minutes before time to leave.' How glad she was that she had not attempted to go to Burgh for the express train. That would have been even more worrying.

Climbing into a second class carriage, she looked for a seat with its back to the engine, and away from the door. The lady bound for Fossthorpe was ahead of her, hesitating over a seat on which lay a book; then, making up her mind, she removed the book to another seat and sat down. Rebecca, seeing that the seat with its back to the engine which she thought looked the most attractive had a newpaper lying upon it, did as she had seen the old lady do, moved the newspaper to another place and sat down. It was quite an at home feeling, sitting opposite to the stout old lady of the shilling fare to Fossthorpe.

'Excuse me, but you have taken our seats.' Rebecca looked up and straight into the face of a cheerful, freckled young man, with reddish hair and a tweed suit, carrying

26

over his arm a plaid and in his hand a travelling bag. He was speaking not only to her, but also to the old lady bound for Fossthorpe.

'Your seats, sir?' exclaimed the older lady. 'Nothing of the kind. This is a public conveyance.'

'But madam, my father placed a book upon that seat and I a newspaper upon this one, not five minutes since.'

'Well, what of that?' returned the old lady.

'It is a custom of railway travellers, to secure seats by leaving something upon them.'

'Nonsense,' said the other firmly, but Rebecca had already risen, blushing and looking round to find another seat. The bent elderly gentleman who had asked for two singles to Kirkby was just behind the cheerful young man and as she moved away he took her seat with a sigh of gratitude.

'I am so sorry to disturb you,' the young man said to Rebecca, his look of indignation gone. He was mollified by her quick response, by her look of embarrassment. 'For myself, it would not matter in the least; but you see, my father is – not an invalid – but of nervous disposition. It takes only a very little to upset him, and he finds it of importance to have the right seat.'

The old lady was not as obliging as Rebecca; she refused to move, so the young man was forced to take his seat next to his father. As Rebecca felt that she could not politely go away when he was busy talking to her, and was still standing there, she at last sat down beside the old lady, opposite to him. The father was in a fuss until the train started. Rebecca was nervous herself, jumping when the guard's whistle shrieked, alarmed at the strange noises, the great clouds of steam and smoke, and the shudders and groans of the carriages as they clicked and clacked into movement.

The elderly gentleman had to be swathed in the plaid which the young man had been carrying. Then he put on a cap made to fit his head, with lappets which he could draw over his ears. Last, he put on a pair of green spectacles.

He had evidently taken a liking to Rebecca, if only for the contrast between her and the older woman, and started talking to her at once.

'You should have a travelling rug, young woman. Or at least a parcel to rest your feet upon, to keep them out of the draught from the door. There is always a draught under the door of a carriage. Edward, where is my parcel? I had better get my feet upon it. The draught will be coming, you know, even if it is not perceptible at the moment. What is your name, young woman?'

'Rebecca Redfearn, sir.' He nodded.

'And a very nicely spoken, well conducted young woman, too. You should have some eye-preservers, though, my dear. Sitting opposite to the engine, you will be in a draught of cold air from the window, and dust and ashes are always rushing in.'

'It is no trouble to me just now, sir,' said Rebecca, who, after her first terror, was finding the movement of the train exhilarating, although frightening, and whose cheeks were beginning to be tinged with colour for the first time in many weeks. The rush of the countryside past the window was deeply thrilling to her; the carrier's cart was nothing to it! Nothing at all! The strange smells of the railway, the sight of the smoke, now white, now black, when it was blown down into sight, stirred her.

'And an aircushion,' continued the elderly man. 'Edward, where is my aircushion? Blow it up, there's a dear boy. Caoutchouc, you know,' he remarked to Rebecca, 'and not at all in the way when not inflated. You might make yourself a travelling cap, but without projecting edges – in case of accident, you know.' He looked at Rebecca's neat bonnet, firmly tied under her chin by its black ribbons. 'And it would keep away tiresome things like toothache, earache and headache.'

'My bonnet is quite warm, sir, and I don't think I will be doing enough travelling to need other things.'

'You never know, my dear. My son and I have become great travellers. Second class. We do not waste money by travelling first. One is almost as comfortable by second, and usually the company is better than by third.' He glared at the passenger in the seat opposite to him, but she was not in the least upset by his remarks. Her eyes were firmly shut, and her chin on her chest.

'A pleasing young woman,' the elderly gentleman said to his son, when they were on the platform of one of the many small country stations, looking for refreshments. 'I always like these unassuming village girls; and she has a certain refinement about her. Yes; that is exactly what it is. If your mother is in need of any servants, Edward, I would certainly suggest to her that she tries this girl for a place.'

'Did you want a glass of wine, sir, or a cup of tea? I think we must order quickly,' was all that Edward said in reply. He looked at Rebecca, though, a good deal. After Fossthorpe, when the old lady got off, Rebecca expected him to take the seat opposite his father, as he had meant to originally, but he waved her to it, smiling, so she moved over with a pleasant little feeling of being looked after, as though some of his care of his father had rubbed off on to her.

The were nearing the end of their journey when the elderly gentleman, in whose mind an idea once planted did not cease to grow, said to Rebecca, 'I do not ask your plans, my dear; but you will allow me to say, that should you ever be in our part of the country and need employment, I would be pleased to tell you of anything we might offer. One never knows; you might need a position.'

She responded readily. 'Thank you, sir. I am going to your part of the country, to Kirkby, and I will not forget your kind offer.'

At her knowledge of his destination, he drew himself up, looking surprised, and a little displeased.

'I knew you were going to Kirkby,' she explained quickly, 'because I heard you ask for tickets. You were just in front of me at Mere Drove.'

'Yes, yes, of course.' Nothing was said for a minute. Then he searched in an inside pocket. 'Here is my card. Do not hesitate to ask. My wife is a kind mistress and our staff are always very happy.' She took the card and found that he was Sir Charles Gilbank, of Gilbank Hall, Kirkby. Reflecting that a man who could afford to travel first class and chose to economize by travelling second, might not be the most liberal of employers, Rebecca was still grateful for his kindness and for the implication of his good opinion. Her feeling showed in a gentle but glowing smile which so lit up her face, even over the worn black pelisse and under the black bonnet, that Sir Charles Gilbank liked her better than ever.

'But no doubt, my dear,' he went on, 'you have already made your arrangements. You will forgive the privilege of the old, in inquiring after the welfare of the young. No doubt you are travelling to a post, or to stay with some of your family.'

Rebecca hesitated. His interest was kindly, and her heart was sore. At his words she began to realize how blindly she had come.

'I'm not quite sure, sir. I'm hoping to find a relative I have never met, who does not know me or that I am coming. I don't suppose he will ask me to stay. I daresay I will find a room at an inn until I know what I am doing next.'

'Someone in Kirkby?'

'Yes, sir.'

'I wonder if I know this relative of yours. Kirkby is not a large place.'

Rebecca, who had been too stunned by the other aspects of her true parentage to think about what sort of man her real father might be, now began to wonder. He must, she supposed, be some sort of tradesman, as she knew he a provided for her mother in the way of money. Perhaps he had been a farmer, visiting another county to buy or sell stock. A baker, a butcher, a candlestick maker. As she had not said what relation she was, she thought there would be no harm in mentioning his name.

'His name is Boville, sir, but I have never met him.'

'What!' Both Sir Charles and his son seemed very surprised by the name she had uttered. Sir Charles had started up, the parcel had gone flying from under his feet. His son's eyes were fixed on her.

'Boville!' This from the son, Edward.

'Edward, it may not be the same. No doubt there are other families in the country by the name of Boville.'

'Not in Kirkby, father.'

'To be sure . . . my dear Miss – Redfearn – am I remembering your name correctly? Are you sure you are related to the Boville family?'

'That is the name I was given, sir, and told I was related.' Rebecca was taken aback by their reaction. Was her father a criminal? A drunkard? Was it a shameful thing to be related to him?

'A distant branch, I have no doubt, Edward; a junior branch, much gone down in the world; hardly a welcome addition, eh, Edward; related to Giffard Boville, heh!' Rebecca imagined the worst. 'You will forget what I said, Miss Redfearn, about a post,' went on the old man. 'Of course it would not be suitable, oh, not at all. We will consider it never said. You can return me my card.' He extended his hand. Edward, looking self-conscious, interfered.

'Leave your card with Miss Redfearn, father. She will surely be welcome if she cares to call, and in any emergency we would be glad to go to her assistance.' What emergency? wondered Rebecca. Is Giffard Boville like a wild bear, that no one may approach him without danger? In her imagination she saw the village drunkard at Cross, reeling along the road in his cups, with everyone keeping out of his way.

After this exchange silence fell on their corner of the carriage, and the three people who had spent the journey in easy chat became uncomfortable in each other's presence. Rebecca felt it lucky that they were so near the end of the journey. Her natural dignity and poise made her able to talk without nervousness to anyone, and she had been grateful for Sir Charles's kindly interest. It was all the more of a shock to be treated to such a change of manner, for no reason that she knew of. Edward, after his first look of amazement, had returned to his former friendly attitude, but he had never taken the lead in the conversation as his father had done and it was his father's change which made them all uneasy. At Kirkby, Edward jumped out first. Sir Charles waited until the train had quite stopped, then nodded to Rebecca rather curtly, and eased himself out of the door of the carriage. Rebecca followed him and as Sir Charles hurried off, his son helped Rebecca down and found her a porter, then smiled, raised his hat, and left her. Somehow, a good deal of the unpleasantness had evaporated. The little courtesies made Rebecca feel, for the moment, like a queen. She watched the Gilbanks go to a carriage waiting by the station entrance and drive away with a certain desolation. After their society for several hours, they seemed more like friends than anyone else in sight. But the porter was waiting; she went with him to the van and saw her trunk lifted out again.

'Is there anywhere I can leave it?' she asked.

'Here, on the station, if thee likes. We'll give thee a ticket for it.'

'I'll leave it, then,' and Rebecca smiled at him shyly. 'Can you tell me . . .' after the reaction of Sir Charles on the train, she hesitated a little. 'Can you tell me where I can find Mr Giffard Boville?'

'Got a job there, have you?' The porter did not seem shocked or surprised at all. 'You've got about a quarter of a mile to walk. Go out of the station, turn left through the town, past the parish church, left again at the Red Bull, and keep straight on till you're in the country. It's a big house on the left of the road.'

Rebecca had already noticed a difference between the railway station and the one at Mere Drove. Both had neat little buildings with patterned and pierced bargeboards finishing off the junction of wall and roof as a lace doily finishes off a cake. Both had the gleaming ribbons of train lines, the proud elaborate engines to pull the carriages, the neatly painted vans and coaches, the clouds of white and grey smoke eddying and billowing as if alive, wreathing the air. There, the likeness ended. Mere Drove had been workaday, compared to Kirkby. Here were flowerbeds, bright as paint, and an air of sparkle and expectation. The crisp air blowing from the moorlands whisked away dust and grime into the valley.

Walking out of the station, Rebecca realized that her experience did not encompass anything like Kirkby. She drew back and to one side, into the shelter of the overhanging roof, where she was unobtrusive. In a rush she felt homesick, an alien in this strange place. The excitement of the journey was over, and she felt sad and alone. Thoughts of her foster father and of Simon Lloyd, both equally lost to her, crowded into her mind. It was a few minutes before she felt equal to looking around her. Her first sight of Kirkby was through eyes brimming with tears.

She was used to flat land stretching out to the horizon, with a great bowl of sky coming down to meet the circular perimeter. Here, the skyline was shaped by the softly rounded outlines of the moorland. The little town clung to the side of a hill, so that every street led up or down. The market-place, sleepy today, was crazily tip-tilted, the rough carpet of cobbles leading up to the Three Tuns, down to the Butter Cross with its circle of pillars, up again to the station entrance where Rebecca stood, down to the huddle of houses and shops at the lower end where the road led down towards the weaving towns of the valley. All lit with a drizzle of sparkling sunlight and quick shadows, on golden stone and rust red pantiles, on grey cobbles and green doors and shutters and on the glimpses of gay gardens and brilliant flowers.

She walked as directed, and was soon passing the low grey parish church crouched against the hillside, with its churchyard at a height of six feet above the narrow road. Turning left at the Red Bull, she had left the town behind. The houses stopped abruptly, and the road seemed full of a bobbing sea; it was a mass of sheep, filling the road from the high stone wall on the left side to the thorn hedge on the right, pushing up against one another and bleating. Again the feeling of being an alien came over Rebecca, for she was used to the Lincoln Longwools, tall, white sheep, with the long fleece hanging clean. These all had black faces, were half the size of Lincolns, and their fleece – what there was of it, to eyes used to the wool which had made fortunes – was grey with dirt, matted looking. 'Like a fen buzzard,' thought Rebecca. She squeezed herself close to the wall to let them pass. The shepherd behind them, tall and gaunt, had his two dogs at his heels. He waved his hand and said, 'Goodday,' as he came level.

'Can you tell me,' Rebecca darted into the middle of the road to him, 'where Mr Giffard Boville lives?'

'Going to service there?' said the shepherd. It was more a statement than a question. 'Through that gate and you'll see it.' Her artless manner, and sweet smile as he answered her, charmed the shepherd, and he watched her as she went over to the gate in the stone wall and opened it.

Passing through the town, she had been troubled by doubts now that she was so near her objective. What sort of man would he be? What should she say? She had thrust down such thoughts and walked on firmly. But now she stood still, with her hand on the gate.

She could see the house, not fifty yards off. It was surrounded by huge trees, and partly hidden in front by a clutter of stables and barns which lay between it and the road. There were roofs edged by fretted balustrades, and in the middle of them a wide tower reared up against the sky, old and grey. She would not declare herself, she decided. Somehow she would see and speak with Giffard Boville and then leave again, not telling him of their relationship. He must be more important than she had expected; looking at the house, she thought he might be the agent for a large landowner. Leaving the gate and walking down the drive, she reached the great bole of an ancient beech near the outbuildings. The tree stretched its boughs over the

34

road and seemed both a barrier and a frame to the view. Across the valley there were bare, bleak moors, with fields on their lower slopes, and at their foot a winding ribbon of trees which hid the river.

Near at hand, the house seemed larger than ever. She was not to know that Mrs Giffard Boville referred to it contemptuously as 'that shooting box' . . .

The drive passed the buildings and veered to the right and to the front of the house, and the abruptness of the open space struck Rebecca like a shock wave, but she did not falter. It was so grey, so grim. There was such an arid spread of gravel to walk over to the front door, such deep crisp-cut steps of grit-grey stone, such a massive oaken door, set in a deep carved porch, such a knocker of black iron. It was with a feeling almost of doom, of fate, that Rebecca stretched out her hand to the thick iron ring held in the teeth of a grotesque beaked head. She grasped and lifted the ring, then let it fall. Standing back, she wondered if the door would be opened by her father.

'I've come to see Mr Giffard Boville,' she said to the man who opened the door, looking at him and wondering, but knowing at once that he was dressed like an upper servant. The butler in his turn saw a forlorn figure standing beneath the carved coats of arms of Boville connections. His voice was harsh.

'What are you doing, coming to the front door, my girl?' he asked, and his fingers waved towards the side of the house. 'Round the back. See the housekeeper.'

For a moment she quailed, and tears pricked at her eyes.

'I've come a long way to see Mr Giffard Boville,' she said doggedly. 'Not a housekeeper.'

'Do you think he sees anyone who comes asking for him?' the butler demanded. 'Servants, at the front door?'

'Can I see Mr Giffard Boville?' she asked again. 'My business is with him.'

There was a look of contempt on the butler's face, but he turned, leaving the door open, and went to a room on the left of the hall. Behind him, Rebecca stepped unbidden

35

into her father's home. The butler's voice could be heard, saying that there was a young person at the door asking to see Mr Giffard Boville. Strange emotions flooded Rebecca, in the dark lofty hall where she stood alone. Yet her thoughts were that she had never seen a floor as beautiful. Encaustic tiles had not reached the cottages of Cross. How easy they would be to keep clean! Her fingers ached at the memory of scrubbing the brick floor of Redfearns' cottage. At last the butler reappeared.

'This way,' he said. There was arrogance in his tone, and contempt in his glance, but he held open the library door. She walked in, and the door was closed behind her.

The room was large and newly built, lined with bookcases to the ceiling. Crossways down its length were two long mahogany tables, solid and magnificent, their tops littered with papers, maps and books. By the fireplace at the far end – and it seemed a very great distance – sat a man in an armchair, and at first he did not turn.

Rebecca stood near the windows and hesitated while a few minutes ticked by that seemed an eternity. At last, unable to bear it any longer, she spoke.

'Mr Giffard Boville?'

The man in the armchair turned quickly, as though he had forgotten that anyone had been shown into the room. Then he rose and moved towards her. Her first impressions were of his height and his air of distinction, and that he was wearing a velvet smoking jacket.

'I am Giffard Boville. Ferguson showed you in – ah, yes; but I fear I did not catch your name. Who are you?'

Whatever Rebecca had originally meant to say, and her later resolve to say nothing, all was forgotten.

She said, simply,

'I be your daughter.'

CHAPTER THREE

Rebecca had only recently known of her father; but her existence had always been known to him. He had supported her mother financially until her marriage to Jim Redfearn. Later he had several times sent money for Rebecca's upkeep, but Jim, healthy and in work, had seen that it was returned. There had been times when his life had seemed bitter and lonely to Giffard Boville, and then his thoughts had turned to Rebecca's mother. The child had been only a name, a vague idea, without substance, and gradually they had become more and more remote. For a long stretch of time they had both been forgotten.

In the last weeks of his illness Jim Redfearn had managed to find a scrap of paper and an envelope, unknown to Rebecca, and slowly written a couple of lines. He had said that he had not long to live and that Rebecca would then be alone in the world. He had addressed the envelope to Giffard Boville and asked Simon Lloyd to post it, and the letter had preceded Rebecca by some weeks into the mahogany silences of the library of Broxa House. After one startled reading Giffard had hurled it into the flames of the library fire. He had become wealthy; he had become a JP; he had become middle-aged and set in his ways.

'I be your daughter' . . . It was the tone and the accent in which the words were spoken which first penetrated his consciousness, long seconds before the sense of them.

The Redfearns had been noted in Cross for being a well-spoken family, using a stately, old-fashioned kind of English. A love of the words themselves and the way they sounded had been taught to Rebecca, and her voice with its rich depth of tone was an ideal instrument for care and exactness of speech. Her accent, one not heard in twenty years, roused in Giffard forgotten memories; and then the words . . .

'What do you mean?' he said at last, almost roughly, coming closer to her as she stood by the window. From a distance he had noticed the poverty of her dress. He had also noticed her height, slightly above the middle, and the erect, supple way she stood, not obsequious, not bold, but with grace and a certain pride. Now he saw what made him falter and reach out for the windowsill and, leaning there, look into her face. For he saw the Boville features, softened and transmuted in her femininity as they had been in his sister's. Conviction grew as he gazed.

'What do you mean?' he said again, but less harshly. 'Come here. Sit down.' He indicated a chair and sank back into his own. He was a vigorous, energetic man, but his legs were shaking. There was a silence. Rebecca felt as though she were drowning on a floodtide of emotion. He was looking at her as though expecting her to speak; she tried to gather her wits.

'I have been told that I be your daughter. My mother was Mary Doling before she was married. I was born twenty-two years ago in the village of Cross in Lincolnshire.' She could think of nothing else to say. In his dilemma his impulse was almost of cruelty.

'What have you come for? Money?'

'No!' Until the day she died, Rebecca never forgot – and could not completely forgive – that remark.

In her highbacked chair she drew herself up and straightened her spine. 'I have enough money.'

'Why have you come then?' So young, he thought. So sad. Heaven help her, she is beautiful. He had not yet denied her. Rebecca, overwhelmed by the situation, was losing her poise. She shuffled her feet on the thick red Turkey carpet . . .

'I came to know what I be.'

'What you are? You are a servant girl and the daughter

38

of one.' She gasped and her eyes beseeched him. Was it true? Was this man really her father?

'Even a sheepdog is judged by its parentage, inheriting its abilities and nature . . . Be I wrong to want to find out what I be made of?' She now faced him with spirit, while her heart yearned for a gentle word. 'Bean't the heritage of a human creature its fate? Moulding its life?'

'Did your mother send you?' Alone in the world, the letter had said; but he must be sure of what had become of Mary.

'Mother died many years ago.'

He leaned back in his chair and did not speak for some time. Before she came he had been sitting in the library, newly and expensively built to his exact requirements, musing bitterly on his isolation from his family, his household, the rest of mankind. There had been a proud regret that he was so, and an inability to do anything but retreat further. Rebecca, walking in, had changed the situation. Shock and emotion had for the time eliminated his normal defence against the world. He mentally searched for the habits of his status and felt that he should be admitting nothing. Looking up again into Rebecca's face, he was struck once more by her likeness to himself and said, 'You are not much like her.'

'Bean't I?'

'What have you been told? What has made you come here and make this claim?' He paused, then thought he ought to add, 'This preposterous claim.' Something in his tone was softer and Rebecca brightened.

'I knew nothing until, the week before last, father—' She choked a little on the word and shot a look at the stranger in the chair opposite. Her love for Jim Redfearn welled up inside her, and her sense of loss . . . 'Father was dying of consumption and before he died, told me that mother was carrying me when he married her and that I was to another man.'

Giffard Boville winced at her outspokenness.

'You realize that what you have just said absolves me

legally from any possible claim.'

She looked at him in shock. Legality or the lack of it was unknown to her in this connection, but his mind, powerful and active, was not softened even in this moment.

'Any child born in wedlock is counted as the child of the woman's husband. You are not a bastard; and you have no legal claim on me.' He matched her in plain speaking.

'For that, as for so many things, I have him to thank.'

'Who have you to thank? Jim Redfearn?' He spoke sharply.

Rebecca's head jerked up. He knew; he had not forgotten. She realised then that her birth had not been without meaning to him, her conception no 'fly-by-night' encounter . . . He saw that he had given himself away and sighed.

'You see,' he said, 'I admit that I have an unknown daughter. What proof is there that you are she? Perhaps your face is proof enough . . .'

Rebecca felt as though her heart and body were turned to water. Her voice would hardly come.

'I have a daguerrotype of my mother,' she faltered, 'and some family papers. Certificates and things.' She fell silent. Then with trepidation, she asked,

'Won't you tell me . . .?'

'I was only a young man, you know,' he said suddenly, with the impulse to defend himself. 'Up at Cambridge. I was not in Hall, the last year. Your mother was the housemaid in my lodgings. I did not set out to seduce her, but she was always there . . . I met her so often . . .' She was a challenge, he thought a beloved challenge . . . 'I would have provided for her,' and jolted out of his reserve, he turned to Rebecca almost in supplication. 'I would have given her an income, gone to see her – she need not have married Redfearn.'

After all those years of forgetfulness, of indifference to his child's existence, now the note in his voice was of hurt, of the hurt of a young man who is left, as well as leaving.

'Surely it was best,' and Rebecca found herself, surprisingly, sounding soothing.

'Yes, it was best.'

Sitting within a yard of one another, father and daughter looked at each other, glances tentative, questioning, learning each other's features, feeling as Cortez did on his mountain when he saw the Pacific. There was quiet in the library.

'So you have not come for money,' he went on, still sounding hard. 'Where is all the money from, that you say you have?'

'I have sold up my home. I have enough money to live for a year without finding work, but I can soon find a place. The money will be a reserve.'

'You realize that I cannot admit that you may be my daughter,' he went on abruptly. 'I have a wife – ah, you had not thought of that. I have two daughters by her.'

'Then I have two half-sisters,' said Rebecca softly; she had always longed for sisters.

'Yes; but they cannot be so to you.'

'No – no.' She was thrust out of that kinship.

'I cannot acknowledge you!' He spoke sharply, as though convincing himself, and Rebecca suddenly had the perception that he would have liked to be able to acknowledge her. For whatever reason – and, realizing that he was rich and had two other daughters, she could think of none – she still knew that he would, just then, have liked to own her as his daughter.

'All I can do—' he hesitated – 'is to own you as a distant connection of the family, as, say, a fifth cousin; fallen on hard times and so come to me. Could you accept that? Could you keep silent?'

'I would be living a lie,' said Rebecca slowly. 'I have come and met you; far better to go to find work in Mere Drove or Burgh, and just know in my heart who my father was, than stay in Yorkshire and say I was a fifth cousin.'

'Have I no voice in the matter, then? Having come – having forced yourself into my presence – are you to go

41

again?'

'Yes,' said Rebecca.

'Not yet, anyway.'

She felt she must say something.

'I do not think I would feel comfortable, meeting Mrs Boville. I had not thought of that – that my father would be married. I should have thought of it.' She shook her head.

'She is away in Italy, Florence, with friends. Her health is not good.' A shadow crossed his face and she wondered at his words. In her world, a wife worked by her husband's side, and she had never heard of one who went away for her health.

'Are you staying at an inn in Kirkby?'

'I left my trunk at the station.' The Rebecca of yesterday would have marvelled at this calm way of speaking of that great wonder, the railway. Today it seemed the most natural thing in the world to say, 'I left it at the station'.

'You will stay for a while. There will be a room in Kirkby. I want to know more of you.' In the neighbourhood, Giffard Boville was known as a grey, grim man, sharpcut as his own house steps, quick to anger and stiff with pride. Yet, as he stood looking into Rebecca's face by the window, inside he had crumbled, softened, given way before her, as a unicorn is said to yield himself to the hand of a maiden, to this country girl. Outwardly, he showed no sign of this.

'I've never been in such a house before,' she said innocently. 'It is grand.'

'New, you know,' he shot a glance at her under bushy brows. 'There is an ancient core to it – the tower – which has been the home of the Bovilles for centuries; but starting ten years ago, I have been building on to it as you see now.' He looked at his gold watch. 'It is growing late if you are to be settled into a room in the town. I will walk down with you, but first, a cup of tea? It is the usual time. We have it in the drawing-room, but Julia and Eliza Ann are out this afternoon.' He rang the bell. 'Tea, Ferguson, in

42

here.'

Ferguson looked incredulous. He glanced from his master to the servant girl. Giffard did not seem to notice his butler's expression as the man went to order the tea.

As if in a dream, Rebecca accepted a fragrant cup of tea in a fine china cup, and a little bread and butter, cut thin as leaves. For the first time she realized that she was really very tired. How strange, to be sitting opposite Giffard Boville and drinking tea! It was hard to think of him as her father, yet she felt something, indefinable, linking them; she had felt it from the first minute in his presence.

He went out after drinking a cup of tea, and returned in a coat and with a hat, and soon they were walking down the driveway together, strangely silent, towards Kirkby. Once in the town, Giffard went at once to the Three Tuns, ordered a room for her, sent a man to fetch her trunk and ordered her a meal, in a brisk, blunt way, as though he were used to giving orders and did not much care how brusquely he did it. She noticed the way he was obeyed and thought that he did not seem very popular, but people jumped to obey him when he spoke. She was a mere puppet in his hands. There was no more of the intimacy which had seemed to be trembling into existence in the library. Just for a little while, when he bid her goodnight, were they once more close. His eyes seemed to be drawn to her; he seemed reluctant to go.

'You will be all right, Miss Redfearn?' (The innkeeper's wife was nearby.) 'You will have everything you require?'

'Thank you, sir, you are very good.'

'You will still be here – I will be down to see you in the morning – you will still be here?' And Rebecca, as once before, was soothing.

'I will be here, sir.'

A meal was served to her in her room, by a bouncing, jolly lass, whose broad Yorkshire accent Rebecca could hardly understand. She was relieved that she did not have to face curious glances in the public rooms of the inn. It was luxurious to be cared for, not to have to wash the pots, to be able, if she wished, to go to bed. It was still early, but her day had been one of emotional turmoil; it would be good to rest in bed.

Once there, she found herself homesick for Cross; the sounds which floated up from the market-place were unfamiliar; everything she knew was many miles away. Her old life, Jim Redfearn ill, Simon Lloyd coming each day with conversation which was like water in the desert, the kindly neighbours – all far away, over. She longed for a few words with Simon, and wondered how he liked the cottage he had moved into, thinking almost with reverence of his clear grey eyes, his thin pale face where the cheekbones showed, the dash of fair hair which so often fell over his forehead. How lucky she had been, she thought, to have been honoured with his friendship. If her heart told her it was more than friendship, she beat down the thought. Friendship, with such a man, was a great thing; to stand high in his regard.

Then she longed for her fosterfather, for dear Jim Redfearn whose name she bore; and it seemed to Rebecca that for the first time she realized what she had lost. All the sorrow washed over her, as though she had never tasted it before. The bouncy maid with the broad Yorkshire accent heard her, as she went upstairs to the attic room, and stood at Rebecca's door and listened to the heartbroken sobbing, until she decided to tell her mistress, and she came up and listened too.

'Poor thing!' she said. 'She has some great trouble, that's for sure. There's nothing we can do, Sythe.' They tiptoed away and Sythe listened for a long time, before she fell asleep.

Simon Lloyd had found the first day after Rebecca left the village hard; but he had expected, when he had allowed himself to think about it, that it would be hard. He had found in the Redfearn family his only real associates in the village. The ancient simplicity of the old people, the upright quietness of Jim Redfearn, the gentle grace of

44

Rebecca, had made visiting Redfearns' cottage a pleasure and now it stood empty, with curtainless windows like eyeholes in a skull from which the soul has departed. He had walked up the path between the gillyflowers, and looked in at the door, for no one locked doors in Cross. The bare room mocked him, for it held not what he sought.

Back in his own home he rested his hand on the dresser, which he had watched Rebecca polish, remembering how she had said, 'Don't you love the grain of oak, Mr Lloyd? When you rub it you can see into it. The little golden lights and flecks seem to be living. How grand the tree must have been in the forest.' She had been alight with the wonder of the world.

He felt that she had given to him her delight and without her that joy had gone from him. He had returned good for good: in lending her books, in talking to her, lecturing her, forming her mind, having her intelligence leap in answer to his own he had done her good – or had he? Would it help her in a world where the ability to pull pints of beer or to bake bread was more likely to be of use than the ability to appreciate a poem or the delicate perception of a Charles Lamb essay?

He was convinced that he had done her nothing but good. If in doing so he had grown too fond of her, so that these last weeks had been an agony to him as well as for her, he had, he was sure, harmed no one but himself. Well, that was soon remedied; he must seek other society; he had neglected his duty to the vicar, who liked him to walk over to the vicarage for a game of whist of an evening; he had neglected his own interests, in not paying more court to Lady Marwood's daughters . . .

'It is a long time since we had the pleasure of seeing you,' said Lady Marwood meaningly. 'You have been neglecting us, Mr Lloyd,' and she tapped him on the arm with her fan; smiled while she chided him, and guided him into the conservatory, where her two daughters were copying verses into their albums. They both looked up and smiled a welcome. He sat down, feeling like the fly in the parlour of the spider. Lady Marwood was beginning to be just a little desperate about her unmarried daughters. 'How lovely that is!' she exclaimed, leaning over the elder girl's shoulder and reading aloud the verse she was engaged on. 'Don't you think so, Mr Lloyd?'

Simon thought it remarkably poor, even in the field of verses chosen for albums; but he smiled and agreed that it was very fine. Both the daughters were well built and buxom, like their mother. Lady Marwood's ample arms, encircled by bracelets, were laid across their shoulders as she moved from one to another, looking at their work. Simon thought she was going to lay her arm over his shoulders, too. He looked at the heavy snake bracelet with its twinkling ruby eye in apprehension, but she contented herself with beaming at him and asking him to stay for dinner.

'What is the news from the village?' asked Maria Marwood. Simon did his best to render a humorous account of the events of the past weeks. He was a good raconteur and made the little incidents of daily life vivid, but he had the minor humiliation of seeing that Lady Marwood, sitting in her comfortable chair under the palm, had closed her eyes. When he spoke of the Redfearn sale and the empty cottage his voice shook, but he hoped that none present would guess the reason.

When Simon began to question Isabella Marwood on the life at the Hall in the last weeks, Lady Marwood at once woke up, nodding at Isabella's remarks and putting in occasionally, 'Very true, my dear! Aye, so we did. Does she not describe that well, Mr Lloyd?'

As the evening wore on, Simon was more bored than he had ever been in his life, but just as he became restless and wondered if he could make some excuse to leave, Maria mentioned 'our uncle the bishop' – and Simon was at once fixed to his chair as though he had been rooted there.

It did not prove a good idea to buy the Redfearns'

furniture, for when he returned to his cottage that evening the young curate felt that he could almost see Rebecca's graceful shape outlined against the cupboard, head bent under heavy coils of hair, and hear her voice with its soft dialect.

'Oh, my dear!' he said under his breath. Sitting by the table and laying his head on his arms he wondered how she was faring in Yorkshire and wished that she had not gone . . .

'Mester Boville to see you,' said Sythe to Rebecca next morning. She had almost added 'miss', but being an egalitarian Yorkshire lass and feeling sorry for Rebecca, changed it mentally to 'love', then omitted it altogether. Rebecca was sitting, very forlorn, in a chair, looking as though she had not the strength to move again. Her face was white and her eyes would hardly open because of her tears of the previous night, and she had refused to eat any breakfast. Looking at Sythe, she managed a faint smile.

'Come on, love, that's better,' said Sythe in a cossetting voice, her good heart breaking through the barrier between a servant and a guest. Fetching Rebecca's pelisse, she eased her up and coaxed her into it, as though she had been a baby. 'Doesn't do to keep Mr Boville waiting,' she admonished.

Giffard Boville, when she reached him in the inn parlour, did not look much better than she did herself. His expression was harrowed and exhausted, as though for him too the night had been sleepless.

'You're still here, then,' he greeted her. 'Come out into the air; it is stifling inside.'

Ordinary words. Yet their meeting was not ordinary. It was full of unspoken things, memories of yesterday, threads weaving between them from the heredity she had from him. They felt close in spirit, the father and daughter, after one meeting. The Lincolnshire country girl and the Yorkshire gentleman. He never felt like this with his other daughters, who had grown up in his presence.

'You must come and stay at the house,' he said abruptly. They were standing in the middle of the market-place, on the cobbles. 'I want to tell you about my family – your family – and show you the places we have been associated with, over the centuries.'

'I had best not stay,' she said.

Her father turned on her with sudden anger, like a whiplash.

'Not stay? Will you refuse to stay under your father's roof?'

She looked up at him and pitied his anger.

'I will stay . . .' she hesitated . . . 'Under the roof of my distant cousin.'

'Come, that's better. We are agreed, then. Stay as a fifth cousin – at least for a while.'

CHAPTER FOUR

'Ferguson!' – the butler had appeared at once in answer to the imperious ringing of the bell – 'See someone fetches Miss Redfearn's trunk from the Three Tuns. Tell the housekeeper she will be in the Striped Bedroom.'

'Yes, sir.' Ferguson looked at Rebecca with eyes that said, as clearly as if he had spoken, 'Oh! You've soon wormed yourself in, haven't you?' Rebecca disliked him even more than she had on the previous day.

'Come,' said Giffard Boville, 'let me show you round. The girls have gone out for a drive, your – fifth cousins; their governess will be sleeping; there is an old uncle of my wife's – he is probably in the garden.'

He led the way out of the hall, and she followed, noticing his tall, slim figure, the set of his head. In appearance, she thought, he was a father anyone would be proud of; and she wondered about those half-sisters she had yet to meet.

She was glad she had come. It would only be for a few days, perhaps a week, and she knew there would be many times when she would feel awkward, and not know the right thing to do or say. But then she would travel on – in a week or so – to somewhere else; packing her new memories, with her old ones of Cross and her dear family there, into a trunk of memories that would always go with her wherever she went. However difficult it might be, staying in this house as a fifth cousin, it would be something to look back on, in years to come.

It was doing her good already. All day her father had taken her round Kirkby and talked to her of the Bovilles

49

and she had been conscious of her triple loss – of father, of beloved and of home – only as a dull ache, and not as a tearing pain. It would come back. Like a creature lying in wait, it would spring upon her, and rend her with its claws of hopeless misery. But while she was distracted, while her mind was soaking in these new impressions, learning desperately in a few days what it could of the father she might in other circumstances have known all her life, then she thought it might remain as a dull ache; she thought this tentatively, as one who looks at the door of his prison and thinks the tormentor will not return for a while. Facing the world was put off. When the time came, her courage would be high. . . .

In thinking this, she had passed in Giffard Boville's wake through the hall she knew already, and into the great dining-room. All the rooms were panelled darkly, a thing she had never seen. The ceiling-high windows in the dining-room had stained glass, with the armorials of family connections, like the curved shields in the entrance porch; no figures of saints, thought Rebecca.

'Do you like it?' Giffard Boville was watching her face, rapt in the dim light of the dining-room. 'We eat on the dais; when there is a dinner party tables are put down here too.' Following his gesture, Rebecca imagined the room full of people eating. Why, it would be like a harvest supper, or a chapel treat. 'There's a minstrel gallery.' She turned and saw the carved gallery, half-way up the wall through which they had come. 'Barry designed it for me.' She could find nothing to say. Dissatisfied at her silence, he led the way out and into the drawing-room, and here he could tell by the look in her eyes that she was impressed. The panelling of the walls was almost hidden by photographs and paintings, and the space round the massive Tudor fireplace was cluttered with sofas, sociables, armchairs of all kinds, little work tables, card tables, a spinning wheel, firescreens. The floor of wide oak boards was almost hidden under oriental rugs, while Delph and china tulip pots stood about. The tables were hidden under flowing covers, the windows each had three sets of curtains, and evidence of the industry of the ladies of the house was everywhere in the shape of embroidered covers, beadworked screens, and cushions of vivid Berlin wool-work.

To one brought up in the spartan simplicity of a fenland cottage, no room could have seemed more beautiful or more luxurious.

'You like this, then?' His air said, 'at last!'

'It's like fairyland,' she breathed.

'I have to go out for a while, soon; I'll show you your bedroom, then no doubt you can look after yourself until tea-time. Come in here, or go into the library, or into the garden. If you could read, I would offer you a book.'

'Of course I can read!' she flashed at him.

'Oh! A learned village miss, eh?' She was not sure if his sardonic voice was meant to hurt or amuse. 'Then help yourself to a book from the library if you wish.'

Rebecca had not yet learned to know Giffard Boville's character. It was a complex one, and her arrival made him more unpredictable then usual. From one moment to another he changed towards her. Now the haughty aristocrat, now the thoughtful host, now kindly and fatherly, now strangely urgent, appealing, as though a soul martyred by isolation had met its kin. Then as suddenly he would hurl at her a barb almost of insult.

The old foursquare tower had been the first home of the Boville family. After the dissolution of the monasteries they had enriched themselves. Stone from abbey buildings had been used to build the flanking wing on the west side of the tower, the ground floor of which was mainly now the drawing-room. Later, in the reigns of the Georges, prosperity had brought another surge of building. The wing on the south front had been added. Now in the heyday of Victoria, Giffard Boville had built on to the east his new dining-room and library, with their accompanying bedrooms over, and remodelled the staircase.

The stair, within the only ancient part of the building,

rose in short shallow flights round four sides of the square tower, the bare oak treads gleaming. On every landing was a window, through walls so deep that the windowsills were the size of small rooms in themselves. Rebecca paused, entranced, by one of them, with a view over to the hills; the view which she had first seen framed in the boughs of the old beech on the drive. Giffard Boville stood beside her.

'You'll not see a view like that in the fens,' he said gruffly.

'No . . . I like it . . . and the air here is like spring water, so refreshing.'

'It is like champagne! But you will never have tasted that.'

She leaned far enough out to look down towards the ground.

'Oh!' was all she said, but he divined her meaning.

'The garden is at its best at this time of year.'

'And I may walk in it?'

'You may, Cousin Rebecca.'

From this viewpoint she could see a group of buildings outlined against the moorland on the other side of the river. A large, muddled mass, it seemed to be, and the sun made it soft gold, where the stone of the house she stood in was forbiddingly grey.

'That's the only other house in sight, from here,' she remarked, trying to find a basis for normal everyday conversation with the man beside her.

'Gilbank Hall; Sir Charles Gilbank and his wife and son live there. You may be adding to your cousinage; Sir Charles and I are talking of marriage between his son, Edward, and my daughter Eliza Ann.'

As they turned and went on up the stairs, she said, 'I met Sir Charles Gilbank and his son on the train. They got on, as I did, at Mere Drove, and were met by a carriage in Kirkby. Sir Charles gave me his card.'

'They have been on a visit to Sir Charles's relative, Lady Marwood. You did not talk to them, did you?'

'Why, of course, sir. They were sitting opposite to me on the train.'

'You did not tell them who you were?' She was surprised at the suppressed anger in his voice.

'I told them I was kin to a Mr Giffard Boville of Kirkby.'

'You did not say what kin?'

'No.' She was apprehensive at his reactions, but he drew a breath of relief.

'Thank God you said no more. That is between you and me only. Do you understand?'

'Yes.'

'Were you travelling first?' He sounded surprised.

'They were travelling second.'

'It is like him! The meanest man in three counties, Gilbank. Otherwise we would have settled the match long ago.'

Rebecca remembered the young man, Edward, who had spoken to her so pleasantly on the train, and wondered if he were very much in love with her half-sister, and she with him, and if the meanness of Sir Charles Gilbank was causing them much distress.

'This is the Striped Bedroom; you will like it, as you are so taken by the view over the garden.' The room had an oriel window, and Rebecca went over to it at once with a little exclamation of pleasure. 'Yes; I thought you would like it.' Her father sounded satisfied. 'You will be all right – happy and safe – while I am gone?' He had spoken in the same tone when leaving her for the night at the inn; she looked at him and nodded. He saw her surprise, and added swiftly, 'We have so little time to grow to know one another. Any relationship must be so brief, so constrained. I am quite anxious that you should not disappear as suddenly as you came.' He laughed self-consciously.

'I will be here.' She went to him and touched his arm with her hand, looking up into his face, feeling that he was not and could not be a stranger. As he looked down at her his face was relaxed, almost tender. Then, resuming his usual command of his features, he nodded curtly and left the room. She watched him go with both regret and relief. She looked around her. To her eyes, the bedroom was the ultimate in luxury. It was a large, light room, furnished sparingly but with slender mahogany pieces, which gave an impression of distinction and grace. There were one or two pictures on the lightly patterned wallpaper, chintz hangings on the four-poster bed, and a bedquilt of white with a garland of patchwork flowers cut from chintzes. She moved about the room aimlessly, touching lightly here and there with her fingers, bending to look closely at the grain of wood or the texture of a printed flower, finally coming to rest on the wide windowseat of the oriel window and gazing out, first over the spread of landscape then downwards at the garden, a composite of colour and pattern. Wide paths were spread with yellow sand. Ordered flowerbeds had the flush of summer just beginning. Walls separated the different sections, so that the whole was not comprehended at a glance, but glimpses of further gardens down the slope of the hill suggested delights to come. Rebecca drew herself up on to the windowsill and allowed herself to float into a state of neither thinking nor feeling, but merely being, while the time drifted past.

She was disturbed by a bumping and a cursing on the landing and corridor outside and came to herself and jumped from the windowsill, crossing towards the door, as it opened and Ferguson the butler came in with two footmen who were struggling with Rebecca's trunk.

Ferguson had a Scottish father and a Kirkby mother. After his father's death the little family had returned to live with his mother's folk; it had been difficult for the boy to fit in with the other lads and it had been a long time before he had felt one of the closed community. When he went out to work and found a place at Broxa House he had been determined to make good and spared no servile effort in his struggle to rise to the omnipotent position of butler.

He resented Rebecca's translation from stray servant girl to house guest. 'She's nowt,' he had remarked to Mrs

Douthwaite, the housekeeper. It was going to be a struggle for him to be civil to the upstart.

'Your trunk, Miss Redfearn,' said Ferguson. 'Where would you like it to stand?' His tone held an obscure antagonism and Rebecca felt under attack as she tried to think what to say. 'Here?' He had not waited for her to decide.

'That will do, yes; I thank you.' Ought she to offer money to the footmen? She had none to spare and did not know what to do, but they were leaving and only Ferguson was still in the room.

It was not clear how it happened. He seemed to be going round the trunk to reach the door and stumbled over it; this was what Rebecca thought afterwards. At the time she thought he deliberately pretended to stumble and so fell on top of her, reaching out to steady himself with hot hands that grasped and held . . .

'Oh!' she cried out involuntarily, making a snatch backwards as she felt herself overborne by the impact of his body and catching hold of the reeded bedpost, holding firmly with one hand and with the other pushing him away.

'So sorry,' he said, regaining his balance. 'My apologies, Miss Redfearn.' His eyes burned her, and he was holding her.

Then, as quickly as it had happened, it was over. He had released her and gone out of the door. She sank on to the edge of the bed, breathless. Had he meant to fall against her? Her mind was full of the impressions of the contact – his open mouth and hot breath so close to her face, the touch of his body and hands on hers, the minute impressions of the hairs on the backs of his hands, the grain of his skin, the smell of another human body. She shuddered, and could still feel his touch.

The longer she thought about it, the more she was convinced that the incident had been deliberate: a threat, a warning, an assault. Yet she could lay no complaint. An accident? The merest accident! And how could she – a servant girl, and the daughter of a servant girl, her own father had called her – how could she presume to complain of that lordly person, the butler of Broxa House? She had barely recovered from the incident when a maid entered the room with a can of hot water.

'Master says, Miss Redfearn, when you have refreshed yourself, would you come to the drawing-room for tea?'

If Rebecca had found Mrs Fox's sister's washbasin and jug, thick earthenware with cold water, a luxury, how much more luxurious was the full china set in this bedroom, with scented soap on a special dish and a shining copper can of hot water! She smiled at the maid, shyly, for if she was seeking a situation she would not have aimed as high as the position this girl had reached, and was rewarded by a friendly look. In the few seconds the maid was in the room, Rebecca was sure that without words she had made a friend and an ally, and she felt better.

So her father – her cousin, she had to try to think of him as that – was back in the house. As she was already wearing her best dress, she had nothing to change into; but when she had washed and combed her hair she felt more able to go down to the drawing-room to tea. At first, when she pushed open the panelled door, they did not notice her, and she had time to take in the room and its occupants.

The afternoon sun was flooding into the room, so that the upper half, the heavily moulded plasterwork of the ceiling, the inlaid panelling with its load of portraits and photographs, and the group of people disposed in it, were all softly glowing. Caught by the surfaces of tables and other furniture, the slanting rays of the sunshine did not everywhere reach the floor, so that, lower, mysterious shadows gathered. There were five people in the room. Near the fireplace was an elderly gentleman dressed in black, large and formless, pudgy fingers holding his teacup as he slopped earnestly over it. A little apart, between him and the tea table, sat a narrow woman in a raucous shade of purple; her back was to the door, and Rebecca only saw the narrow shoulders, and the back of her cap.

56

Round the tea table in the sunny window she saw two girls, younger than herself, and felt a surge of hopeful anticipation. Sisters! Half-sisters . . .she had never seen girls dressed as they were dressed and she felt an unaccustomed shyness and wonderment that such radiance could be in some measure related to herself.

Giffard Boville was sitting pushed back from the tea table, with its pretty fripperies, into the bay window. She saw no expression on his face, for it was against the light; but from the hunched aspect of his shoulders, she guessed, though she had known him so short a time, that he was feeling irritated and displeased.

He was not the first to notice her entrance. One of the girls looked round and taking her for a servant, exclaimed in a haughty voice,

'I did not ring!'

At this Giffard Boville looked up and caught sight of Rebecca; he rose to his feet and went over to meet her, and taking her hand, escorted her to the tea table. Was it an illusion, that she felt he was cheered and calmed by seeing her?

'Julia, Eliza Ann, I would like you to meet a cousin of yours – a fifth cousin; Miss Rebecca Redfearn. She has been left an orphan recently and has come to consult me, as head of the family, about her future life. I want you to make her welcome during her brief stay with us. Miss Redfearn, may I introduce my daughters, Julia – Miss Boville, the eldest—' Julia, in a lavender day gown of five yards' circumference in the hem and a wonder of tucks and lace edgings, nodded frigidly; 'and Eliza Ann, the younger—' Eliza Ann, in palest rose with tucks and lace, bent her head; 'their governess, Miss Sutor, and Mr Machereth, uncle to Mrs Boville.' Rebecca was stared at by the two older members of the party, and Mr Machereth spilled some tea on his waistcoat, having had his attention distracted for a moment from the process of drinking it.

Julia Boville was just twenty years old and her sister almost seventeen. They had been petted and spoiled as children, but as they grew up life had not been so easy. Quarrels between their parents had frightened and bewildered them; the bright and secure became dark and insecure. Their mother's ill health and more and more frequent absences were troubling. Julia in particular had become the prey of moods which she could not understand. She was the most like her mother in looks, with dark brown, passionate eyes, and could be by turns enchanting and tempestuous, charming and furious. She wept sometimes, when she was alone, and wished she could understand the world and herself; but then to that world was brave, abrupt, unspeakably arrogant . . .

Eliza Ann was calmer than her sister and had a little more of the Boville about her looks. Her eyes were grey like her father's and her disposition was more docile than Julia's.

After gazing at Rebecca for a minute and frostily indicating a chair, Julia Boville put her face close to her father's ear and spoke very low. Rebecca's cheeks flamed. Her cottage manners would not have countenanced this.

'I'm afraid she must,' replied Giffard to Julia, and went on, to Rebecca, 'have you a dress suitable to wear for dinner tonight, Cousin Rebecca?'

'This is my Sunday dress,' answered the girl, and held her head high, as Eliza Ann broke into giggles she did not try to hide.

'And do you have a new one once a year?' asked Eliza Ann.

'Julia! Rebecca is without tea!' Giffard's voice cut across the titter which had run round the party.

'Yes, father.' At once Julia took up a pretty Derby cup and saucer and began to go through the little ritual. 'Cream, Miss Redfearn? Sugar? Eliza Ann, please pass Miss Redfearn the bread and butter. These scones are very good.'

What Rebecca had never known of exquisite discomfort, she was made to feel during that hour of afternoon tea, on her first day in her father's house. How it ever dragged to an end, she could not have said. But at last the footman came to clear the tea table. At last her father dismissed her with the words,

'We dine at six, Cousin Rebecca,' and at last she was able to escape to her room, to anticipate the humiliations of the evening meal. What relief she felt that the following week she would be leaving, she expected for ever! Lonely, an outsider in a family none of whom had asked for her arrival, even in this bitter hour she was not sorry that she had come.

Since Jim Redfearn's death she had acted almost as though directed by another will. Her own seemed locked within her, shocked, grief-stricken, unable to decide. Somehow, she was carried through . . . it was thus, with involuntary will power, that she was able to go down into the great, dark-panelled dining-room and up on to the dais where the long table was set for dinner. With her worn black gown, pale face and work-roughened hands, she sat down among a company who seemed to draw together to exclude her.

The inadequacy of her gown had come home to her when she returned to her bedroom after afternoon tea; the maid had been there, looking round rather helplessly.

'I was sent to lay out your gown for dinner, Miss Redfearn,' she had said.

'I must wear the one I have on,' Rebecca had replied, proudly, refusing to dissemble.

'Oh.' The maid looked at her, not scathing, not pitying, but just wanting to be helpful. 'Should I press it?' The gown had been pressed and brushed, and Rebecca had discovered that the maid was called Alice and liked her more than at their first meeting, but that did not lessen her difficulties as she walked up to the dinner table.

There was only one chair left empty, so she took it.

The butler was in attendance and as he began to super-vise the service of the meal Rebecca knew that he had looked at her sardonically and exchanged glances with the footmen, who were trying to hide their amusement.

Seeing the way her half-sisters were dressed, Rebecca understood.

The shadows of evening had gathered around the high mock-medieval roof-tree, enforcing the ancestral gloom which seemed to grip those round the table. Dark, menacing, Mr Machereth seemed to loom up, a mountain of a man, across the table from her; Miss Sutor, after one deprecating glance, averted her eyes as though the sight of Rebecca was too painful. Miss Sutor had a blade-sharp body and wore a quantity of blade-sharp ornaments on a gaudy, over-youthful evening gown. She resented the advent of another dependant, seeing her own comforts threatened by dilution, and withdrew into superior silence.

The footmen circled with the soup and Rebecca, who had never had her dinner served to her in this manner, felt that she never knew when the servants were going to pop up at her elbow, or what they were going to do next. A dread swept over her of bumping into them if she moved her arms, upsetting something they were carrying.

The hardest thing to bear was that her two half-sisters, towards whom she had felt such tender yearnings, regarded her as a figure of fun and were ashamed to be sitting at the same table with her. Her natural self-respect held her above an abyss of misery into which they would willingly have plunged her. When the sisters looked at each other, it was to exchange wordless comments on her pale cheeks, the way she handled her fork, the way she tucked in her napkin, or her simply coiled hair.

Mr Machereth, opposite, never spoke to her. He was too much occupied in looking after the soup, the fish, the entrée, the roast, the sweet, the savoury, the dessert, to spare those few words which might have eased her isolation.

With the dessert, the servants withdrew. Rebecca was left with a delightful dessert plate in front of her, hand-painted in the centre with fruit, bordered by a band of a heavenly colour between blue and green. Looking round, she saw that on helping themselves to the glowing peaches in the centre of the table, her half-sisters then peeled them and ate them with a knife and fork. Left to herself, she would have picked one up and bitten it. The grapes were offered to her; she saw, just in time, that grape scissors were provided to cut off a portion of the bunch; having taken some, she was about to put one in her mouth when she saw that Miss Sutor was washing hers, in the water of the finger-bowl, before eating them and, prickling with relief that she had noticed, Rebecca did the same.

Giffard Boville, at the head of the table, ate morosely and in silence for the most part and it was not until the dessert that he spoke to her directly.

'Cousin Rebecca,' he said, 'you must have some decent clothes.' It was said with a look which made her feel lower than a servant girl; a mere beggar-maid in rags for his bounty. She thought evil shades hovering round the table laughed, and were glad.

In her pride, she answered, 'What I have, sir, is quite sufficient for my station in life.'

'I cannot have you at my table looking like a scullery lass. I will buy you some new clothes.'

'I could not take them, sir.'

'Not accept them?' His quick temper was rising.

'I can buy myself what clothes I need for my daily life.' They were speaking to one another down the length of the table and everyone else was looking and listening.

'Look here—' and everyone except Mr Machereth looked up, with Rebecca, and their silence intensified – 'who is the head of this family? I am. Do you deny that?'

'No, sir.'

'If I choose to clothe one of my poor relations, I have a right to do so.' Mr Machereth looked up reproachfully. 'Do you deny me that right?' Looking helplessly around the table, Rebecca found that she had no allies. Eliza Ann was shrinking into herself in terror of her father's cold anger. Even Julia looked frightened, and the other two were looking towards Rebecca with pained expressions as the cause of the trouble. Julia's little Maltese terrier, Floss, went under the table and hid behind his mistress's feet.

Giffard Boville had not raised his voice in the slightest. If anything he had dropped it. The words he spoke came more slowly than was usual with him. He could often be testy and a little abrupt when dealing with those around him; but it was only when his anger was really roused that he spoke so quietly and slowly in so restrained a fashion. This apparent calm and reticence did not stop everyone who witnessed if from wishing that he would express his anger more openly, that he would shout, or thump on the table. Anything rather than the chill of his rage.

Rebecca had stopped looking at him. Somehow she must end it. She remembered her fear on the train, that her father might be a drunkard, and decided that this dominating temper was not much better. She had never been governed so at home. The chandelier above them seemed to her to tremble.

'You forget, sir, that I am leaving in a few days. There will hardly be time for you to buy me new clothes, or for me to wear them.'

'Nonsense!' he hissed the word so that Rebecca imagined the black bats flitting in the twilight outside heard him and swerved in fright. 'Nonsense!' Then, more normally, 'Of course you will stay longer than a few days. There is no need to go away before we have had the chance to get to know you.' Rebecca was aware that the others were disavowing any need or desire to get to know her as hard as they could without actually saying anything. She read it in their looks. 'You will stay,' and his voice began to drop again, 'as long as I wish you to. You will stay some weeks.' He tapped his finger lightly but ominously on the table to emphasize his words.

She spoke, desperate to appease him.

'Very well, sir.' He stopped tapping the table. 'I will stay longer and accept new clothes rather than distress you. But only on the condition that they be discreet, sober and suitable.' She was thinking that it would be of little use to her to be tricked out in muslin covered with lace, or a silk

62

evening gown half off her shoulders and breasts, in her future life as a housemaid in a farmhouse or hostelry.

He was mollified.

'Decent and sober as you like. Julia will see to it.'

For the first time, Julia looked at Rebecca without contempt. Shopping, Rebecca was to discover, was an art and a passion with Julia. Her mind immediately took off.

'Forty yards, I think, for two day dresses, of sprigged or checked muslin; silk for evening; we will send to York for patterns; a shawl; a crinoline; forty yards of cashmere for two winter dresses, and eighty yards of velvet trimming; a cloak; at least two bonnets—'

'Stop!' cried Rebecca. 'I cannot possibly . . .' she saw Giffard Boville's brow darkening, and caught the apprehensive looks of the rest of the party, and subsided, beginning to realize that the temper of an autocrat can brood over a room like a thundercloud. 'They must be very plain,' she murmured at last, and everyone relaxed.

'Forty-eight yards at one penny farthing a yard,' said Julia, whose thoughts had travelled on to underclothes and their trimming, 'that will be . . .'

'Five shillings!' cried Rebecca, horrified.

Giffard looked down the table at her in surprise.

'And the muslin will probably be twopence three farthings. Say forty yards—'

'Nine and twopence!' cried Rebecca, unable to stop herself.

'I have spent a fortune on my children's education,' said Giffard Boville, 'and neither of them could reckon that without pen and paper, and half an hour to rectify mistakes.' He looked hard at Miss Sutor, who found it was now her turn to be uncomfortable, and acquired a grievance against Rebecca.

'I beg pardon, sir, I should not have spoken,' said Rebecca, who could see that this speech made everyone antagonistic to her. 'But in my station of life, good arithmetic is needful. Our schoolmaster was always telling us that we had our way to make in the world. For ladies, it is not necessary.' Eliza Ann looked gratefully at her, and as they left the room and went to the drawing-room, the feeling between them was warmer. Julia and Eliza Ann began to discuss her new clothes.

'They must be black, you know,' said Rebecca with some trepidation, for Julia had a way with her, a decisive, haughty way, which made Rebecca aware that in this world she herself was of no account. 'I am in mourning for my father.'

When the two men arrived, and set up a chess table, Rebecca saw that her true father did not intend to take any further notice of her that evening; she understood him. It had all been a great shock; they needed time to adjust to the idea of one another, to grow to know each other with the gradualness of everyday contact. That was the natural way of things.

In a few minutes, the maids filed in. The fire had been lit earlier, by the footmen, and the lamps lit. One, on a large table, gave light for most of the maids, Julia and Eliza Ann to sit round it; another was on a smaller table for the head housemaid and the underhousemaid, whom Rebecca recognized as her friend of the copper water can and the clothes brush, and these two occupied themselves with household mending, while those round the big table sewed at red flannel petticoats for the poor.

Julia did not sew, she read aloud out of the Bible.

For a while Rebecca, like Miss Sutor, took no part in the proceedings; then, although shy at seeming to put herself forward, Rebecca could bear to be inactive no longer, and asked if she might help. Sewing was a thing she had no aptitude for, and hated; but that night she was pleased to do it, sitting in the lamp's glow, hemming, and listening to Julia's voice. This room had none of the powerful gloom of the central tower, or the grim dining-hall and the presence of the maids tempered her feeling of isolation.

Later that night, in Julia's bedroom, Miss Sutor, Julia and Eliza Ann were gathered for a few minutes' private talk before bed. The two girls were wearing soft wraps and had let down their hair. They were both holding ivory-backed hairbrushes, and now and then gave their hair gentle strokes with them. The conversation had centred on Rebecca.

'I am sure that she is not what she seems,' said Miss Sutor.

'You mean that she is not a poor relation?' asked Julia.

'I mean that this is not your father's first acquaintance with her. Judging by the way he looks at her, they know one another very well.' She paused significantly, but neither of the girls seemed to take her meaning. 'Very well indeed.' Still the two girls' expressions were innocence itself. 'It is my conclusion that she is your father's mistress,' brought out the governess at last.

'Father would not have a mistress!' said Julia indignantly.

'Any man would,' countered Miss Sutor, who had a low opinion of the male sex. 'Particularly with his wife away.'

'How can you suggest such a thing?' remonstrated Eliza Ann. 'Anyone can see that she is a Boville.'

'I perceive no resemblance to the Boville family at all. In any case, that need make no difference to an immoral relationship between them.'

'What a horrible idea!' Julia put her hands over her face, dropping her hairbrush with a clatter into the hearth. 'What a degradation, if it should be true, and she has been invited under our roof!'

'You mark my words,' said Miss Sutor, and malice shone in her eyes.

'I hate her,' whispered Julia. Later, when their governess had gone and left the sisters together, Julia said to Eliza Ann, 'We must destroy her.'

'Oh, Julia!'

'First we must seem not to hate her, to find out if what Miss Sutor says is true. Can we do that?'

'Pretend to be friendly?'

'Yes. Then we will plan to get rid of her. Somehow to make her go away for ever.'

It was agreed.

CHAPTER FIVE

Finding that breakfast was not until nine o'clock, Rebecca walked to Kirkby. In this period of leisure in her life, she wanted to spend time getting to know the little town, and today was market day. The long rows of rectangular windows, separated by mullions of dressed stone, seemed to her very picturesque, and she had asked Eliza Ann about them on the night before. After receiving a stare of surprise at her ignorance, she had been told that they were the windows of weavers' cottages; before the advent of the big mills in the valley, the weavers had worked their looms in the upper floor of their homes. She wanted to stand and gaze at them, and imagine the generations of Kirkby folk who had busily thrown their shuttles and worked their heddles in the light of those ranges of windows.

In her shabby clothes, no one took any notice of her, and she revelled in the strangeness of the little crooked town perched on its sloping hillside, and arrived back in plenty of time for breakfast.

After the meal, Julia summoned her to the Grey Dressing-room, where the dressmaker from Kirkby was waiting. Eliza Anne was shut up with Miss Sutor, at her lessons.

The dressmaker could supply a good black woollen cloth, quite suitable for a cloak and hood, and Julia ordered one for Rebecca.

'How can you go out in that?' she said, of the old thin pelisse. 'You could not even walk through Kirkby in that.'

Rebecca assented, meekly. The measuring for, and ordering of, the gowns took all morning, and when twelve o'clock struck, Rebecca felt as though she had already lived through two days since waking and wondered what to do in the afternoon. She seemed to have endless hours of spare time. She expected to have a further talk with her father, but he was preoccupied by his agent, a young, pleasant-looking man called Henry Camm, who joined them at the luncheon table. Giffard Boville talked to him throughout the meal, and as Julia – now that the interesting topic of Rebecca's clothes was temporarily at an end – had resumed her haughty indifference, Rebecca once more felt very much alone.

She tried to talk to the massive pillar that was Mr Machereth, but he was too much occupied with the contents of his plate; Miss Sutor refused to reply to her remarks, and merely stared at her when she spoke. Mr Camm, who looked as though he would be willing to talk to anybody, was monopolized by his employer, who did not speak through the meal to Rebecca, but looked at her sometimes with intent eyes. Rebecca felt that he noticed her every action, and heard her every word. She was not to know that Miss Sutor, Julia and Eliza Ann also realized this . . .

Eliza Ann was too far away across the table for Rebecca to try to talk to her. Again she felt the sardonic gaze of the butler, and felt uncomfortably during that meal that she would rather a thousand times have been in the noisy, crowded kitchen of the Bells' cottage than in the panelled dining-room of Broxa House.

'Thank goodness I have finished with lessons for the day,' said Eliza Ann as they left the table. 'I am going into the garden; have you seen it, Rebecca?'

'Not yet.'

'Then come with me. There will be no talking to Julia this afternoon. Did you not notice how silent she was? She will sulk until dinner time, because father is too busy to take us out driving, and we had been planning to go over to Gilbank Hall.'

'Would that make Julia sulk?'

'Don't you know?' Eliza Ann stared at her. 'Didn't father tell you one of us is to marry Edward Gilbank?'

'He said—' Rebecca felt she hardly knew Eliza Ann well enough to be forthright – 'I understood him to say – that there might be a match between Mr Gilbank and yourself.'

'Oh, me, Julia, it is all one. He and Sir Charles Gilbank want to join the estates but they cannot agree on terms. Julia wants the match for herself, because she longs to get away from here and be her own mistress, and she would like to be ruling over Gilbank Hall one day. Besides, she is the eldest. But Edward talks more to me, so I am the current favourite in father's plans.'

Rebecca was amazed at how lightheartedly Eliza Ann talked. She was leading the way out through an ancient doorway in the foot of the tower, and Rebecca was following her. The sun lit up Eliza Ann's black, glossy curls and bright face, and she accorded badly with Rebecca's ideas of a young woman who was to be disposed of in marriage as casually as one might sell a horse.

'But do you love him?' She could not help feeling deep concern, for Eliza Ann was, after all, her own half-sister, and she knew that she could grow to care for her very much.

'Love him? Who could help loving Edward Gilbank?' was the cheerful answer. 'You do not know him, Cousin Rebecca. There is not a better man in the country. Everyone loves him.'

'But you cannot marry a man just because everyone thinks well of him and your father wishes to join the estates!' cried Rebecca, far exceeding her role as a fifth cousin.

Eliza Ann looked at her curiously.

'How odd you are, Cousin Rebecca. Everyone does these things. Why, mama and papa married because their fathers wished it, because of the land. How else could an estate be built up? These things work very well.'

Rebecca longed for more information; if Giffard Boville and his wife had married to please their fathers, was the marriage happy? Somehow she thought not. But Eliza Ann needed no prompting.

'I believe,' she went on, 'that they were very happy at first; mama has often told me of it. They do not get on so well now, and of course mama's health is so bad. I shall enjoy it when it is my turn to have an establishment, and I should get on very well with Mr Gilbank. So would Julia. Everyone gets on well with him, he is so easygoing; one would never have to coax, or wheedle, as mama does when she wants something.'

The time for confidences was over; Eliza Ann seemed to recall Rebecca's inferior position, assumed a pompous little air of patronage, and began to point out the different flowers. They were walking among the formal beds at the back of the house, on the paths of yellow sand. Rebecca exclaimed at the immaculate surface, and Eliza Ann explained that the sand was brought up from the river in carts, and the gardeners raked it every morning. At the end of the garden they came to an archway in the wall and, on passing through it, saw the gardens going on down the slope towards the valley, changing in character as they did so.

'Come this way,' and Eliza Ann went over to the left, and through a yew arch, and they were suddenly in a garden of quite different character to the formal bedding of the largest garden. This was much smaller, and the plants were larger, encroaching on the air over the paths, leaning forward to display oriental blooms. 'It is the newest of the gardens. Mama wanted it, an Oriental garden.'

They walked into the centre, where a pool with water lilies was surrounded by paths and seats. Rebecca was thinking about Eliza Ann and Julia; if she had ever seen a Pekingese dog, and been a lover of them, she might have found in the sisters a parallel attraction, with their hair of black silk, their rounded foreheads, like babies', the short noses, the well-lashed wide apart eyes, the determined chins. She thought them attractive, and was looking in admiration, sideways at Eliza Ann, when she cried out. On the left – behind the short figure of Eliza Ann, rearing up among bamboo – were two dragons, of bright green.

Eliza Ann laughed.

'You're not frightened, surely! Those are terribly rare and expensive; everyone admires them. Mama bought them, and they were the inspiration for this garden. They weigh a tremendous amount. They came all the way from China. By ship, of course. Mama called them Ming and Ting.'

Rebecca was shaken, and the mindless frivolity of calling these impressive and powerful creatures such names as Ming and Ting left her wordless for a moment.

'I haven't seen anything like them before.'

'No, of course not. They are very exotic.'

'From China!'

'Come up and have a closer look at them. All the plants are Chinese or Japanese too. Mama wants a little oriental pavilion. If she sees one on the continent, she will bring it back with her.'

Rebecca, in spite of Eliza Ann's reassurances, persisted in finding something weird about the dragons; she could not like them. Yet there was something she did like in the spirit of this little garden, its opulence, its seclusion from the rest. When she was ill at ease, she thought, it would be a place to come, to hide away from the hate she felt round her in the house.

They lingered a little while, and Rebecca thought that Eliza Ann liked her, and wished they could have the prospect of growing dear to one another.

When they returned to the house, it was time for afternoon tea; Giffard Boville had had his tea sent into the library, where he was still busy with Henry Camm. Rebecca remembered that on her first day in Kirkby it had been she who shared his afternoon in the library. She wished he was not so busy today, and was surprised to see two men in the drawing-room as they entered. Mr Machereth was talking to a young, tweed-clad man with a retriever at his heels, and as Rebecca followed Eliza Ann, he turned, and Rebecca recognized her companion of the train, Edward Gilbank.

'Come over here, Mr Gilbank, for your tea,' called Julia, and there was no trace of sulkiness in her voice, it was completely welcoming. Edward, however, ignored her, and came over to greet Eliza Ann. Rebecca shrank back, shyly, and did not expect him to notice her. However, in spite of another call from Julia, he came on from Eliza Ann to where Rebecca hovered a little miserably near the wall by the door and, stretching out his hand, took her own.

'We have met before, Miss Redfearn,' he said kindly. 'Do you not remember our journey together? How do you do?'

Blushing a little at being picked out, when Julia was standing impatiently by the teapot, Rebecca thanked him, said she was well, and somehow discovered that when he turned to go to the tea table she was accompanying him on his left side. He drew out a chair and held it for her to sit down, remarking to Julia, 'Miss Redfearn and I are old friends; we have been cooped up together for hours on the Parliamentary train.'

'How is your father, Mr Gilbank?' asked Rebecca, anxious to say something to break the stony silence which she knew must follow.

'Very well; he stood the journey better than usual. He loves travelling, but it is always a worry in case it affects his health.'

'I thought it very exhilarating to travel by train,' she said boldly.

'Yes, I am sure it is a tonic, and my father finds it so. That is why we make journeys so often. But there are still the hazards – draughts – bad water – damp beds – though of course on a journey to our connections in Lincolnshire they are not so likely to trouble us, as they might on the Continent.'

After this he spoke more generally, to the rest of the company, and Rebecca was glad to fall into silence. She knew by the frown on Julia's face that she was not pleased

71

to have the poor relation noticed, and thought she read disapproval on the faces of Miss Sutor and Mr Machereth; but Eliza Ann did not seem to be worried by it, and Rebecca's heart warmed towards her even more.

Pleased to have lapsed into obscurity again, Rebecca put down her hand to Mr Gilbank's retriever, which was lying on the floor by her chair, and fondled its ears.

'I wish you would not bring Bounce in with you, Mr Gilbank,' said Julia, pettishly, noticing her action. 'Poor Floss is quite terrified of big dogs, and his feet are so muddy.'

Floss, quite unconcerned, was sitting on a cushion by his mistress, being fed with fragments of cake.

'His feet cannot be muddy today,' replied Edward Gilbank, 'as we have not had rain for a week. But I will leave him outside in future.' Julia felt that she had said the wrong thing and, being annoyed with herself in consequence, blamed Rebecca; it was all her fault, and as Edward talked to Eliza Ann, Julia hated Rebecca anew.

That evening Giffard Boville called Rebecca into the library after dinner, and talked to her, about her life, about her education, about her plans. He was kind, and not upsetting; she had been rather dreading her next talk with him, but at the end of it she felt that she knew him better, and liked him. She realized that he felt remorse for his indifference in past years. They had things in common, which she had never had in common with any other person, and she began to see that she had inherited his strong, passionate nature, and that with a different upbringing she too might have given way to temper, and dominated, as he did. There were vague, childish memories of tantrums, and how gently and firmly she had been guided out of giving way to them. Those impulses, when they came now, were controllable. She could help herself through them and, struggling with herself, remain in command.

Rebecca felt that in her father's house she was like a stranded bird, perched half-way up a wall, in some cranny;

not quite at rest, not belonging, open to every gale or gust of rain which might sweep her from this harbour; yet clinging on, longing to reach shelter, yet half longing, too, to give up the struggle and take flight.

'Did you see that nice young girl – the one we met on the train – Redfearn, wasn't it? Miss Rebecca Redfearn?' asked Sir Charles Gilbank.

'Yes, I did see her.'

'How was she? Are they being good to her? Close that door, Edward, your mother is in a draught.'

'The breeze from the garden is very pleasant, Sir Charles.'

'Nonsense, my dear. Shut it, Edward.'

Edward thought of the contrast between the pale, slender girl in black, and the two buoyant Boville girls.

'I felt rather sorry for her, father. But as far as I can see, they are not unkind. She came in with Eliza Ann, from the garden, I think. Perhaps Julia was not over-pleasant to her.'

'Huh!' snorted his father. 'I thought not. Proud, the Bovilles. Proud as Hades. It won't suit them to have a poor relation to stay. Well, it might improve our position, dear boy. Maybe Giffard Boville won't strike so hard a bargain now the world sees not all the family are top drawer. Yet – I liked her a good deal better than most young women. Neither servile nor pert. Your mother would like her. Pleasant young girl, my dear,' he yelled at Lady Gilbank.

'Yes, Sir Charles, I hear you,' answered Lady Gilbank placidly, going on with her knitting.

Sir Charles had misrepresented matters when he told Rebecca on the train that his wife was a very kind mistress to her servants. She had been so, before age and increasing infirmity made her virtually a recluse, but now the household was governed by her husband and her only son, and she had very little to do with it. Kind, though, and forbearing, she undoubtedly was, and she put up with closed doors when she wanted them open, and many other minor misarrangements of life, rather than disturb her husband by insistence. She was a little hard of hearing; but she never protested when Sir Charles treated her as though she were stone-deaf.

'Did you ask them over?'

'Yes, father. They are to drive over tomorrow.'

'I hope they bring her. Yes, I would like to make her acquaintance again. You will like her, my dear,' he shouted at his wife.

'I invited her, particularly,' said Edward, and the sight of Rebecca's face, as she held back shyly after entering the room, and of her profile as she sat beside him and rubbed Bounce's ears, was in his mind as clearly as though she were still present.

'I liked her, when we were talking in the garden,' said Eliza Ann as she sat in Julia's room later that day. 'Do you think Miss Sutor can possibly be right? I'm sure she's not. It's time Papa said I was too old for lessons, anyway.'

Julia considered.

'The way she carried on with Edward Gilbank was enough proof for me,' she said. 'Don't be deceived, Eliza Ann.'

'It wasn't carrying on.' Eliza had some sense of justice. 'You know how kind he always is to anyone poor or in trouble.'

Julia picked up Floss and caressed him, and thought with resentment of Rebecca fondling Bounce's ears.

As Rebecca went to her room, she heard a scuffle, behind a half-open door. She went over and pushed it wider, in time to see Ferguson going down the stairs, and a very flushed and dishevelled Alice emerging from the door at the top. These were the narrow spiral stairs, the original Peel tower stairs, which Alice had to use carrying the hot water.

'Was that Ferguson?' asked Rebecca, unnecessarily.

'Oh, Miss Redfearn,' Alice entreated, 'don't tell.'

'Come in here and calm down.' Rebecca was on home

ground. She might be out of her depth in dealing with Julia and Eliza Ann, but as a young girl in service she had gained enough experience to help Alice. Once in her bedroom, Rebecca made the girl put down her coal-scuttle and rest for a minute. 'Is he like that with all the maids?' she asked.

'Oh, yes, miss; he will catch us, if he can. I watch out for him as a rule. I don't want to go the way one or two others have gone.'

'Mmmm.' Rebecca did not need to hear more.

'It's good of you, miss,' said Alice after a minute. 'I'm all right now. I'd better get on. Those stairs are killing even without him lying in wait.'

'Why don't you complain to the housekeeper?' asked Rebecca.

'That wouldn't do no good, miss. She's hoping he will marry her; and she won't take notice of the way he behaves with the maids.'

'Isn't she jealous?'

'She doesn't seem to be. She knows she has something more important to him than we are.'

'What's that?' Rebecca hardly needed to ask, knowing how life was.

'Her savings,' replied Alice, and with an impish smile at Rebecca, she went out of the door.

CHAPTER SIX

Rebecca was not faring too badly in Yorkshire. A fortnight's idleness had already made her hands paler and smoother; she looked at them in amazement every morning as the change progressed. The bracing air blowing from the moors was invigorating her and bringing back the delicate colour to her face, the ample food was taking away excessive thinness. Before three weeks had gone, she was looking much better.

The gowns and cloak had arrived from the dressmaker. In good fabrics, they were all plain black, with touches of white, but even so revealed her grace so well that Miss Sutor became more bitter than ever.

'Somehow we must discredit her,' Julia said to Miss Sutor. 'But how?'

'Can we prove that she comes from a bad background? That her people are cheats, or paupers?'

'That would reflect on the Boville family, would it not?' said Julia.

'Every family has its black sheep. No distinguished family is without them.'

'I suppose there must be something like that in her background, or her branch would not have sunk so low.'

'Perhaps she is deceitful. May I suggest that you ask Mr Boville what he knows of her; cast doubt upon her character.'

'If, as you think, he is enamoured, he will admit to knowing of nothing but good, and any fault will be excused . . . Oh, what a thing it is to suspect my father of! Yet I would not have believed that he would have sat at

76

table with one as badly dressed as she was at first, or one who did not know how to hold a knife.'

They sat and pondered the problem.

'She must be proved to be false, obnoxious.'

'She could be made fun of. We could hold our knives as she does, ape her accent. That flat twang!'

'I could write to mama.'

Miss Sutor, who was enjoying Mrs Boville's absence and was putting herself forward in all kinds of ways, fussily unsurping whatever little powers she could, and generally making hay, could not encourage this.

'Oh, that would never do! How distressed she would be, may I say! Just when she is so happy with her friends. Her holiday is doing her so much good. To be recalled to this house! You know she blames its situation for her ill-health. She would feel that she was unable to go away, and would pine and grow ailing – you would blame yourself so much, dear Miss Boville – the distress such suspicion would cause her! It would be enough to send her into a decline, of itself. It is not to be thought of.'

'Probably you are right.'

'The woman is friendly with Alice; could it be said that she upsets the servants' discipline? Makes them high, and above themselves?'

'I haven't noticed that.'

'Could we make her disgrace herself? Become drunk, perhaps?'

'A very little wine is all she will take.'

'I expect she has never been used to it. If we were to prime her glass with brandy?'

'It would not please papa if she were to slide under the table!' Julia could not help laughing. 'No; the footmen or Ferguson pour the wine. We could not manage it.'

'In her coffee? Perhaps not brandy. Perhaps something to make her ill?'

But Julia was not lost to all humanity. She cried out in horror, 'What are you suggesting, Miss Sutor? You forget to whom you are speaking.'

In the end, Julia, who now felt that Miss Sutor was too dangerous an ally, thought of her own plan. She tested it out by imagining all the ways in which it might go wrong, and then, thinking it foolproof, decided that when the time seemed right she would put it into practice.

Miss Sutor was soon faced with an opportunity for empire-building, beyond her wildest dreams.

'The devil take him,' said Giffard Boville. He was at the head of the breakfast table and reading a note which the footman had handed to him.

'What is it, papa?' asked Eliza Ann, looking inquisitively at her father's black expression.

'Devil take him. Ten thousand devils take him!'

'Who, papa?'

'That damned Camm. He's fallen off his horse and broken his leg.'

'Oh, poor Mr Camm!' It was Eliza Ann again. 'Is he very bad, papa?'

'Bad enough. He can't come to work and we're nearly at quarter day.'

'Is he going to be all right? Is he very ill?' Julia frowned fiercely at her sister, trying to make her see that such questions were folly; but there was no stopping her. 'How did he do it, papa?' Giffard ignored her.

'I don't suppose there is another clerk at liberty in Kirkby.'

'But why look as far as Kirkby, dear Mr Boville?' It was Miss Sutor. 'Here – if the dear girls will spare me – is one who will be only too willing to help out in this difficulty. You will remember the credentials I brought with me. My training was excellent. I may be of a humble background, Mr Boville, but we are impoverished gentry; our blood is not inferior to your own. My training – I may say – is superior to Henry Camm's; my attainments no whit less than his.'

'Well . . .'

'Look no further, I beg! The inconvenience is nothing, may I say. If the dear girls will spare me.'

'Julia, Eliza Ann?'

'Of course, papa.'

'Very well, then, Miss Sutor. Pray come to the library, after breakfast.'

'But poor Mr Camm?' persisted Eliza Ann.

'I ought to send word. Will you be out walking, Eliza Ann, as you will not be having lessons? You could represent me. Call and see how he is. Tell him Miss Sutor is helping out for a while.'

'May I tell him how sorry you are to hear of his accident, papa?'

'Oh! Well. Say whatever you think proper.' Rebecca looking at the radiance about Eliza Ann both then and later that morning, could not help remembering her calmness, when she remarked on her possible marriage to Edward Gilbank.

Eliza Ann was carrying a basket of good things from the kitchen, jellies being a well-known cure for broken legs, and likewise fresh cream.

Now, thought Rebecca, over a visit to her father's agent, she can look like this. Is it wise, to send her? He might be confined to his bedchamber. Would Miss Eliza Ann Boville mount the stairs, regardless of propriety, and see a young man in bed? Would she – wearing that vulnerable look – sit by his bedside? Rebecca ran and slipped on her cloak and hood and set off after Eliza Ann.

'May I come with you?'

Eliza Ann was disposed to love everybody that morning. She saw herself as a Florence Nightingale, a Lady of the Lamp – or at the very least, the lady of the calves'-foot jelly. She agreed, and the two walked on together. Even Miss Nightingale needed assistance.

Henry Camm was downstairs after all, with his feet up on the sofa. One leg was strapped to a stout stick, firmly bound, and his face was interestingly white.

'Papa is so sorry to hear of your accident,' Eliza Ann cooed softly, 'and says you must not on any account worry. Miss Sutor is to be secretary, until you are quite

79

well.'

'There are some things I need to tell him, Miss Eliza Ann.'

'Write them down. Or tell me. I promise not to forget.'

The two girls spent half an hour in his company, and by the time they left Rebecca was convinced that if Henry Camm were in Edward Gilbank's shoes, Eliza Ann would not be so indifferent to the prospect of his marrying Julia, as she had appeared when they had talked about that projected match.

Henry Camm was, Rebecca thought, a very pleasant young man.

'You are not to hurry back,' Eliza Ann assured him again, as they stood by the door about to go. 'Get quite well. Do not worry.'

There is nothing more inclined to make an employee, totally dependent upon his post, worry, than to be told that he is not to hurry back; that he can be managed without; that he is to take his time in getting better. By the time he was helped to bed that night, Henry was almost feverish with anxiety.

Miss Sutor, meanwhile, was discovering that poor Henry apparently was quite incapable at his job. The accounts she declared to be a hopeless muddle, and not kept at all according to the best models. Poor Mr Camm's inferior education, of course, was to blame. He did not know, it seemed, how things should be set out, and Miss Sutor was in quite a fuss about it. Her high, sharp voice chattered along in the corner of the library, exclaiming and condemning, as her pen scratched busily. Giffard Boville grew silent. Had he then been so deceived in Henry's character? Was he then so useless? Might money have been lost by his inefficiency? Would it be necessary to let this superior person – Miss Sutor – with her manifold attainments and obvious ability – stay on to do the secretarial work, instead of pleasant, quiet Henry Camm? It seemed a pity that Miss Sutor was able to find so much wrong, when he had not suspected it . . .

The visit to the Gilbanks which had been planned for this week would have to take place without Miss Sutor. She would be too much occupied in putting matters in order. Giffard Boville felt it his duty to go and it was arranged that she should stay behind and get on with the work.

'What an opportunity, Miss Boville!' she exclaimed to Julia. 'With your father absent, I can look among his papers, and find anything relating to Miss Redfearn. It has not been possible, you know, with him always about. If there is anything incriminating, you may be sure I shall find it.' Julia agreed, but without enthusiasm. The idea of Miss Sutor scrabbling about among her father's private papers was distasteful, particularly since he would, in such perfect confidence of her trustworthiness, lock nothing away and attempt no concealment. The fine parts of his character would lay him open to this abuse of his confidence. She was enough her father's daughter to dislike this furtive spying, and the nature of the person who could think of doing it. Her own plan and projected behaviour, she thought, were justified . . .

Rebecca was discovering how much the two families saw of one another. Unless either family was away from Kirkby, they met every Sunday at church. If the weather was bad and the carriage was used, it was only a brief exchange of words in the porch after service; but if it was fine and dry enough, they used the more direct way of a footpath through the garden and the fields and into the town, through the churchyard, a walk which joined that taken by the Gilbanks, so that if they did not meet on the journey in, they would walk together on the journey back, until the parting of the ways.

Every few days Edward, usually out with the dogs, would appear at Broxa House and stay for a few minutes, or for half an hour. He might drop in to the library with a message for Giffard about fences or sheep, or into the drawing-room with something for Julia and Eliza Ann, a cutting from one of his mother's plants which they had admired, a hank of silk he had been commissioned to collect for them on a visit to Leeds or Manchester, or some other trifle of the kind which cements the relationship between neighbours.

Julia and Eliza Ann responded by calling on Lady Gilbank, tatting little mats and presents for her, taking over a sitting of eggs from their special black hens, and piecing together scraps of silk and velvet to make a smoking cap for Sir Charles.

It was the first time Rebecca had gone to Gilbank Hall; Miss Sutor's presence had on previous occasions ensured that the carriage was full. Today Giffard insisted that she go, when Eliza Ann and Julia had obviously been about to set off without her, so she too had climbed up into the carriage. Today was an arranged visit of state, not a casual dropping-in kind of call, so they were to drive for close on a mile instead of taking the few minutes' walk across the valley. They were squashed in the carriage, with three voluminous skirts. In their crinolines it would have been impossible.

Julia flatly refused to be pleasant to Rebecca, looking out over the countryside with a mulish expression and not speaking a word to anyone, but Eliza Ann was talkative and the drive was not unbearable. Once through the town they were passing through territory new to Rebecca. The hills and outcrops of rock which she had grown to recognize were all seen from a different standpoint, and she found that they were like friends, revealing different facets of themselves as they became better known. Black Crag she saw for the first time as the crest of a long wave of moor, not an isolated outcrop. Hangman's Brook, rushing down from the height of Gibbet Moor, was only seen from Broxa House as a patch of hanging woodland on the side of the hill, but close to, as the road went over a round-arched stone bridge, it could be seen as a brawling, sparkling, singing stream. It was so noisy in its tumultuous way that for a few minutes they could not hear one another's voices. It came crashing down over rocks and boulders among vivid green ferns and mosses, leaned over by slender silver birches and rowans, cleaning out a space beneath the roots of a majestic oak and laying down there a tiny beach of sand. Here still for a yard in a sudden pool between great rocks, it then went spilling through a narrow outlet and cascading down in a spray of silver, caught in a shaft of sunlight between the trees, which could only flourish in a sheltered crack in the upland like this.

It enchanted her; she longed to be free of the carriage and its occupants, to be alone by the brook and to climb up, jumping from stone to stone, wetting her feet accidentally on the wet moss-covered stones, trailing her fingers in the cool water, feeling the dappled leaf-filtered sunlight on her cheek. For the first time since Jim Redfearn's death real, thrusting, exultant life erupted in her, and she glowed with the excitement of it.

The huddle of buildings which she had seen from across the valley and which had been pointed out as Gilbank Hall, was also quite different to her expectations. The road continued past, but only as a cart track to the uplying farms. Here, the macadamed surface ran in between two outbuildings, which looked like a defensive gateway, and into a large courtyard. Ahead of them lay the main block of the Hall and on either side were ranges of stables and cottages, barns and dairies, all with their windowless backs to the world outside and their living selves showing to the courtyard. It was untidy. None of the raked walks of sand here, but a kind of daily life with lack of show which, Rebecca felt, took the visitor to its heart.

The Gilbanks' coachman came running out of his house at the side to take the horses' heads, lead them to the stables, and generally assist the Bovilles' man, and the visitors descended.

Edward Gilbank was already in the courtyard to meet them, coming to bend his head courteously over Julia's hand, then to reach out to help Eliza Ann, and finally to take hold of Rebecca's elbow to help her with the high step down to the stone flags and cobbles. She would have jumped down without a second thought, but – as once before, on the station – his manner made her feel like a queen. Ahead of them was a great stone trough, fully eight feet long and three wide, fed by the pump which stood at its head, and a cart-horse drinking there lifted his head and gazed at them in majestic wonderment, while the sparkling drops of water fell from his hairy lips on to the tiny bright mosses and liverworts of the shady side of the trough.

Julia looked still crosser and more impatient. When she was mistress here there would be no such slovenly ways. The outbuildings would be done away with, a domestic area built somewhere out of sight, and there would be none of this living hugger-mugger with one's servants. The place would be re-fronted, of course; suitably Gothic, to go with its venerable age, but showing its aristocracy. She could not understand and had no sympathy with the sentiments of the Gilbanks, which led them to cherish the home of their fathers as it had always been. The daily contact with the families around them meant to them what the clansmen had meant to the ancient Scots lairds.

Gilbanks of Black Crag, Moores of Huntingtower, Hutchinsons of Bradshaw, Bovilles of Broxa Moss, they were of their land, and at least the Gilbanks and the Moores and Hutchinsons had clung to that identification. Their world had its roots here, even if the Bovilles had defected and taken to oriental gardens and pretentious ways. Sir Charles Gilbank might love travelling; but more, he loved coming home; it was all the dearer for absence. Once here, he would start planning more forays. It was with him as with some bandit in a fastness of rock, the world outside an open invitation.

Rebecca's innermost spirit had sat apart, weeping in a high tent, for weeks. Now, with the upsurge of life, the crack of the carapace, her sorrow began gradually to change to something more bearable, and her joy in life to be renewed. It had started on the morning when she had run for her bonnet and cloak to go with Eliza Ann, on her visit to Henry Camm. Then, she had felt concerned for Eliza, and the positive need to help her. Now, standing in the courtyard of Gilbank Hall, she looked over at Julia and wished she could do something to improve their relationship. She had lived through the idea that the household disliked her, Julia in particular; she granted them the right to do so – but that it should make Julia look sullen and forbidding, even when Edward Gilbank was there! Just when she should have been showing him that she could be generous to a poor relation, to be so pettish, and make him think ill of her! It was a shame. Rebecca read Edward Gilbank's reactions with such ease that she did not realize Julia was not able to do so. She looked over at Julia and smiled gently, hoping that she would accept the gesture as a peace offering, as Edward spoke.

'Miss Boville, would you like to see our new litter, before you go indoors? My Newfoundland, Lass, has eight pups and they are just here in the kennel.' The kennel was the building at the end of the stables; a large room kept for the dogs. But Julia was not to be persuaded to be pleasant. She tossed her head.

'Oh, Mr Gilbank, you cannot wish us to go trailing in dirty kennels when we are in our new delaines, to show your mother!'

'I would like to see the pups, Julia,' said Eliza Ann.

'We will go straight in to Lady Gilbank, Eliza Ann,' and Julia led the way to the bottom of an outside stair, and began to climb it. It led up to a doorway on the first floor, and was covered in against the weather.

Eliza Ann reluctantly followed her sister, but Giffard Boville said, 'Let them go, Edward. You and I have a value for Newfoundlands, and I insist on seeing them. What about you, Cousin Rebecca?'

Rebecca looked after Julia wistfully, willing her to change her mind, to come back and be pleasant, but it was of no use. Why should she herself miss the pleasure of seeing the pups?

'I would like to,' she said.

Leaning over the partition which cut off the nursery from the antics of the other dogs, between her father and Edward Gilbank, looking and talking and laughing, Rebecca seemed a different girl to the sad stranger they thought they knew. For a few minutes she was a child again.

'Look at that littlest one! How cheeky he is! Did you see him with his brother? Oh! What sauce!'

The puppies tumbled over one another, and fought, delightfully.

When they all recollected their duty and turned to follow the two Miss Bovilles, it was with a feeling of something shared, an innocent joy in the world, and an intimacy seemed to have grown between them. Standing at the bottom of the stairway, Rebecca, laying her hand on the stone and examining it, turned to Edward.

'Why is it, Mr Gilbank, that your walls are so different to those of Broxa House? They are grey, and look hard. Yours are hard, of course, but the colour is different, and they do not feel the same.' She drew her fingers across the surface of the stone wall.

'Why, the stone is from a different quarry, that is all, Miss Redfearn. There are three types of stone in use round here. Haven't you noticed the difference in Kirkby between one type and another?'

'No,' she said, 'I haven't.' She felt as though her eyes were opened by his casual remark to a wealth of knowledge; she had not thought of stone as being hewn from the earth, in a quarry, or of there being different kinds. Stone was stone, wasn't it? But now she knew that it wasn't, and that there was more to know.

'Would you like to see our quarry? It is on our own land. We sell the stone, and there are always men working there.'

'I would like to,' answered Rebecca, but she thought that Julia would not like to, so there would be most likely no such expedition.

They followed one another up the outside stair and in

through the door, and were in a large hall, open to the heavy oak rafters, which soared to a ridge in the centre. On the left was a wide fireplace, but it was too hot for any fire today, and the hearth was filled with pine boughs which gave their redolence to the spacious room. It was furnished with heavy old furniture and pale faded carpets, but Rebecca did not have time to do more than feel the atmosphere of the place, for Edward was holding open a door on the other side of the Great Hall and waiting for her. There was another stair, down, and a room at the bottom with a murmur of conversation, long windows looking out on to a little rose garden, and, it seemed, a host of people.

Sir Charles Gilbank rose to greet them, Julia looked up with hostile eyes, Eliza Ann was talking happily to a faded-looking older woman in a high-backed carved chair, and . . . there was no one else. It was the impression of a crowd, more than the number of people. Rebecca subsided from her previous high spirits. She was introduced to Lady Gilbank, who patted a low stool beside her and said, 'Sit down, my dear. I have heard so much about you.'

Sir Charles Gilbank spoke to her across the room.

'You are looking much improved, Miss Redfearn! You will forgive an old man his freedom in saying that. Are you in a draught there? These flimsy summer dresses you young ladies wear are not much protection against cold winds, and in a room of this aspect we get them from the moors.'

'It is a very warm day, sir. I do not feel any unpleasant draught. It is welcome.'

'Well, well.' Seeing Rebecca, his mind went back to his journey from Lincolnshire. 'When we met you before, Edward and I were on our way back from a visit to my step-sister Lady Marwood; you would not have heard of her, I daresay. But we have had a letter this week. Where is that letter, Edward? Oh, here it is. I wonder if there is any news which will interest you, Miss Redfearn, as you are from that country. They went to a ball in Stamford. Do you know Stamford? No. Maria, the eldest, is engaged – that is just a family matter; but maybe you have heard of the young man. Do you know Cross at all, Miss Redfearn?' Rebecca could not answer; she inclined her head, and Sir Charles went on. 'It is a pretty village as Lincolnshire villages go, though not to be compared with Yorkshire. Maria is engaged to the curate at Cross, Simon Lloyd, but you will not know him, I suppose. They are planning to marry next year.'

Rebecca said nothing.

'Miss Redfearn, I am sure you are in a draught. I am positive that I saw you shiver just then. Edward, we will have the door into the garden closed.' The rest of the company had to put up with losing the stream of rose-scented air from the garden and Sir Charles had achieved his objective of closing the door. He had done his best, he felt, to make Rebecca feel welcome and at home, so he turned his attention to Giffard Boville.

Rebecca had shivered. She had shivered as though a breath of air from some underground vault had struck her. The shock of the news now seemed to turn her body to ice. As she sat on the low stool, she bowed her head and turned it away from the centre of the room, and looked at her fingers. They looked white, and she could not stop them trembling. There had never been any real hope that Simon Lloyd would marry her, but to hear that he was to marry someone else was a blow. It was so final. The only thing more final would have been to hear that he was already married. Lady Marwood's daughter Maria! It was suitable. She recognized the suitability, the inevitable quality of it. But it was as though the rosiest memories of life in Cross were suddenly hidden from her by a black shadow, as though even her treasure of memory was transmuted and lost. Sir Charles might have stopped the gentle garden breeze from blowing on to her, but she felt chilled to the bone, and longed for solitude to pass through that time alone.

When, feeling that she was behaving in a very bad-

mannered way, Rebecca made herself look up at Lady
Gilbank and try to speak, she found that her voice was too
soft to be audible to the older woman and she did not feel
equal at that moment to the effort of making it shriller.
Julia's piercing tones and Eliza Ann's high ones could be
heard in every particular, so Rebecca fell back thankfully
into silence. Lady Gilbank made up in nods and smiles for
their lack of communication on other levels and presently
Rebecca found herself an occupation, untangling Lady
Gilbank's ball of thread, which meant that she could keep
her head bent and stay out of the conversation. Somehow,
the visit passed. Of all the company, Edward Gilbank was
the only one to see that something troubled her.

Julia agreed with the idea of an outing to the quarry, to
see stone being cut. Everyone was surprised that she did;
they could not know that the idea had at once sprung into
her head of falling against Rebecca and sending her over
the edge (everyone knew that quarries had dangerous
edges) or, alternatively, she thought that Rebecca might
slip on some treacherous pathway. Her former plan could
wait and be used if this failed. While they had no Miss
Sutor to consider – she would certainly be against the idea
– an outing to the quarry might very well take place.

When they were home and she was alone in her room,
Julia bumped up against pieces of furniture, practising how
it might be done, and, with both her little hands outspread,
pressed against her cliff-like wardrobe. Not to hurt
Rebecca too much, of course. (Unless accidentally . . .
more than one meant . . .) Just to frighten her, to make
her go away and let it seem as though she had never been.
There were times when Julia was afraid of herself, that she
could suspect her father and hate Rebecca. What was this
creature that she was turning into? Miss Boville had never
been like this before. Looking back on herself, she knew
that she was not perfect; she could even, at times, agonize
over her faults. Now she knew, and had to admit to
herself, that she was giving in to her worst traits of
character. It was as though there were two Julias. Often

she did not wish to be wicked, was frightened by what she was contemplating, and even began to wonder if Rebecca's visit was not quite innocent, and if she did not rather like her. She was a gentle presence in the jangling house, and now that she looked more presentable, often had a glow about her, as though to be alive was a pleasure, which was infectious. Not that it had been very noticeable since the visit to the Gilbanks; she had been very withdrawn since then.

But the bad Julia would come up again, as though she were a presence whispering in the good Julia's ear, and in no time she would feel all bad, and give the chest of drawers such a shove – it could no longer be described as a push – that if it had been Rebecca on the edge of a quarry, there would have been no hope for her.

Henry Camm was improving slowly and hoped to be soon back at work. Eliza Ann and Rebecca had kept him well supplied with books to read and good things to eat, and had been careful not to tell him what Miss Sutor was saying about him.

When they had returned from their visit to Gilbank Hall, Miss Sutor had drawn Julia aside, in an important manner, and spent a long time whispering in her ear, even though no one else was within earshot. There had, it seemed at the end of it, been nothing to indicate any guilty connection between Giffard Boville and Rebecca; no revealing letters, or mysterious payments to an unknown bank. After taking an hour to narrate it, it amounted to the fact that Miss Sutor had found nothing but was as convinced as ever.

Julia burned with shame at this way of treating her father and had to convince herself by repeating over and over her many imagined proofs and grievances, that she was in the right to have allowed it.

Retribution, however, was on its way to Miss Sutor, and arrived on Quarter Day, when all the Boville tenants, gaitered and bewhiskered, had arrived and were standing in the hall waiting to go in and pay their rent.

'Anderson of Cow Wath,' Giffard Boville said to Miss

90

Sutor, after shaking hands with him and spending a couple of minutes chatting about foot-rot.

Miss Sutor, in a sharp, important voice, announced the amount of the account due.

'I beg your pardon, missus,' said Anderson of Cow Wath, towering above her with the top of his head a startling pale pink and white where he had removed his hat, 'but yon's noan right. I know what I'm due to pay, and it's no more and no less. I know to a farthing. Here it is, right and tight, done up in its bag.'

'Yes, Miss Sutor,' said Giffard Boville. 'Anderson's right. You must be looking at the wrong man. This is Anderson of Cow Wath, not Anderson of Sycklebrook.'

'I have it here,' said Miss Sutor loftily, and her eyes snapped at him.

Giffard Boville went round and looked over her shoulder at the account book, and said, 'Well, you've got it down, Miss Sutor, but that doesn't make it right. There must be a mistake somewhere. Please write down what he's paying, and you can find out what's wrong after.'

This was not going to prove so easy, as the morning wore on. One tenant after another protested about his rent, or the charge for this or that; and as the rent had been the same in many cases for several years, Giffard Boville knew they were right, and Miss Sutor's book-keeping, some-how, inexplicably, wrong.

There was one tenant who agreed hastily with the amount asked and fumbled furtively in his pocket on drawing out his rent bag, so that Giffard was forced to think that this man was being let off lightly and had been extracting a guinea or two from the proper amount. Generally, it was one long protest, and by the time everyone had been seen, Giffard was exhausted. Never, while Henry Camm had been doing the books, had there ever been a problem! Nothing like the murmurings in the hall as one disgruntled farmer went out and told those waiting what had happened. Nothing like the stubborn looks on the faces which were usually so forthright. This was going to be a black mark against the name of Boville, not just for a day, but in these Yorkshire folk's minds, for ever. Giffard began to sweat slightly, although the library was always cool, and looked in anger at Miss Sutor, who was as sharp and pert as ever.

'You haven't got the slightest idea,' he said when the tenants had gone. Usually there were cheerful goodbyes, promises of 'see you at harvest', and gruff shouts of farewell. Nothing of that today. Giffard was standing leaning on his clenched fist on the table, looking like a thundercloud. 'You haven't the slightest idea how to do book-keeping.'

Miss Sutor bridled.

'Mr Boville, all morning you have supported those stupid farmers against me. I have worked like a slave on your estate books, may I say. That Camm had left them in such a pickle they were nearly impossible to correct.'

'I never had any trouble on a Quarter Day with Henry Camm.' It was easy to believe that Miss Sutor would stand unconcerned in the path of an avalanche; she certainly appeared unconscious of her employer's emotions.

'I have done my best for you and never complained, Mr Boville.' Her tone was self-righteous.

'Your best—' he was keeping his temper under control, but the deadly quiet was creeping into his tones – 'is not good enough. And I am doing the complaining.'

'I am not going to be spoken to like that.' She rose to her feet. 'I'll have you know I'm doing you a favour by stopping, against my own interests,' went on Miss Sutor, shaking all her little ornaments to give emphasis to her words. 'Lady Sayers has asked and better asked me to go to her as governess to her children. I could have a post there tomorrow, much better than this. It is only love for dear Miss Eliza Ann which has kept me here so long.'

'She is too old for a governess,' said Giffard. 'At seventeen a girl should be thinking of marrying, not be still cooped up with a fussy old hen, with no more brains than one.'

'Oh!' cried Miss Sutor, for the first time looking directly at him and seeing the expression on his face. 'You make it impossible to stay!'

'Good,' replied Giffard, and his tone was biting. 'Go as soon as you like. Lady Sayers is welcome.'

'Oh! No gentleman would speak so! I'll not stay another minute!' And in fact, though she hovered a little inside the door to see if he would change his mind, there was no help for it. With a shake, a jingle, and a crash of the door behind her, Miss Sutor gave up her post at Broxa House.

There was much apparent distress at losing their governess both from Julia, who had long been out of her control, and from Eliza Ann, who had been longing to be free. Damp handkerchiefs were flourished pathetically and there were many promises of writing frequent letters. But when the wagonette had driven off to the station, the two Boville girls turned back into the house with cheerful faces and there was an air of holiday. Rebecca felt that a bad influence had left the house, and Julia was quite pleasant to her over dinner. If only there could be kindness between them, Rebecca reflected. If, for however short a while, they could be like sisters to one another! But the rapprochement was not to last.

'Rebecca!' shouted Giffard Boville. His voice rang up the well of the stairs and reached her even through the thicknesses of both the landing door and that of her bedroom. Hastily, she put the last pin in her hair and ran downstairs. His voice had sounded furious with impatience.

'Rebecca,' he said more quietly, soothed by her quick appearance, 'I need some help. That wretched woman has made a fine muddle of things and Henry Camm won't be back yet. You can do arithmetic; can you write a fair hand?'

'I think so, sir.'

'Then you can help me. I keep copies of all the letters I write, and somebody has to copy them out.'

93

She had been at leisure long enough to enjoy some occupation. Giffard had tired of having somebody sitting in a far corner of the library and keeping up a fusillade of sharp remarks; he sat Rebecca down next to him at one of the long tables and told her what to do, expecting her to do as she was bid, meekly and docilely, and then checking to make sure that she had done it to his satisfaction. On that first morning she was merely doing as he had asked, copying letters. She wrote a very clear script and he found that she did it well – there being many ways in which a copyist can make a mess of so simple a task as copying a letter. He felt paternal pleasure in having her there, working beside him, and there was an unusual air of serenity in the library. At lunchtime, finding out where Rebecca had been all morning, Julia was bitterly jealous, but Eliza Ann was grateful for her father's good humour. Giffard announced that neither he nor Rebecca would have time to take part in the expedition to the quarry, there was too much to catch up on; Julia and Eliza Ann must go alone . . .

Rebecca had loved school and been sorry to leave, and as the days went by she found that all her skills were needed. At first she felt very rusty and afraid of angering Giffard by making mistakes, but as she saw that he was pleasantly surprised by her ability, she grew more confident and by the time that Henry Camm appeared to resume his duties, her father was reluctant to give her up.

'Miss Redfearn will go on helping me for the present, Camm. Before your accident, you were always complaining that there was never enough time to do all the supervision out of doors. All that side of the work has had to be left. You can catch up on it while Miss Redfearn is with us.'

It was not only copying his letters; Rebecca found that an estate, with coal mines, and public duties in addition, demanded all kinds of paper work. Her father made no allowance for inexperience and if she did not understand at once what was wanted he soon showed a little testiness, but once she realized what was wanted and carried it out, he would grow calm and show that he was pleased. Her intelligence was equal to his own and she had the adaptability of youth, so she took care that she remembered her instructions and kept her wits about her.

As the days grew into weeks their harmony in working together grew, until it became a positive pleasure for Rebecca to think each morning that she would be working in the library after breakfast. Giffard equally looked forward to it. He could not remember when the necessary work had been so rewarding. If often they talked of other things, apart from the day-to-day affairs, if he found himself going over to the bookshelves, reaching out for a favourite book, and reading a passage out to her, or showing her on a map some neighbouring spot about which he had been telling her one of the old legends of the countryside, then did it matter? If he tried to freeze her marrow with stories of boggarts and bogies, or amuse her with one of the local folk-tales, spoken in his unerring version of the local dialect (which he could speak when he chose as well as any of his tenants), then did it matter, if the work was always done, just the same? One day soon he would have to do without her blue gaze and parted lips, waiting breathless to hear the point of some anecdote, and her face, soft with compassion at the tale of some old tragedy. One day soon this companionship with the daughter who was coming to mean most to him, would end.

Julia was intent on ending it.

While Rebecca was gradually becoming an accepted part of the household, the butler, Ferguson, could not accustom himself to it. When he and the housekeeper, Mrs Douthwaite, were alone, sharing their pot of tea after a meal in the servants' hall, they would sometimes talk about Rebecca. Before she came, their talk had been mostly of their plans for the future. When they had saved enough they were planning to marry and set up in business in a little country public house. Ferguson was growing tired of subservience; he looked forward to the time when he would only have to be servile for his own gain, and could just as well be surly if he wished.

Since Rebecca's coming, however, her sudden rise had become an obsession for him. People who appear to change class are often resented by those who are left behind, and he longed in some way to show her that he still regarded her as inferior, just as inferior as she had been on that day when she arrived at the front door. His thoughts revolved around her to an extent which was in danger of undermining his concern for his own position and future. In one way he was used to dominating over the maids; he took what freedoms he thought fit.

One night, when Rebecca went to bed, she was surprised by seeing him on the landing.

'Will you come and look at this a minute, miss?' he asked, holding open the door of the room which was used to store the hip baths, when they were not in use. She went in, quite unsuspecting, thinking there was some minor mischief such as mice, and at once was gripped strongly in his arms, and he was attempting to kiss her.

'Oh!' she cried, pulling herself away, and slapped him across the face. His reaction surprised her. He was one of those men in whom the satisfaction of lust is so close to the infliction of violence that the two are almost merged into one. The look in his eyes seemed to change in a moment to the glare of hate, and he gripped her wrists.

'What!' he hissed. 'After the looks you've given me at meal times this week?'

'Let me go!' She shook her arms and broke her wrists free of his grasp. 'I can't think what you mean. I don't recall looking at you. How dare you do this?'

'All the servant maids are mine if I want them,' he said.

'Well, I'm not. I will tell your master.'

'You won't, or I shall tell him you've asked me into your room, before now.'

'Oh! Oh!' cried Rebecca again, and somehow got out of the room and away from him. 'He needn't think he can treat me as he treats poor Alice,' she thought to herself, rubbing her wrists. She intended to tell Giffard the next morning. But then – suppose he believed Ferguson against her? Rebecca had been brought up to know that if she had been a servant girl in Broxa House, Ferguson's word would have been taken against hers. What had her own father called her: a servant girl, and the daughter of one. Her father was coming to mean very much to her. Soon, inevitably, she would be leaving. Did she want to spoil their time together with the sordid story of this incident? The blush rose in her cheek at the very idea. There was humanity in it too. If she accused him and was believed, Ferguson might well lose his post and not be given a reference. He might be unable to find another post. Was she to be responsible for that? All for something she felt quite confident she could deal with herself? She had had to deal with unwelcome advances before. She decided to keep silence.

Ferguson could not sleep that night. He wondered what Rebecca would do, and at times dimly saw that he had acted stupidly. At other times he thought of her nearness. He was relieved when he realized during the following morning that she was going to take no action against him, but it made him despise her more than ever. Because his senses had been aroused, by the afternoon he was in pursuit of Alice.

Alice should not have been on the first-floor landing at that particular time of day – the bedrooms were finished while the family were at breakfast, that was the invariable rule – and no maids went into them after that until early evening. She should certainly have been nowhere near the landing or the corridor, and Rebecca was in the garden with Eliza Ann. The south wing should have been quite deserted as Julia went into Rebecca's room. It would have been, if Alice, trying to escape from Ferguson, had not run up the back stairs, desperate for refuge, and slipped into the corridor just as Julia walked into the Striped Bedroom, quite confident of being unobserved.

97

She was observed, and Rebecca was told as she was dressing for dinner. Alice sobbed over the latest episode in her sad little saga, and something was known to be afoot . . .

After dinner Julia took advantage of Rebecca's absence in search of a workbasket to tell Giffard that valuables were missing from her room. It was a very simple little plan. Julia was not hardened in crime. She was like any other creature with an intruder in the nest, anxious to be rid of them and in quiet possession once more; but she was not criminal enough to think of anything more subtle than pushing Rebecca into a quarry or accusing her of stealing. She had nerved herself at last to carry this out.

'That woman has taken things from my room,' she said to her father. 'I want you to search the Striped Bedroom to see if they can be found. She may be some sort of poor relation, but we should disown her. As well as being a beggar she is a thief.' So far she had proceeded almost in a breath with her accusation. Then she paused and another thought rose to the surface. 'She is setting you against your own daughters.'

Giffard had looked appalled when she commenced her attack; now both he and Eliza Ann looked surprised. Relations between Giffard and his two Boville daughters had never seemed more tranquil than in the weeks that had passed since Rebecca began to spend her mornings in the library.

Rebecca came back into the drawing-room and everyone looked in her direction. Julia went up to her.

'Thief! Thief!' Carried away by her own drama, her voice rose and she spoke in Rebecca's face. 'You have been stealing from me.'

'I?'

'Don't deny it. Nothing was ever stolen until you came.'

'What have you lost?'

'Things I inherited as the eldest daughter . . . things which were mine by right!'

Rebecca went white, and looked over at Giffard. Eldest

daughter? Then a flush swept up over her cheeks. What did Julia mean? Did she mean that she would have liked to help Giffard with his morning work in the library? Surely not. She knew both of them well enough to realize that in the space of one morning the two haughty spirits would have been in conflict.

'I don't know what you mean,' she said defensively.

'You see that blush, papa?' cried Julia, who had worked herself up into a passion. Her old nurse would have known how to deal with the situation. 'Let us go now and search her room. I want my property.' Rebecca remembered what Alice had seen and began to guess what was coming.

'Do you mind, Cousin Rebecca?' asked Giffard, looking helplessly at the nearly hysterical Julia. 'It would be the quickest way to settle this.'

'Of course.' Rebecca could do nothing to stop it. The four of them went to Rebecca's room, leaving Mr Machereth alone. After his dinner it would take more than his niece's hysterics to take him from the fire and leave his coffee and brandy glass behind.

Once in the Striped Bedroom, Julia ran about in a frenzy. She tossed the contents of drawers on to the floor and tipped out things from the glove and hat boxes in which Rebecca's new possessions had come from Kirkby. At last she snatched Rebecca's workbasket from her hand and tipped that upside-down too.

'Look at this!' she almost screamed, her face red, and her eyes wild; she looked beside herself.

Out of the workbasket, in front of Giffard's appalled eyes, and those of Rebecca and Eliza Ann – for they were all standing as though turned to stone – came a crumpled piece of lace, and from the glove box, a disc of carved ivory.

'The collar of coralind Venetian point lace,' cried Julia, 'which has been in the family for three hundred years, priceless, given to me on my seventeenth birthday! The collar that was Marie Giffard's, the friend of Queen Anne of Denmark. And this is the ivory mirror-case, most

99

cherished possession of the Bovilles down the centuries, brought back from the Crusades, they say, which mama coaxed you to give to me, papa, because I love it so. Here,' snatching something up from among Rebecca's petticoats, which had been thrown down higgledy-piggledy on the bed, 'is the glove of Lettice Boville who so bravely defied Cromwell's troopers in the Civil war.'

Julia had prepared her speech well, or she could not have brought it out while she was so carried away by temper. She had chosen those treasures of the Boville family which had special significance for Giffard. When he had not grown bitter against his wife and against his fate in life . . . when the old tower had not been made grandiose . . . there had been a time when he loved to take his little girls upon his knee and tell them the old proud stories of the Bovilles, showing them the tracery of the lace, the exquisite carving of the ivory, and the sad beauty of the faded satin glove.

'I have never seen them before,' said Rebecca in a small voice. It was chilling to see what depths Julia would descend to in her dislike, and to witness that pretty face distorted and the little hands clawlike, pouncing. She picked up the lace collar and spread it out in her fingers with awe. It was so fine she would have needed a magnifying glass to see all its beauties, which had once been worked under the clear Italian skies by young women singing the pretty lace songs as they wove fairy-like thread with their shining needles into this intricate design resembling coral. 'I have never seen this before,' she repeated.

'Then how do you account for it being in your workbasket?' asked Giffard, his voice reluctant.

'As it happens I haven't used this workbasket today. I keep my knitting in it, which I have been working in the evenings while Miss Boville reads aloud. It is the first time it has been in my hands since the day before yesterday, because last night, if you remember, Mr Boville, you were trying to teach me to play chess. Even if I had picked it up, I would very likely not have noticed this lace. It was right at the bottom, I saw that when Miss Boville uptipped the basket; it was the last thing to fall out.'

'This was among your gloves,' sneered Julia, holding out the ivory mirrorcase. 'How do you account for it?'

'I can only account for it by thinking that someone put it there to make it appear that I took it.' Rebecca felt that all this was beyond her. Julia had the advantage. Her father would believe Julia, and not herself. How could it be otherwise? The anticipation of defeat bowed her shoulders. The thought of how much Julia must hate her, saddened her expression.

'Pick up your things, Julia, and take them away,' said Giffard. 'Let us go back to the drawing-room.' He turned and led the way. Once back, they stood in an inert group, wondering what was to happen next. When Julia returned from restoring the treasures to her room, Giffard asked Rebecca what she had to say. She had decided to fight back, but unwillingly. She asked that Alice, the maid, be questioned, as to whether she had noticed anything unusual taking place, or had seen the treasures during her routine care of the bedrooms. Giffard rang the bell, and Alice came in. Rebecca turned to the fire, and went to stand near Mr Machereth.

'I will take no part in this,' she said. 'Will you ask, please, Mr Boville?'

'You take care of the bedrooms, I believe,' said Giffard to Alice, while Julia stood with her head high, and Rebecca with hers bowed. 'Have you noticed any disturbance in them lately? Anything out of place? Miss Boville found that one or two items of value were missing from her room.'

'I wouldn't touch anything I weren't supposed to touch,' said Alice indignantly.

'We weren't suspecting you. Just asking if you saw anything suspicious.'

'Oh!' cried Alice, enlightened. 'Was that what you were doing in Miss Redfearn's room, Miss Boville? Looking for something you'd lost? If you'd said, I could have helped you look for it.'

'Whatever do you mean?' said Julia, looking self-conscious.

'Just now we have all been in Miss Redfearn's room,' said Giffard.

'Oh, not just now, sir, I don't mean. This afternoon about three o'clock it was. I saw Miss Boville go into the Striped Bedroom, and heard her opening the drawers.'

'Today?'

'About three o'clock, sir. I told Miss Redfearn when I was helping her dress, that Miss Boville had been in, but I didn't know what it was about. Do you want me to go on looking, miss? What is it that's been lost?'

'You knew this, Rebecca?'

'Yes.'

'Why didn't you stop all this performance before? Alice, you can go. It is all right! The things which were missing have been found.'

Rebecca forced herself to speak, but without looking up from the carpet.

'I didn't know why Miss Boville had gone into my room. I didn't know what she was meaning when she called me a thief. How could I have stopped everyone going upstairs, or her turning everything upside down? There was no time, and I didn't know the lace and glove and mirror case were there.'

Giffard turned on Julia.

'Is this how you treat your relative and guest? I think you had better apologize at once.' But Julia did not apologize. Chagrin at the failure of her plot, reaction after her state of high tension, even sorrow that she had played such an unseemly part and was now disgraced in the eyes of her father . . . all this was too much for her. Her eyes brimmed over, and she buried her head in her hands and sobbed as though her heart would break. Rebecca remained by the fire, and Mr Machereth had long since fallen asleep. Eliza Ann and Giffard Boville, after hesitating for a few seconds, went to her, put their arms round her and comforted her with Eliza Ann's eau de Cologne.

'You had better get her to bed,' Giffard said quietly to Eliza Ann. 'Order a hot drink. Don't leave her. She will sob herself out, then fall asleep. Do your best for her, there's a good girl. I will come up presently.'

When the younger girls had left the room, Giffard went over to Rebecca.

'Can you forgive her? I had no idea she felt such dislike for you, or that she would do such a thing. I am ashamed of her.'

'She's young,' replied Rebecca. It seemed to her that eons of time separated her and her half-sister, instead of the two years. 'But what if Alice hadn't happened to see her? She isn't supposed to be around the bedrooms at that time of day. It was very out of the way that she went there. Or she might not have remembered seeing Julia. In that case you would have condemned me, and I would have been considered a thief for ever.'

The breakfast table next day was an uncomfortable place. Everyone ate in silence, except, at the end of the meal, Giffard, who was reading a letter from his wife. He announced aloud that Mrs Boville was finding the Italian climate so beneficial that she proposed to go on to Rome, perhaps for several months. Julia and Rebecca both wondered how they could stand it, if they had to go on facing one another every day, for much longer.

103

It was a few nights later that Julia was awoken from her first sleep by her Maltese terrier, Floss. Floss was never far from Julia, by day or night. He had a basket in her bedroom, but usually preferred to sleep curled up on her bed, sometimes near her shoulder, almost on the pillow, sometimes in a ball at her feet. The weather was still warm, and that night Floss had been restless; he had been too hot on the bed, and had jumped down to the floor, and there stretched out at full length on the coolness of the floorboards, until he decided he was too far from his beloved mistress, and returned to lie on the corner of the sheet.

The smoke had woken him from his unsettled dozing. It had curled into the room, over the top of the door, and gradually mushroomed downwards; but long before it had filled the top half of the room, Floss was scrabbling and pawing at his mistress, whining desperately, and Julia, difficult to rouse from her first slumber, was murmuring and beginning to wake.

By then it was perhaps three-quarters of an hour – perhaps an hour – since Mr Machereth, who slept in the Spotted Bedroom, between Rebecca in the Striped and Julia in the Grey – had finally gone to sleep. He had enjoyed his dinner; he always enjoyed his dinner. He had enjoyed his coffee and brandy, and his game of chess with Giffard Boville, and sitting by the drawing-room fire. The Bovilles, who owned a mine working one of the finest seams of coal in the area, were never without their evening fire, except in the very hottest weather. The mine had been part of Mrs Boville's marriage portion, and she liked to see the brilliant black lumps and clear flames, and reflect that the mine gave her her hold over Giffard – for most of their income came from it, more than from the hill farms with their thin soil. Those evening fires were one of the comforts of Mr Machereth's life. His life was full of comforts: the sun in the garden, which he would follow from one sheltered seat to another, the fire in the evening, the breakfast, luncheon, tea and dinner, so plentifully provided at Broxa House, the nightly game of chess with Giffard Boville, then the soft bed, the ample supply of pillows and blankets. He relished each one of his pleasures, as it came his way, indolent, supine, harmless. That night he had lain for a long time. Mr Machereth, proceeding slothfully from one greedy pleasure to another, was not harmless. He lay propped up on his pillows in his big bed, his huge frame relishing the comfort of it, his mind musing over the slow delights of the day, and looking forward with more pleasure to the coming time when he would drift into sleep, and know the sleep of the just for nine delicious hours of slumber. His candle was standing on a low table, between the bed and the window, its golden flame steady, its fat, white, expensive column translucent with light for the top inches. The table was beautifully made, well polished, a delight to the eye, and the light shone on the richly patterned wallpaper, the upholstered chaise longue, the heavy brocade curtains, the matted floor, giving everything the effect of subdued richness.

Even in his drowsy, contented state, Mr Machereth could not drift into sleep and leave the candle burning, but he had been lying for an hour gazing at it and lacking the inclination to get out of bed. Once again he decided to ask for the table to be moved nearer so that he could reach it without effort. He had been meaning to ask that, every day for months. With a shadow of discontent, he sighed, and at last did what he so often did, reached out a massive arm for one of his spare pillows, and hurled it at the candle. The light was extinguished, and Mr Machereth closed his eyes.

The candle, knocked over on to the chaise longue stuffed with horsehair, did not instantly go out. Horsehair smoulders, burning slowly, with smoke that fills a room, minute by minute, collecting near the ceiling, first thinly, then with increasing density until it becomes a cloud, spreading out, drifting over the whiteness of the limewashed ceiling, to the walls, to over the window, to over the door, then downwards, over the moulding, to the picture rail, down, in an impalpable cloud, to the top of the door, and there, finding a space through which its softness can escape. It crept from the room to collect first under the corridor ceiling, then, edging down to the moulding, and the picture rail, and the top of the doors, soft, grey, remorseless, entering first the Striped Bedroom where Rebecca lay sleeping, then, a little later because the door was positioned a little further away, the Grey Bedroom, where, stretched at full length, Floss was twitching in his fidgety sleep. By the time he had fully awoken Julia, even the Grey Bedroom, the last to be affected, seemed to be full of smoke.

The whole of the south wing of Broxa House had been gradually permeated.

Julia stumbled out of bed, and at first could not realize what had happened. Half dazed, and clutching Floss, she went out on to the corridor. The little dog was excitedly licking her throat and uttering tiny sharp whines and barks of dismay. Julia had no experience of fire or smoke outside their usual confines. Her first sensation was the eeriness of it: uncanny quiet, like the quiet of a snowfall which deadens footsteps. In the same way the smoke produced a hush, and confused her, so that even though she had many times gone along this short corridor in the darkness without a hesitation, now her steps were unsure. At the door of Mr Machereth's room she choked, and knew that the smoke was thicker; she stumbled past and opened the door leading out on to the main staircase, connecting the wing to the body of the house.

It was a stout, well-fitting door, and the staircase was lit by shafts of moonlight coming in at the windows; the air there was clear. Julia never knew afterwards why she closed that door again, and so, though she did not realize it, confined the smoke to one area. There was some thought in her mind – more instinctive than conscious – that upstairs in the ancient tower were the rooms of the women servants. While it did not form itself into words, there was in her mind an image of smoke sweeping up through that stairwell, and the helpless screams of the trapped.

She shut the door and, half bending, crouching against the wall, crept to the door of Rebecca's room. She could have gone through the stairs door into the main body of the house, shut it after her and raised the alarm; she did not. At that moment Rebecca was entirely in her power. For weeks she had been hating her, planning her disgrace. She had accused her of theft, ignored her, not spoken to her. Now, standing outside Rebecca's door, she could have abandoned her to be smothered in her sleep by the insidious smoke. Better than a push in the quarry . . .

Julia bent, choking, near the wall for a tiny space of time, trying desperately to wake enough to think. Rebecca's eyes seemed to be looking at her out of the darkness, sweet, sad eyes, unflinching.

The idea of abandoning Rebecca to her fate fled from her mind. Without any more hesitation, she felt across the door of Rebecca's room until she found the handle, turned it and flung herself inside and on to the bed, reaching out with both hands for Rebecca.

Rebecca woke to Julia's sharp shaking, feeling that she was in the grip of a nightmare. Floss scrabbled at her, and Julia's voice, half weeping, was in her ears.

'Cousin Rebecca! Cousin Rebecca! You're not dead, are you? Say you're not dead . . .' Julia's face was pressed to her cheek, wetting it with tears. 'Quickly, oh! quickly! you will know what to do . . . oh, Cousin Rebecca!'

'What is it? Oh, Lord!' Rebecca's arm went round Julia, and she opened her eyes into the tangle of the other girl's hair.

'Come quickly. There's a fire somewhere; there's smoke. Quickly, oh, quickly! Help me! What are we to do?'

'Oh, Lord, what's happening . . . Julia . . . Julia . . . oh, my dear . . .' For a moment the two girls clasped each other in their arms, then Julia half dragged Rebecca out of bed and held on to her, supporting the girl drugged with smoke out to the landing, where they collapsed together into a heap. The smoke, disturbed, thickened in some places, thinned in others, baffling, deadly, spreading downwards, slowly. The smouldering chaise longue was getting hotter, and at any time the temperature would rise to the point where, at the least addition of new air, flame would flash across the room, engulfing curtains, reaching Mr Machereth's bed. It only needed a fresh current of air; and the danger would change into one more rapid, more immediate, if not more deadly . . .

Near the floor on the landing the air was better, and Rebecca began to recover from the effects of the smoke. She and Julia were still clinging to one another, and now and then murmuring each other's names, and in the midst of peril they felt strangely happy; the enmity was over, and if they were to die, they would die together . . .

'You've saved my life,' said Rebecca, wondering, and then, rousing a little to action, 'what's making all the smoke? We must do something. Where's Mr Machereth?'

'Uncle Machereth!' choked Julia. She remembered that the smoke was thickest near his door. She remembered wanting Rebecca urgently, wanting her help – to do what? It had been on contact with the thicker concentration of smoke near Mr Machereth's door that the girls had collapsed on to the floor; they were huddled near his door now. If it was worst there, his room must be the seat of it. He was in danger, and might die if they did nothing.

'You're supposed to wrap a wet cloth round your face, when there's smoke,' Rebecca whispered. 'There's some water in my jug.'

'My room's clearer.'

They crawled to Julia's room, which was clear enough for them to stand upright, dipped two of her petticoats into the water from the washstand, then wrapped them round their heads and faces.

'We'll have to get him out,' Julia had said, but they had already agreed that without words. They went back, once more crawling along the short corridor, and, reaching up to the doorhandle of the Spotted Bedroom, opened the door. There was an inrush of the clearer air of the landing, and flame shot across the room, seeming to explode into the air. At the four corners of Mr Machereth's bed, the curtains burst into flame, and the air became too hot to breathe.

In the darkness, heat, smoke and flame, the girls felt with their hands over the surface of the bed, pushed back the bedclothes and, still kneeling on the floor beside the bed, shook the stout old man and tried to wake him. They pulled at his nightshirt and, desperate, gasping, at the end of their endurance, he was pulled out of bed to the floor and on top of them. They all lay in a pile, the two girls gasping and choking. Mr Machereth had been overcome by the smoke, and lay tumbled, an unconscious body. Neither Julia nor Rebecca could have spoken. Without a word they acted together, pushing and pulling him along the floor, and dragging him between them through the doorway.

Rebecca pulled the bedroom door shut after them. She wanted to shut out the glare of that leaping flame, to cage it, to confine it, to stop herself seeing it. Julia opened the door on to the staircase, and together they pulled him through, into the pale penetrating moonlight, and on to the gleaming bare oak boards. Floss, who had almost been forgotten in those last minutes, had been cowering in the short corridor, miserable and unhappy. He came through the door with them and, as Julia closed it again, he at once felt better. On the landing he began to frolic about, barking shrilly, while the girls slumped silent on either side of Mr Machereth. They thought he was dead.

'I'll fetch papa,' gasped Julia, crawling away, then, realizing that here there was no smoke and she could stand freely, she pulled herself up by the banisters on to her trembling legs and went off towards Giffard's room, leaving Rebecca crouched by the unconscious Mr Machereth. At first she did nothing; then, noticing that Floss was licking Mr Machereth's face and whimpering, she was stirred into life; if the dog did this, could they be sure he was quite dead? Taking off the damp petticoat, she dabbed at his face with it; then, growing less dazed and more convinced that there might be hope, she attacked the motionless man, shaking his shoulders, slapping his cheeks, rolling him from side to side. He let out a groan, and she was encouraged, and pummelled him more fiercely. By the time Giffard, roaring down the stair-well for the servants, was coming towards her along the landing, Mr Machereth was definitely breathing, though in a rough, shallow fashion, and Rebecca was half sobbing as she rubbed his wrists.

In seconds, it seemed, Ferguson, the two footmen and the men from the stables had all arrived. There was a muddle of shouted orders, but somehow the women servants were being woken, the men from the stables were carrying Mr Machereth downstairs and laying him on the sofa in the drawing-room, and the footmen were collecting all the buckets and starting to form a chain to the pump in the yard outside the kitchen.

'Shall I send for the fire engine from Kirkby, sir?' asked Ferguson. Boville considered.

'By the time they get here . . . and that leather hose of theirs is worn out, they've been asking the parish to pay for a new one . . . the engine is in Sutcliffe's barn and locked up and he'll be asleep . . . they've to harness the horses . . . damn it, by the time they get here and show how useless they are, either we'll have put the fire out or the whole place will be burning. Send the knife boy, though, for the doctor; Machereth looks badly to me.'

The housekeeper set Alice to looking after Rebecca, Julia

and Mr Machereth in the drawing-room, and rushed to help with the buckets; suddenly alone again, they could hear the excited movement as the buckets were passed from hand to hand, as the door from the landing was opened and the first water used to soak the swelling, blistering door of the Spotted Bedroom, just in time before it collapsed outward. From their arrival on the main landing the whole thing could not have taken more than minutes. The maids and men were hardly dressed; a few outer clothes had been pulled on raggedly, a few shawls thrown round shoulders; Giffard Boville was in nothing but his nightshirt; the housekeeper was discovered to sleep in a large gathered white cap, and Alice in curlpapers.

It was Julia who was being practical, and taking the initiative. She sent Alice to make hot drinks, and herself found blankets and brought them to wrap round Rebecca, who sat on a low stool drawn up close to Mr Machereth on the sofa, and Uncle Machereth himself, who had not opened his eyes. Rebecca was shivering uncontrollably, and her one idea was to go on rubbing Mr Machereth's wrists and now and then shaking him or slapping his face. Julia wrapped him in a cocoon of blankets, and poured a few drops of brandy between his lips from a spoon, then settled down herself, to wait for the doctor's arrival. Alice brought hot tea, and the brandy was added to it lavishly; then she went off to help with the buckets, and the three were silent in the oasis of one lamp, until the doctor, medicine box in one hand and riding whip in the other, came into the room.

The disturbance, and the doctor's loud voice, made Mr Machereth open his eyes. He saw Rebecca's face floating near him in the dim light, her features softly outlined, and looking at him with concern, and felt her fingers round his wrist, her other hand rubbing the back of his hand . . . wherever he was, it seemed to him a good place to be. Warm, with visions. But his chest hurt; and as his mind cleared, he realized that his body felt badly bruised, and not as comfortable as he had thought at first. The doctor

111

was saying something; praising Rebecca and Julia for saving him; asking them for details. Mr Machereth lay and listened with horror to the account of the smoke, the flames shooting across the bedroom, the girls pulling him out of bed and to safety. Mr Machereth's mind was not as slow as his body and, lying on the sofa, his eyes fixed with deep gratitude on Rebecca's lovely face, he was pondering deeply.

It was fortunate that so little time had been lost after the outbreak of fire, for it did after all prove possible to confine it mainly to the Spotted Bedroom. The other two rooms would have been alight in matters of seconds, if there had been seconds more. As it was, the smoke had left its legacy.

Before dawn, Alice came back, and took Rebecca up to her own bed again. The window was wide open, to let out the smell of burning, but the bed was as comfortable as ever and much better than sitting in the drawing-room, now that the emergency was over. Alice held a cup of hot milk to Rebecca's lips, and then tucked her up as though she had been a baby. There was only time for a smile of thanks, before Rebecca fell asleep, exhausted.

Mr Machereth was put in Giffard's bed, and he too dropped gratefully into sleep.

Julia had borne up well, until she too was taken up by the housekeeper. Then in her own room, which was so blackened as to be scarcely recognizable, she all at once gave way to hysteria. Alice had been looking in the cupboards and drawers for a clean nightdress for her, and was revealing the sad state of everything; gowns covered with broad bands of black, underthings like the back of a grate. Julia sobbed and shook, and could not be comforted. At last at their wits' end Alice and the housekeeper took her along to Eliza Ann's room. Of all the household, Eliza Ann was the only one who had slept through the fire. It had simply never occurred to anyone to wake her. Julia was persuaded to creep into bed beside her sleeping sister, and Floss went in too, and settled down in her arms.

'Floss, Floss,' wept Julia into his silky coat, and until the doctor's prescribed dose of laudanum took effect, she went on crying on to the little dog, with her back to Eliza Ann.

It was many weeks before Broxa House was really back to normal after the fire. Confined though the effects had been, they proved to be far-reaching. Builders had to come in, to practically rebuild the Spotted Bedroom, and their work in the central one of three associated rooms inevitably affected both the others. Julia went on sleeping with Eliza Ann, and Rebecca was found a little room usually used as a dressing-room. Mr Machereth kept to his bed (or rather Giffard's bed) for a week, to recover, and Giffard had a truckle bed made up in his dressing-room, for himself. Everything was very awkward and uncomfortable for all of them. Clothes had to be washed and cleaned, and furniture and walls washed down; in the end both the Grey and the Striped Rooms were completely repapered, and Giffard grumbled about the expense.

At the end of a week, Mr Machereth reappeared on the ground floor, looking none the worse. The fire had been a trauma, and he was quieter than usual. But it was remarked that on his first day down he passed Rebecca the butter without her asking for it. On the second day, when he recommended a particular fruit as being remarkably fine and worth her attention, Julia looked with raised eyebrows at Rebecca, and smiled. It was generally thought that he was showing a little gratitude, which was unusual enough; but if so, he should have shown it equally to Julia, and he took little notice of her.

There had been a little strangeness between Rebecca and Julia during their first meetings after the fire. These were fleeting, for they both were shocked and shaken for several days, and as the doctor kept them much of the time sedated and in bed, they only met now and then for a few minutes. They smiled tentatively at each other, spoke both shyly and tenderly, and felt awkward. But the shyness wore off and by the time Mr Machereth was beginning to show Rebecca these little attentions, she and Julia were in that happy phase of growing friendship when each is discovering new pleasures in the company of the other.

Mr Machereth's remarkable display of preference for Rebecca grew so noticeable that it became quite a settled feature of life. He sat beside her, even when her seat in the garden was in the shade; he told the footman to give her a second helping of soup, whether or not she wanted it; he insisted that she try a glass of his brandy, and he was loud in praise of her skill at knitting.

Rebecca had endured humiliation, and she now knew the pleasure of being petted and made much of; the autumn was passing with great comfort and pleasantness.

'It is too cold for you out here, Miss Redfearn,' said Mr Machereth earnestly, on a day when autumn was decidedly turning into winter. 'May I fetch your shawl?'

With surprise, she agreed. He brought the shawl, from the back of a chair in the drawing-room, to where she sat in the garden. The seat was next to the south-facing wall of the house, which seemed to harbour sunlight and warmth even in winter. With his fat, boneless fingers, he draped the warm shawl round her shoulders, then sat beside her with a sigh as of work well done.

'Thank you, Mr Machereth,' she said.

'Do you think—' and he turned his mild blue eyes upon her – 'Do you think, Miss Redfearn – Rebecca – that you could call me Marc Antony?'

'Why, Mr Machereth . . .'

'Marc Antony, please.' His look pleaded, but she hesitated. 'If you could bring yourself to do that, it would give me great pleasure.'

She looked at him and smiled, a little doubtfully, and there was a pause in the conversation. When Mr Machereth was at the chess board, his knights pounced, in a most unexpected manner, and his rooks were capable of sweeping and devastating descents. With that same surprising speed he now said:

114

'If you could bring yourself to call me Marc Antony, perhaps we could be married.'

'Married, Mr Machereth?'

With more of the unusual exertion, he turned rapidly to face her, and almost snatched her hand up from her lap, to hold it tenderly in his own.

'I have been a widower for a long time, Rebecca,' he said. Then she remembered Julia once saying that her uncle had been married, for a short time, as a young man; his wife had died and passed out of human memory – even, it seemed, his own; and he had appeared happy since then without anyone, in the house of his niece, his brothers, anyone who would have him to stay. He had been fixed for an unusually long spell at Broxa House; most years, he moved on to his brother's, in Manchester, for the winter.

In his soft clasp, Rebecca's hand felt as though it were plunged between damp, warm woollens on washing day. She could not find the heart to repel him unkindly.

'I do not think we would suit, Mr Machereth,' she answered gently, sliding her hand out of his grasp.

'Oh, but we would!' – and he repossessed it.

'No, we would not,' and she was a little firmer. 'I am a penniless girl, a poor relation. Soon I will be earning my living again. I am not at all suitable to be your wife.'

'You are suitable to be anyone's wife,' he replied, gazing at her adoringly.

'You must forgive me; I do not wish to cause you pain; but I really feel that we would not suit one another.'

At dinner, Mr Machereth's unhappiness was obvious to everybody. He would not take any second helpings, and fixed his mournful eyes on Rebecca whenever he could lift them from his plate.

'Rebecca,' said Julia afterwards, 'whatever have you done to Uncle Machereth?'

'I refused him; he asked me to become Mrs Machereth.'

'Oh, no!' Julia covered her mouth with her hands, and tried to stifle her laughter.

'That is most unkind, Julia. Why should it be funny? I

115

receive the first proposal of my life, and you think it laughable.'

'You dear creature!' said Julia. 'Of course it is laughable, to think of anyone inspiring passion in Uncle Machereth's heart.'

'It would have been a very good match,' said Rebecca pensively.

'Rebecca! You will make me die of laughing!'

'You are an unfeeling girl,' said Rebecca, but she could not help laughing herself, then saying, 'Oh, dear, poor Mr Machereth. I hated having to make him unhappy.'

It was not to be borne. Without his second helpings, Mr Machereth – Marc Antony – would be pining away; his broadcloth would sit loosely on those massive shoulders; the soft hanging outlines of his face would become still softer, and lose their glow. He followed Rebecca around the house for a week, and persisted in his suit, while she gently but as persistently refused it; then with dignity he accepted defeat, and signified that his move to his brother's house in Manchester was imminent.

Giffard had not interfered in the affair. From many points of view, his eldest daughter was being foolish in refusing Mr Machereth; he had money, and would in all probability have died long before her, leaving her a rich widow. But Rebecca was not the stuff of which adventuresses are made. He knew, from her general attitudes, that to marry for love was her ideal, and it had not been possible for her to consider for a moment agreeing to the match. Giffard had stood aside, and let her make her own decision . . . could he have urged her to become his own aunt by marriage? He thought not; and the danger of their true relationship being found out would surely have been increased. He bade Mr Machereth goodbye, and saw him safely ensconced in a railway carriage, with relief.

Mrs Boville was still putting off her return, so Giffard was able to ask Rebecca to stay on, and the party at Broxa House settled down to spend the winter together. It was an enriching time. Never had any of them found daily family life more rewarding. Rebecca's different ideals and standards reacted with those held by Giffard and Julia, and prevented boredom. Eliza Ann, whose opinions were yet to be formed, listened, learned, and tried to contribute. There was always something to learn, something to talk about, over the tea cups and the knitting needles.

They were very serious sometimes, and had long discussions. They spoke of the hidden springs of life; and Giffard found himself talking things over with his daughters as though they were equals, and they to know him for the first time as a person. At less serious times they were joyous in each other's company, and found cause for laughter, for almost childish glee.

Edward Gilbank often joined them. Rebecca had liked him from the first; and she liked him increasingly as time went by. He never met her without giving her that indefinable feeling of being treated – as she would have expressed it – like a lady. When he was there, she felt an added glow of self-respect, that marvellous feeling of being approved of, of being regarded as someone rather above the common way. She felt humble as she found increasingly that this man who gave her deference was himself above the common way; that, gentle and kind as he was, there was within him a holding to the best, and a high principle, which was like steel in its steadfastness.

The winter wore away and became spring, and it would soon be almost a year since Rebecca had appeared at the door of Broxa House.

'We will be having visitors,' said Edward Gilbank one day. 'You remember our relations in Cross? We have spoken of them once or twice, and of Miss Marwood's fiancé, the Reverend Simon Lloyd; they are to come to stay. I hope you will all come over to dine, and meet them.'

Rebecca responded only with a nod and a smile, and left it to Julia and Eliza Ann to ask questions. Soon afterwards, Mrs Boville wrote to say that she was coming home, and would be travelling by easy stages. The winter of their content was over, and change – wide-reaching, engulfing change – was on its way.

CHAPTER EIGHT

The Marwood party had been at Gilbank Hall for three days before the dinner at which they met the Bovilles took place. Lady Marwood revelled in being able to show off Maria as an engaged girl. It had been so long – she had thought that they were both on the shelf! It might be thought that a poor curate was no great catch, but he had prospects and might end up a bishop. Thanks to the Marwood interest, he had prospects. Already a living, a fat, comfortable living, was in the offing.

Simon, the devoted fiancé, was irreproachable. He danced attendance, smiling. If the conversation bored him, he did not show it. His family were delighted . . . If, at Gilbank Hall, it was a relief to go out with Edward Gilbank, a gun under his arm and a dog at his heels, he did not make it too apparent to his intended. If he did not love her – if his heart were sterile within him – what did that signify? The fat living and the preferment, were, it seemed, assured. Marwood House would go to her surviving son at Lady Marwood's death, but there would be money to inherit.

Rebecca had some time to prepare herself to meet Simon, but he did not expect to meet her. 'The Bovilles' were spoken of, as coming over; Sir Charles mentioned 'our dear neighbours the Bovilles, with whom we hope for a closer connection . . .' Simon heard the names of Julia and Eliza Ann, and Lady Gilbank spoke of 'their cousin – such a sweet girl', but no one named the poor relation and he had forgotten that Boville was the name Rebecca had mentioned to him as they stood under the Marwood window in Cross church.

Compared to the pain of leaving him and the pain of hearing that he was engaged, Rebecca felt the pain of meeting him again would be bearable. She almost looked forward to it. Seeing him attentive to another woman would end her preference for ever. She had never really dared hope to be his wife, yet when the news had come that he was to marry Maria Marwood it had been bitter. Now, she thought she could meet him with equanimity. Ever since she knew the meeting to be inevitable, she had been steeling herself. The day had come; she would see his aquiline features, his bright, intelligent grey eyes, his way of tossing back a heavy lock of fair hair . . .

Rebecca wore the crimson tabinet.

'You must have flowers,' said Julia critically, entering Rebecca's room and looking her over. The crimson tabinet was so wide that Rebecca took up twenty square feet of floor space, and stood looking like a great rose, her slender waist rising from the full sweep of skirt, her creamy breasts half revealed by the low-cut bodice, her hair in high coils. 'Alice, fetch the roses I did not use – they are on my dressing-table.'

'You look beautiful, Cousin.' Rebecca's voice was warm, as she looked at Julia in her ivory and yellow brocade, the woven bunches of flowers enhanced by the tiny real bunches in her hair and at her low bodice, and in the posy holder at her waist. Julia did look brilliant, and she smiled lovingly at Rebecca as she fastened a deep red rose in her hair and one at her breast.

It was a moment – one of those moments, so rare, so cherished, which are remembered for ever. Rebecca, behind her two half-sisters, sailed down the stairs of Broxa House and the consciousness of beauty possessed her. It was the first time in her life that she had been dressed to perfection and she knew that she was the personification of youth, life and beauty. She thrilled with the pleasure of it, and if the knowledge of the coming meeting with Simon Lloyd had an effect, it was to add the heightening of danger. She placed her feet carefully, in their elegant high-heeled shoes, on one step of the staircase after another, and swung her crinoline round the newel post, managing it with her creamy hands as though those hands had never done anything more onerous; she held her head poised high.

Giffard Boville, waiting for them in the hall below, felt his heart throb in delight and pride as he looked up and saw Julia, Eliza Ann and Rebecca coming down the stairs towards him.

'Do we not look well, papa?' cried Eliza Ann. 'Rebecca – have you seen Rebecca?'

'It is good to see you in a proper evening gown, my dear,' said Giffard Boville, and his voice came grudgingly from a throat tight with emotion. As a father, that was his supreme moment, just as, as a beauty, it was Rebecca's.

They went out to the two carriages that were needed to hold three wide crinolines. Julia and Giffard rode in the first, Eliza Ann and Rebecca in the second, which was a hired one from the inn at Kirkby.

They arrived and mounted the steps to the Great Hall, where the table glittered for dinner with plate, crystal, china and garlands of smilax. They were greeted by Sir Charles and Lady Gilbank and Edward, introduced to Lady Marwood and her daughters, and Rebecca came face to face with Simon Lloyd.

He had not forgotten her; but he remembered a village beauty, worn with toil and sorrow; suddenly, in the home of these relatives of his betrothed, he saw a girl so radiant, so glowingly splendid, that he had never seen her like before. He had loved her a year before, but that had faded into the past and now, in one instant as she stood unexpectedly before him, he fell in love as he had not known he could. At first he did not even comprehend that she was the same person – his breath was swept away by the vision. A dream of fair women. Had she been a dream of his, he could not have imaged forth such calm, lustrous eyes, such

120

delicately rounded contours of cheek and neck and breast, shadowed by soft hair, decorated by deep red roses. He was caught and held by the aura of peace which seemed to radiate from that lovely face, but he was also aware of the graceful arms, the slender waist, the wide bell of the crinoline.

Rebecca looked at him, and thought him changed. He seemed stiff and tongue-tied. That was natural, of course, she soon reflected, when she had left him in such different circumstances to those in which he now found her. She was pleased to see him again; her heart did not bound as once it would have done and as the dinner and the evening passed, she found him less talkative than she remembered him, more chill. When he spoke, she found herself comparing his comments with those of Edward Gilbank, and preferring Edward's. In fact in the intervening year, she had been open to such different influences that the unspoken, unadmitted love for Simon Lloyd had, by degrees, lessened.

Neither of them spoke of their previous association. None of the Marwoods had really known Rebecca in Cross; they were not much given to good works in the village, holding themselves rather aloof, and if they had seen her, on entering or leaving church, the shy village maiden and this county beauty seemed to have no connection. They did not recognize her, and it would have been awkward to say, in that company, that she remembered them. Simon did not mention it; nor did she. Edward and Sir Charles had not really known from the conversation on the train that she had come from Cross. Her past had been little discussed since she came to Kirkby. No one watching them could have guessed that she and Simon were not strangers.

As the evening wore on – and Rebecca was without doubt the belle of the night, and attracted a good deal of attention from the gentlemen – she got over any little disturbances the sight of him had caused, and was much more inclined to forget him for ever by the time they bid one another goodnight, than she had been before. A few more months, and her two years as Simon Lloyd's pupil in ideas and culture would recede into memory and she would feel nothing stronger than deep gratitude.

With him it was quite different. The longer he was in company with her, the more violent the attraction which he had first felt on being introduced. He listened to her voice, which had always been exceptionally musical, and found that it had lost all its country accent; she had unconsciously taken on the intonation of Giffard Boville. Her hands were delicate and pale, and moved among the furnishings of the table with ease. He was not to know how many small humiliations she had gone through to reach that state. She nodded and smiled and chattered to her dinner neighbours with easy composure and seemed to have as much social grace as Julia or Eliza Ann. She had rather more, for when they moved quickly, their skirts endangered small tables within yards, but her expanse of tabinet was under perfect control.

The two Marwood sisters, Maria, Simon's fiancée, and Isabella, seemed to him mere lumps in comparison to her, and Simon felt a passion so consuming – so physical and violent – that he almost trembled with it.

The rest of the company thought Simon unusually silent. They had not been suddenly smitten with Rebecca themselves, and had no reason to suspect what had happened so disturbingly to him.

To Lady Marwood, no other girl could hold a candle to her daughters. She pronounced Rebecca a pretty-spoken girl, with no real interest in the matter. Giffard Boville was proud of all his daughters, and though this evening his eyes were as always drawn to Rebecca, he also looked with enjoyment at Julia and Eliza Ann. Sir Charles thought Rebecca his own little protégée and gave her a good deal of attention, in his old-fashioned way; but one or the other of the Boville girls was to become his daughter-in-law, and the Marwood girls were his relatives, so they all had so large a place in his estimation that he smiled upon them all

122

with benevolence and avoided giving offence to any. Lady Gilbank happily took a back seat on any social occasion; if she found Rebecca's gentle manners more to her taste than the overpowering Marwoods', or those of piquant, perky Julia and Eliza Ann, no one ever bothered about what Lady Gilbank thought.

It was Edward's duty to be attentive to the guests and he worked hard to ensure that no one felt alone or uninvolved, but he considered that he could give himself some reward, so he made sure that Rebecca was near him at dinner. He was able to talk to her over the meal and hear her conversation with others, and no word of hers went unheard. Later, when Lady Gilbank was dispensing tea, Rebecca found Edward bringing his cup over to the chair beside her and sitting down with every intention of staying.

'Don't you want to hear about Lass's pups, Miss Redfearn?' he asked.

'How are they?' She smiled at him. 'I do wish I could go down to see them.'

'Come along, then; let us slip away.' His eyes twinkled at her over the edge of her fan, which he had playfully taken from her hand and opened. 'If you don't see them today you may miss them completely. We are beginning to pack them off to their various homes.'

'It was on my first visit to Gilbank Hall, last year, that I saw her last litter,' Rebecca remembered. 'I'd like to see these, but I can't go down in this dress.'

'They were a jolly set, weren't they? You did not care about your dress then.' Rebecca felt that she did not care so much now; she would have risked a muddy hem for the sake of a few minutes laughing with Edward over the Newfoundland puppies.

'It would not be good manners,' she said regretfully, and gave him a teasing look as she repossessed herself of her fan.

'Edward,' said Sir Charles, coming up looking worried, 'come and help find the music. Isabella will sing that new

Scottish ballad, but someone has tidied it away and we can't find it.' Edward appeared to have no intention of moving.

'You must go,' said Rebecca softly, with a gentle tone of reproach in her voice. He looked at her and smiled. The instant he left his chair it was taken by Moore of Huntingtower. Whenever Rebecca was in Edward's company, she felt as though she were under his protection. It was the same throughout the dinner party, although he was not able to sit by her again.

The other men at the dinner quite frankly considered her the beauty of the evening and clustered round her, holding her glass, fanning her with her fan, pressing on her all those attentions which gallantry can devise. But as none of the people who mattered in Rebecca's life cared a jot what Hutchinson of Bradshaw did, or Moore of Huntingtower either, no jealousy was aroused by their attentions.

Even Simon, consumed by a love so intense and frightening that he was almost speechless, did not care about their obvious captivation. He wanted her; that was the only thought in his mind. He wanted this woman more than anything else in life: more than Maria; more than the fat living and the preferment; more than the approval of his family; more than money; more than life itself . . .

Two days later the family at Gilbank Hall and their visitors came over to Broxa House to play croquet on the lawn at the front of the house. Simon looked for Rebecca with palpitating longing. He had the view pointed out to him. The building, with all its saga of Gothic styles, of carefully chosen battlements, of re-use of the great oak door of the tower with its ancient knocker, was explained to him. Standing at the side of his Marwood fiancée, he listened with an acquiescent smile to Giffard Boville's proud explanations, and bowed politely over the hands of Julia and Eliza Ann, but until Rebecca appeared at the door nothing had any meaning for him. Dull wastes of time separated his arrival and her appearance, where nothing mattered. But as soon as she, in a simple cream muslin sprigged with tiny lavender leaves, stood at the doorway before joining them on the lawn, it was as though the sun had come out, sap had started rising after a winter, the landscape had changed from grey to glowing green. Now his only worry was, would she come and stand by him? How long would it be before he could speak to her? To see her, which a minute before had been enough to make his heart sing, no longer satisfied him. He wanted to be close to her, to hear the tone of her voice, to have her turn and smile at him, fix those eyes upon his face.

They disposed themselves for play and soon the crinolines of the women and the checked trousers of the men were passing over the closely shorn grass. The click of the mallets and cries of success or despondency added another dimension to the summer air.

Simon was near to her, had looked in her face. His fever of the dinner evening was no less; it held him firmly. As he achieved his previous ambition, to walk and speak with her, another more violent longing took its place. He wanted to hold her, to kiss her, to crush her in his arms. Regardless of the fact that he was in the presence of his intended, he looked round, blindly seeking like a bloodhound on the scent, for some way of getting Rebecca to himself in a secluded spot, where he could seize her and embrace her. There was no such opportunity. Consumed inwardly by the longing to make love to her, he had to walk decorously round the lawn, woodenly taking part in the game and trying to respond to those who had become less than the dust.

She thought him constrained and strange, but did not realize the cause. His eyes burned, and she found their gaze resting on her constantly, but apart from making her uneasy, she did not take a great deal of notice of it. The emotion which was consuming him in no way transmitted itself to her. Feelings, locked within us, are often not suspected by those most affected.

The sun warmed her; her present happiness in her

father's companionship and the friendship of her sisters made her glow inwardly; the drowsy hum of insects in the air, the scent of new-mown hay, the pattern of intricate movement of balls and mallets and people on the shaven lawn around the little hoops gave her a sensation luxurious and dreamlike. Edward was there; she had learned to look forward to his presence with pleasure, and at every turn she saw some little mark of his thoughtfulness and care for her. They exchanged a word, a half-smile, a look, which gradually built up, as each tiny brick contributes to the construction of a large building, to a warmth and happiness in each other's company which had grown so gradually they had hardly realized it was coming into being.

The croquet party, decided Julia, had been a great success.

There were to be no more meetings between the two families while the Marwoods and Simon Lloyd were staying at Gilbank Hall, because of a week of torrential rain, which began on the day after the croquet party. Day after day pouring rain from grey skies made it impossible for the ladies to venture out of doors. They talked of going round in the closed carriage, but decided every morning that such weather could not last and put off their social life for another day. It did last. The curtains of rain came sweeping across from the hillside and threw themselves against the grey stone walls of the house with a swish and a sizzle, streaming down the window panes and doing their best to creep under the door. The hay in the fields lay sodden and rotting, and farm workers and estate men stood about in barn doorways, whistling and smoking, wishing they could get on with things.

Lady Marwood at last decided that she could not stand it any longer. This weather, she declared, was worse than Lincolnshire, forgetting the winters when the wind swept in off the sea. She might as well be uncomfortable at home, as away; so, on the last day of heavy rain and bitter wind, she, her daughters, her maid and Simon Lloyd were seen off by their relatives, who were not too sorry to be rid of them. Lady Marwood was a dominating guest and although the girls were popular and pronounced 'very genteel', they were a little too spoilt for the taste of the Gilbanks. Until the day of the dinner party, Simon had been quite a favourite; he and Edward had enjoyed long conversations on books and opinions. But latterly he had grown abstracted, and taken to long silences, and they were not sorry to say goodbye to him too.

The travelling coach which was to take them to the railway station drew up outside the door. In the interval of a few minutes when the rain slackened slightly, the ladies picked their way between the puddles and climbed into the coach. Even as the footman slammed the door and Simon fastened the window tight from inside, the rain poured down again, and the noise of it on the carriage roof stopped them talking.

At Broxa House, everything, subtly, had altered since the arrival of Mrs Boville's letter announcing that she was on her way home feeling much stronger. The housekeeper and the butler began a grand inspection to make sure that everything in the house was as it ought to be, and her bedchamber, unused for more than a year, was thoroughly cleaned.

Julia bathed Floss and spent a morning drying him and then carefully combing out his hair. Rebecca considered his flowing coat beautiful, and now touched it and trailed it over her hand, wondering at its lightness and silkiness.

Eliza Ann spent days shut up in the schoolroom, going over her exercise books erasing blots and tidying them up, pinning her water colours to the wall, and putting out her embroidery. Julia spent a good deal of time practising the piano.

Giffard Boville, turning from the window of his library where he had been contemplating the rain, remarked to Rebecca: 'I'm afraid you may find it – awkward – when Mrs Boville comes. Things cannot be on quite the same footing that they have been.' He looked at her seriously.

'No.' She had been thinking of it. 'I do not wish to cause you any discomfort. Do you want me to leave before she arrives?' It was a sacrifice, but she felt she must offer it.

'No! No! I don't want to lose you. You have become dear to me, Rebecca. Your help has suited me better than help I have had from anybody else. But I think my wife might not like it if she realizes how close we have become to one another. We are truly father and daughter, are we not? We think alike, work alike; no one suits me as you do, Rebecca. In losing you I will lose my right hand, and the nearest companion I have ever had. But we knew at the beginning, didn't we, that it could not last?'

'It has meant a great deal to me too,' she said softly, 'father.'

'Bless you, child,' said Giffard Boville, taking her hand. 'I wish we could be openly to each other what we can only be in our hearts. I hope you will like Mrs Boville. Perhaps we need not think of you leaving us; she might take to you, as Julia and Eliza Ann have done, and then you could stay on.'

'Perhaps,' said Rebecca, smiling tenderly at him. But she knew that a phase was coming to an end. It was most unlikely that Mrs Boville would want her in the house. She must just be grateful for the good fortune which had given her this year, this oasis in what she knew must be a life of toil. She would carry with her always her memory of her year in Kirkby. That very day, when she went upstairs to dress for dinner, she began to think about leaving.

When Alice came with the hot water can, Rebecca said to her, 'Alice, my trunk has been put away somewhere. Could you ask the housekeeper for me to have it got out and brought in here again?'

'Oh, Miss Redfearn, you aren't going away?'

'Not – not just at the moment, Alice; but now Mrs Boville is returning, my services will not be so necessary and I would not be surprised if my visit came to an end fairly soon. This isn't my home, you know,' she said,

128

laughing. 'Do look more cheerful, Alice. I will tell you my address, when I go, and you must come to see me, or write. I will be just Rebecca to you then. We will still be friends.'

'It looks very like going, Miss Redfearn, if you want your trunk.'

'I have so many more things now than when I came, that I think I may need a second one, or at least a bigger one. And if I do decide to leave and take a position somewhere, I want to be prepared so that I can go with no fuss, and quickly. Do you see what I mean?'

'Oh, yes.' A look of understanding passed between the two. 'One thing,' said Alice reflectively, 'you can better yourself now, can't you. You can be a companion, or a governess. You could pass anywhere.'

Rebecca thought about this. Had she changed so much from the peasant girl who would only be hired to clean or do general work? She remembered thinking that Alice's job was higher than any she herself could aspire to.

'You think so?' she said doubtfully.

'Oh, yes!' Alice's tone was enthusiastic. 'In your good clothes and with your lovely manners, you would find a job anywhere. Besides, Mr Boville would give you a good reference.'

'He would – yes, he would. How odd, Alice, I hadn't really thought of doing those kind of jobs.'

'We have lots of companions and governesses to stay here, at times,' said Alice, 'and they aren't a patch on you.'

Rebecca laughed, and blushed and, for want of a reply, went over and kissed the girl.

Leaving! It would be painful; but as she thought back, she knew that it would not be the blow to her that it had been to leave Cross. Her position here had had deception in it and for that alone she would be better pleased to be out in the world, honestly earning her bread, than living under false colours in her father's house. As she went to the window and gazed out through the rain at the formal flower beds, where the roses were all hanging their heads and their petals were balling in the wet, the main show of the summer ruined, she felt almost exhilarated at the idea that a new part of her life would soon be beginning.

A day or two later, large crates and boxes began to arrive at the house. Julia and Eliza Ann rushed to and fro in excitement, wondering what their mother had brought. They did not have long to wait to find out. The carriage and Giffard Boville went to the station, and returned with Mrs Boville.

Rebecca stood to one side, in the drawing-room, and watched with interest as the two girls met their mother. She saw a dark, fashionably dressed lady, very much like an older version of Julia, with the same firm chin and softly rounded forehead, dressed in dark brown, with a frill of black lace inside her bonnet. Her face did not look like that of an invalid – she appeared to radiate health; but her voice was pettish, Rebecca thought.

'Dear girls!' she cried, giving them a peck on the cheek. 'Have my boxes arrived? What a journey I have had! I am quite exhausted. Julia, ring for tea.'

'This is Miss Redfearn, whom I mentioned to you,' said Giffard Boville, leading Rebecca forward.

'Oh! I have heard of you, Miss Redfearn. I declare, Boville, she is very much like your family. The Boville dingy colouring and long face. Are you to stay long?'

'Rebecca has been most useful during her visit here,' said Giffard.

'It is so nice having her, mama!' cried Julia. 'Like another sister.'

'Cousin Rebecca is so clever and helpful,' put in Eliza Ann.

'Yes, I have no doubt. Do you leave soon, Miss Redfearn?' asked Mrs Boville again.

'My visit is almost at an end, madam,' replied Rebecca.

'Oh, yes. I expect so. We will be shutting the house up and going to London and you would not want to be here

130

alone.'

'I don't know that I can go to London just yet,' said Giffard. 'The estate—'

'The estate and the mines can manage without you, Boville. My health will not stand much of this northern climate, you know.'

'Mama!' broke in Eliza Ann. 'We have been longing to know what is in the boxes.'

'They've arrived, then? That's good. Just something I saw in Paris. The sweetest little oriental pavilion . . . it is a pity we do not have continental weather, to go with it. I want to see it erected in the Oriental Garden before we go.'

For a few days, all was flurry and excitement as the workmen erected the pavilion. Fortunately the weather had improved. In no time, it seemed to Rebecca, a space was cleared in the Oriental Garden, the plants carefully set on one side wrapped in damp sacking and watched over by the head gardener, and foundations were laid for the little pleasure house. All the family were to be found in the garden at intervals during the day, either wandering down to see progress, or on their way back from checking on what was happening. For the first time in many months, Rebecca was superfluous. No one seemed to want her. Everyone was absorbed in Mrs Boville's affairs. There seemed to be a constant ferment and yet much of it was all about nothing. Rebecca met Alice a thousand times a day rushing about the house. Every day Alice looked more tired and strained until, on going to her room in the middle of the morning, wanting to be alone and out of the fuss, Rebecca found the maid there, slumped across the bed, half fainting.

'What's the matter?' Rebecca rushed to her in alarm.

'I beg pardon, miss.' Alice heaved herself to one elbow. 'I was dusting your room and I came over funny.'

'Stay there,' said Rebecca, pushing her down again on the bed. 'I'll fetch you a drink of water.'

She brought a cup of water and held the girl's head as she sipped it, then soaked a handkerchief in eau-de-Cologne and smoothed her forehead with it.

'Better?'

'Oh, much better.'

'Stay there – don't go getting up.'

'I must get up. Mrs Douthwaite will be after me if I don't get on.'

'You've been doing too much. Let me loosen your stays.'

'It's just this last week. I've been feeling that sick in the mornings. You know what I'm afraid of, Miss. I should have been poorly a month sin'.'

'Oh, no!'

'It looks like it, Miss Redfearn.'

'He'll have to marry you, Alice.'

'He says he'll be damned if he does.'

'I'll do something! I'll speak to Mr Boville. He'll be dismissed if he doesn't marry you. That'll bring him to his senses.'

'If you don't mind me saying, Miss Redfearn, it ain't no good speaking to the master now that the mistress is back. Not about any of us servants, that is. When she's at home, it's Mrs Boville who is over us.'

Rebecca was taken aback. She had no desire to tackle Mrs Boville, though she would have been sure of having Giffard on her side. For a while she said nothing, while Alice gradually regained her colour, and then sat up, gratefully sniffing at the handkerchief.

But what else was there to do? Alice was in a position where she could not help herself. Discovered to be pregnant, she would be instantly dismissed; her only hope was to get in first with her accusation of Ferguson and swing her employers to her side, so that pressure was put on him to marry her. Alice herself would never summon up the nerve to do it; Rebecca could . . .

If she waited, she would not be able to do it. There and then, she went along the corridor and knocked at the door of the boudoir. The high, fretful voice called her to come in. On entering, Rebecca found to her surprise that not only Mrs Boville but also Giffard Boville was in the room.

'I'm sorry – I'll come back later,' she stammered.

'It's all right, Rebecca. Come in.' Giffard came forward hastily and took hold of her elbow, almost dragging her into the room.

'Yes, Miss Redfearn?' asked his wife, frostily, looking at Giffard's hand on Rebecca's elbow with a lift of the eyebrow. The girl swallowed a lump in her throat and spoke up, clearly.

'Mrs Boville, I'd like to speak to you about the conduct of your butler, Ferguson.'

'Ferguson?'

'He has behaved in a very shocking manner. He is not to be trusted with the maids. He has seduced one of them – not by kindness, but by threats – and she is now carrying.'

'Which girl? She shall be sent packing at once.'

'She resisted him. The fault is his. And now he refuses to marry her.'

'I think this girl has played upon your feelings, Miss Redfearn, and imposed on your lack of experience. Ferguson is a most respectable man. No doubt it is one of the grooms. She only wishes to blacken Ferguson's character for some reason of her own – some grudge she wants to pay back. He has reprimanded her, perhaps.'

'I'm sorry, Mrs Boville, but I cannot agree with you!' Rebecca burst out. 'This man's character is far from good. All the younger maids go in fear of his advances, for they are afraid of being dismissed if they complain. Even – even—' she had noticed the look of unbelieving disdain on Mrs Boville's face, and brought out the card she had hoped not to use – 'even I have suffered an insult from Ferguson.'

'You did not tell me of this!' exclaimed her father. 'What? What has he done? The fellow shall go instantly.'

'Mr Boville,' cut in his wife icily, 'pray let go of Miss Redfearn's arm. I am sure she can stand on her own. Do not forget, so far we have only Miss Redfearn's word for all this. Your concern – pardon me – your concern appears a little excessive.'

133

Giffard let go of Rebecca and turned away, saying sullenly, 'Miss Rebecca Redfearn is my cousin; her concerns must concern me. If she has suffered insult under my roof, I must redress it.'

'A fifth cousin—' and then Mrs Boville repeated herself, with increased emphasis, 'a fifth cousin, Mr Boville, cannot have so large a share of your regard, surely, as those with longer and nearer claims. Miss Redfearn has been known to you for a year, I think you said. Ferguson has been our valued servant for eighteen years.'

'I have known of Miss Redfearn's existence for the whole of her life,' said Giffard. 'Ferguson only works for me. I trust my own blood, and what I know of Cousin Rebecca's character.'

'Oh, well!' Mrs Boville waved an airy hand. She did not gainsay him. 'Let us at least hear his side of the story. In any case, Miss Redfearn, what did he do to you that has caused such distress?'

'He—' she hesitated. 'He attempted to seize me on one occasion. It was my impression that he intended to kiss me, if no more. I was firm, and he desisted, but the maids are defenceless. I am a guest in your house, and could have appealed to Mr Boville.' Giffard was heard to mutter that he wished she had.

'I suppose the maid wants him to marry her.'

'Yes, madam. And I think it would be best for the staff as a whole. Once married, he would have a curb on his activities.'

'Fetch her in,' said Mrs Boville, with a sigh.

Rebecca fetched Alice, supporting her with her arm. She could tell at once, by the atmosphere in the room, that angry words had been exchanged between husband and wife while she was out of it; Giffard had a hang-dog look, and he met her eyes miserably. Then she had an intuition. As if she had heard them, she knew the accusations his wife had hurled at him – not knowing of their real relationship. She thought he was too partial, even perhaps in love with her. Rebecca burned at the thought. Without revealing the truth – and that was impossible – she realized they had no defence against that suspicion, be it real or feigned for the purpose of having a hold over them. By remaining under his roof she exposed her father to misery and to all the taunts an unloving wife could hurl at him. The sooner she was gone, the better . . .

'So.' Mrs Boville pursed her lips and looked Alice up and down. 'It is you who is in trouble, is it? And blaming Mr Ferguson?'

'Please, ma'am, it was Mr Ferguson. I didn't want to. He said if I didn't he'd see I lost my place.'

'Well, you've lost it now, haven't you?'

'Yes, ma'am.' Alice hung her head. No one else said anything.

'You're not a child, you knew what would happen! You could have complained to Mrs Douthwaite.'

'Yes, ma'am,' said Alice, who had tried that without receiving any help.

'Fetch Ferguson,' said Mrs Boville with a sigh. Rebecca at once went out of the room. Downstairs she found Ferguson and told him that he was wanted in the boudoir. He came without speaking. Even after a year, he could never quite treat Rebecca as he should have done. Her position rankled; it irked him. They went upstairs in silence. As always, he astonished her, because she could see clearly both sides of his character. The Bovilles and their visitors formed high opinions of the man as the most deferential, obliging and efficient of butlers. Those of the servant class knew him as a petty tyrant who could not be trusted with the maids. Both views of him were true ones. Rebecca had to agree with Alice that he was a well-built man, but she considered that he had a certain loose-jowled vulgarity, and carried too much flesh. Now, walking in front of her, he had an air of the most complete self-confidence. He walked into the room, bowed, and asked Mrs Boville what he could do for her, in a most attentive manner.

'You had better have the banns put up, I think,

Ferguson, for you and Alice,' replied Mrs Boville.

'Banns?' On entering the room and seeing Alice there, he must have guessed something was in the wind. He rocked back on his heels. 'I don't understand.'

Giffard, from the other side of the room, reinforced the order.

'You are being let off lightly. Unless they are read for the first time this Sunday, I shall dismiss you my service.'

'But I don't understand, sir. I am engaged to marry Mrs Douthwaite. The question of my marrying Alice does not arise.'

'If it is your child she is carrying, then it is your duty to marry her. That should be made a rule in all cases,' said Mrs Boville. 'If she was not your first choice, then you should not have behaved as if she were already your wife.'

'I appeal to you, sir,' Ferguson said, turning to Giffard Boville. 'Alice will confirm that I never promised her. Mrs Douthwaite and I have been agreed some time.'

'Think of your child, Ferguson,' said his employer. 'Would you want it to grow up without your love and care? Even unknown to you?'

'Madam,' Ferguson turned back to Mrs Boville. 'Please send for Mrs Douthwaite. She will tell you that she and I are betrothed.' Again, Mrs Boville found Rebecca useful.

'Fetch Mrs Douthwaite,' she said to her curtly. 'Don't tell anyone why I want her.'

When Mrs Douthwaite entered the room, she knew by seeing who was present that something was the matter.

'Did you know about Mr Ferguson and Alice?' asked Mrs Boville. Her housekeeper gave the housemaid a comprehensive look.

'Men will be men, ma'am,' she said comfortably.

'Mr Ferguson tells us that you and he were intending to marry.'

'Oh, yes, in a couple of years, ma'am.'

'Alice is going to have a child, so Mr Ferguson will have to marry her instead. If not, he will lose his post.'

Ferguson and Mrs Douthwaite had not yet reached their

aim in their savings. Another two years and the little country inn would have been just within their reach. Four years, and they could have taken their pick. They could have snapped their fingers at their employers then, and left, shrugging off the responsibility of Alice. Now they both thought of the difficulty of finding another good position if they left without characters. To leave now would be catastrophic, to stay not less so.

'She could go on the parish,' said Mrs Douthwaite hopefully.

'She will do no such thing,' said Giffard Boville. Mrs Douthwaite put her handkerchief to her eyes.

'This will ruin me,' said Ferguson.

'Not at all.' Giffard Boville slapped him on the shoulder. 'Marry Alice and I keep you on. Don't marry her, and you go.'

'I will have to look for another place,' sniffled Mrs Douthwaite.

'You should soon find one,' replied Mrs Boville abstractedly, noticing in the looking-glass that her hair was out of place. Ferguson thought of being shamed before all the countryside. He drew himself up and put his chin high.

'The banns will be put up, sir and madam.'

'That's settled, then. I want to hear no more about it. You may all go,' said Mrs Boville in a sad, failing voice, picking up her comb. 'All this is bringing on one of my headaches. Mrs Douthwaite, send up my maid at once.'

'Yes, madam.'

A disconsolate little procession left the boudoir. Even Alice did not really look happy. Rebecca followed the three servants. Ferguson paused at the top of the stairs and spoke under his breath to Rebecca, his eyes furious.

'Just you wait.' She ignored him and went to Alice, kissing the girl and pressing her hand.

'There, my dear. Now you must be spared the heavy work. Mrs Douthwaite will be finding a replacement, won't she? Then if you are training a new girl it will be easier for you. No married servants are allowed on the staff

137

together, are they?'

'No, miss, that's a rule. Oh, Miss Redfearn! It was good of you.' They were alone on the landing. Rebecca patted Alice's hand.

'It's nothing. But I don't envy you your husband.'

'He has his good side.'

'I haven't seen it,' said Rebecca wryly.

CHAPTER NINE

From this time Rebecca was even more unpopular with Mrs Boville. She ought to have been looking round for a new position, and would have found it hard to say why she was not.

'I wish you would stay until I am married, Rebecca,' said Julia one day as they were sitting together in the Oriental Garden, enjoying the delights of the new pavilion. 'I would like you to help me with my clothes and all the arrangements. But at least you will come back for the wedding.' They had been talking about Rebecca's future, and Julia had been thinking of all kinds of fantastic situations for her. Rebecca could not help thinking how the other girl had changed, in the brief time they had known each other. Julia was softer, and kinder; she was more considerate to the servants, and it was only at intervals that she showed a hint of her old arrogance.

'Are you to be married soon? I didn't know it was decided,' she said, and felt distressed, but would not ask herself why.

'It is not decided yet, though when I was walking with Mr Gilbank in the woods last Sunday I thought he was about to ask me,' Julia replied dreamily. Rebecca had noticed Edward's attentions. They had all been on their way back from church. There had been something she particularly wanted to ask Edward herself, but he had seemed almost to avoid her, and had stayed firmly by Julia's side. She had been surprised, even piqued, because so often it had been by her side that he had walked, on the Sunday meeting of the two families. She had always

139

appreciated the courtesy of his attentions to her, the poor relation, and assumed that he did not yet want to show his preference for either of the two Bovilles, and that she herself was a safe harbour. When he had deserted her for Julia she had supposed – with some sadness, missing his company – that he had made up his mind at last, and evidently Julia thought so too.

'Are you happy?' asked Rebecca delicately. 'Will not Eliza Ann be upset, if he chooses you?'

'Oh, no – she won't mind, really. Mama will find her someone and she will soon think of Edward as a brother. It did look, did you not think so, Rebecca, as though he had made up his mind at last?'

'I thought so.'

Julia turned on her a face at once hopeful, laughing and tender.

'Perhaps mama has been dropping hints to the Gilbanks – you know she is becoming impatient, and talks of Moore of Huntingtower for me; Edward would not like that.' Rebecca was surprised that Julia should be so ready to show delight in Edward's advances; she had thought the whole arrangement a lukewarm thing, and wondered at it; now, looking at her half-sister's face, she felt something which she did not care to analyse.

'Do you love him?' she asked.

Julia looked over the flowerbeds, and out to the profile of the moors.

'Yes . . .' she said, very quietly. 'I think I have always loved Edward, since we were children. I dared not show it, in case he chose Eliza Ann. But last Sunday, it did look, didn't it, Rebecca, as though . . .'

'It did.'

It seemed to Rebecca that she must waste no more time, but she no sooner sat down to work out her letters of application than her emotions were set in turmoil, and every action made impossible, by the receipt of a letter.

'There's one for you, Rebecca,' said Giffard curiously, as

he gave out the letters at breakfast. 'With a Cross post-mark. One of your old neighbours, I have no doubt. But the writing is in an educated hand.' He sat for so long with the letter between his thumb and fingers that Rebecca thought he was never going to give it to her. Mrs Boville had long since begun to open her pile of letters, many of them from abroad. Julia had read hers, from a cousin in Worcestershire. Giffard's lay unattended in front of him.

'May I have it, Mr Boville?' asked Rebecca at last. He passed it to her without any further word, and Mrs Boville, who had glanced sharply at Rebecca, was able to take the attention of the table with her discussion of her own mail.

One glimpse was enough to tell her that the letter was from Simon Lloyd. That handwriting was familiar from a thousand incidents in the past. She declined to open it in the publicity of the breakfast table. Whatever Mr Lloyd could be writing to her about, it would not be a matter for the Bovilles . . . she slipped it on to her lap and finished her breakfast, listening with composure to the conversa-tion of the others. If her receipt of a letter had surprised them, it was a very minor surprise and forgotten already, except by Giffard, who kept looking at her curiously. Maybe, she thought, one of her old friends was ill, or needed her help, and had asked Mr Lloyd to write on their behalf. It would solve her problem. Now, she felt strong enough to return to Cross. She would return, and help, and be again the person she had been before, only en-riched. It did not occur to her that she could never again be the same Rebecca Redfearn who had so innocently left Cross a year before.

Once alone in her room, Rebecca opened her letter. Not feverishly, not with her heart beating unduly fast, but quite calmly, and with a mild curiosity. That calmness did not outlive her first glance at its contents.

It was a declaration of undying love.

Simon had, he wrote, broken off his engagement to Maria Marwood. This alone would have astonished

Rebecca, but that she was the apparent cause of it . . . that Simon should say he loved her . . . the letter dropped to the windowseat while she gazed into space, blank with shock. The old times at Cross, when the sight of him had made her day complete, when their conversations, eager, lingering, had been the breath of life to her, returned to her now in memory. Had he loved her then, when she had known him all the world to her and feared the strength of her own feeling?

She turned again to the letter. He did not say so. It had all come, apparently, when he had seen her again, in Yorkshire. His love had burst upon him like a flame, and he was able to think of nothing else. To know herself beloved, to read those words, passionate, burning the very paper, and know that they were meant for herself alone . . .

Yet he had been cold to her when they had met, had hardly spoken, had not mentioned their previous friendship, had let it appear as though it had never been. She was chilled, as before she had been warmed. Then, too, she had felt nothing, when she had seen him. He had no longer roused in her the previous overpowering feelings. In fact, she preferred the society of Edward Gilbank. It had seemed that her feeling for Simon Lloyd was over. Now, to receive such a letter!

It took some time for her to recover from her first shock and flow of sensation.

He loved her – she at once believed it. He would not have written so – no one could have written so if he did not fervently mean what he was writing. And he had jilted Maria Marwood. This was harder to believe. How could he do such a thing? He had offered marriage to Maria, been accepted; how could he go back on the contract? Her first reaction was repulsion, when she considered this. To go back on one's word, particularly when the happiness of another human being was at stake, was bad; all her early training rose up and condemned the man who could do such a thing. She returned to the letter and read the

142

sentences again. He had jilted Maria because he could not bear to marry anyone but Rebecca, she was the cause of it. For a moment she rebelled. Why was she blamed for his action? Why must she take the responsibility? It was none of her doing. Proposing to Maria Marwood, falling in love with Rebecca, jilting Maria – she did not feel herself to blame. Had she made him propose? It was his own action, his conscious decision. Had she tried to make him fall in love with her? Sitting on the windowseat, Rebecca flinched as she imagined what Maria, what Lady Marwood, would say. They would say she had trapped him, enticed him. She remembered the few, stilted sentences they had exchanged while he had been in Kirkby, the feeling she had had that he was now nothing to her, and absolved herself from that suspicion, but she knew that the world, knowing her to be poor, would not absolve her.

Then she returned again to the letter and realized that in jilting Maria, whose uncle was his bishop, he had done far more than break the heart of a girl; he had ruined his chances of preferment in the Church of England. Jilt Maria, and remain for ever a parish curate.

'I must marry you,' Simon had written. 'What will become of us, I know not; but I do not care what happens to me, as long as you are mine.'

Oh, Simon! Your worldly ambitions, the fat living, the vision of a stall in the cathedral, all gone, for the joy of a woman's arms? A woman whom you once – when she was all yours – allowed to walk away from you, out of your life, and face the world alone, rather than yourself give up the good things of the world?

'I have resolved,' he wrote, 'to go abroad as a missionary. Will you marry me and come with me? It will be a hard life, but we will have one another. Write; say you will; I wait only for your word. I can be with you in a day, and we can marry in Liverpool before sailing.'

Then, as she re-read the words, she did not want to leave Kirkby. Simon seemed like a stranger, and the idea of foreign countries was repugnant. Dear, wild Kirkby,

143

where the wind off the moors blew heather-scented, where the clear sparkling cloud-shadowed light of summer shone on the valley and on the little town clinging to the hillside above the deeper valley, where the winter gales drove down battering Gilbank Hall and Broxa House in their passing and then hurled themselves against the weavers' houses! Where, looking across to the majestic roll of moor, veiled by the finest of hazes, she could see one field, among all the grey-green, which was brilliantly emerald. Where those she had come to love lived out their lives. She did not want to leave it.

Now she knew why it had taken her so long after Mrs Boville's return, when she had once more been made to feel unwelcome, to plan out her efforts to find a post. It was working against the grain. She had put down roots here, in this short year. Whatever she had inherited from Giffard Boville – and she knew now how much that was, of looks and of temperament – it appeared to have included a love of this upland countryside. Her ancestors of his family had lived here for many hundreds of years, in one part or another of this gritty, rolling backbone of England, and it held her; more, it seemed, than Cross had done, where her mother's family had tilled the soil unsung. The high lands had romance, adventure, infinite change on a bedrock of millstone grit and coal . . .

It was impossible to make an immediate answer to the letter. She put it into the bottom of her box, where already she had been packing her winter clothes, ready for going away. Slipping her hand down the side, she would be able to bring it out again instantly. She must think.

There was a need to hurry in making her decision. Simon had placed her in a quandary, for he had already taken action. For better or worse, he must leave Cross now, at once. Rebecca could imagine how the vicar would have received the news of the engagement, and then of its breaking. It would be impossible for Simon to remain for more than a few days. Her reply must go if not tomorrow, then the next day at the latest. How she would have welcomed this, at one time! How overwhelmed she would have been by happiness! But now her forehead showed her perplexity. To think that she had been expecting the letter to bring news of some old body in the village who needed nursing, or some young children left motherless! She had been expecting it to offer her a situation. Well, it had – a situation as a wife, as a wife to a missionary. A shiver ran through her. She did not want what life was offering her – what, a year ago, would have seemed like heaven: the chance to work at Simon's side. Yet could she write and tell him so? At the idea of the cruelty of such an action she shrank from doing it. She could not put pen to paper and tell him he must be a missionary alone.

Fortunately, if anyone noticed her distraction during the rest of the day, he or she did not remark on it. As far as possible she avoided the rest of the family, and spent her time packing her trunks. The old one had not been big enough, and the previous week she had bought a second one. Gradually she packed all her possessions, leaving until last those things which she was using. She was surprised at the contrast between the scanty possessions she had brought to her father's house, and the comfortable wardrobe she now had. She had not realized until now how much Giffard Boville had given to her, and in her heart she thanked him again for his love and kindness, as she folded the warm merino and the broadcloth cloak. On an impulse she fetched some mothballs and strewed them in among the warm winter clothes. Why? Had she already decided to marry Simon and go with him as he asked, to hot countries where those garments would not be needed? She paused with the last of the mothballs in her hand and looked down at the trunk, wondering.

All that day she found she could not come to a decision. In the late afternoon, Ferguson had words with Mrs Douthwaite. The coming Sunday was to be another calling of the banns for him and Alice, and the difficulties of the relationship in the kitchen were coming to a head. It was impossible to the housekeeper and butler to abandon the

145

hierarchical practice of retiring to take their pot of tea in the housekeeper's room, and equally impossible for them to enjoy it, or linger over it. Many times it was drunk without words, or Mrs Douthwaite might break the silence only with sharp remarks. They both hoped something might happen to alter the course of things.

As her husband-to-be, the other staff expected Ferguson to seek out Alice and spend his free time with her, and to an extent he did this. There was a little house in Kirkby belonging to the estate which they were to have and the arrangements were made for it. Ferguson did not find conversation with Alice interesting. The topic of the public-house-to-be with Mrs Douthwaite was superseded by the topic of the baby-to-be with Alice.

On the day Rebecca received her letter from Simon, Ferguson had done an unusual thing for him. He had retired into the butler's pantry with one of Giffard's bottles of brandy. The difference in him was not perceptible when he superintended the evening dinner; but when the family went out to enjoy the rest of the summer evening in the ȝarden, he went back to the bottle of brandy.

After a whole day when Rebecca could not be alone to think, she went into the garden with the others and, leaving them seated in the Oriental pavilion, walked further by herself. She had long since become familiar with all the surrounding footpaths and tonight she made for her favourite walk. Down through the garden of Broxa House, out of an unassuming gate at the bottom, she followed a path which led through the meadows to the river which, bordered on either side with trees, separated the Boville and the Gilbank properties.

The gentle sound of the river calmed her, and she walked steadily upstream on a narrow path which led to a rustic bridge over the water. This was the path which they used when, on informal occasions and in fine weather, they walked over to see the Gilbanks.

Tonight, walking the familiar path, Rebecca realized how much she had come to love it. Every yard was familiar and, in being so, dearer. Here a kingfisher was often seen; there, a trout; under the bridge a pike some-times lay waiting; and the river itself was like a friend.

Standing on the bridge, leaning over and gazing down into the water, she read her letter again and tried to make up her mind. Simon had already burnt his boats and could never again be the curate of Cross and Maria Marwood's fiancé. A life as a missionary was probably the best course open to him. But to her? Oh, Rebecca, at one time you would not have reasoned so, if Simon Lloyd had told you that he loved you!

There was a quick step on the other footpath and Edward Gilbank greeted her; Bounce was at his heels, and jumped up at Rebecca, sure of his welcome.

'Get down, Bounce, you bad dog!' she laughed, catch-ing his paws in one hand and stroking him with the other. 'Cannot you control him, sir? He is a disgrace. He would never retrieve a bird, he would be too busy pawing at the chests of the gentlemen of the party.'

'He does not do it to anyone but you,' was the answer. 'You encourage him, Miss Redfearn.'

'Me! Encourage him! When I have just told him what a bad dog he is?' She caressed the dog as she spoke, looking down at him with tenderness, and a smile on her lips.

'You should have a dog of your own,' he said.

'Oh! I would love one. Perhaps one day. That is a dream, I think; but one day my circumstances may allow it.'

'You could have one now.' He dropped twigs idly into the water, and leaned beside her on the rustic parapet.

'What? When I am just about to leave?'

'You're leaving?' He looked at her intently. 'Are you unhappy?' She felt warmed by the concern in his tone. But it was always so. She remembered being struck by his affectionate care of his father, on the train, the first day they had met, and ever since he had always championed those who seemed to need it. No wonder, as Eliza Ann had once said, that everyone in Kirkby loved him.

Everyone in Kirkby . . .

'I did not expect to see you,' she said, suddenly feeling

some constraint in his company.

'I was restless tonight, and Bounce had not had a walk all day.'

'And I,' she sighed, 'have to make a decision. I came here to think.'

They leaned side by side on the bridge and both watched the fragments of twig as Edward dropped them into the water. For a long time there was silence between them. The soft colours of the valley deepened, and the colour of the sky turned from rose to silver grey.

'I also have a decision to make,' said Edward quietly. His normal cheerful friendliness had gone; his voice was deep and serious. Rebecca glanced sideways at him and saw the depth of emotion in his eyes. They had been leaning shoulder to shoulder on the parapet. Now he reached out a hand and gently brushed her hair with the backs of his fingers, in a light caress.

She dared not look at him.

'I must go. It is growing late.' Her manner was nervous. To steady herself she gripped the parapet rail of the bridge. Then she half turned and said goodbye to Bounce, who thumped his tail and looked pathetic. 'Stay, good boy.'

'Does that apply to me, too?' asked Edward. He had drawn back a little and was looking at her intensely. 'Or may I escort you to the house?'

'I must be alone to think,' she pleaded, smiling nervously and avoiding his eyes. 'Thank you for offering.' She turned away from him and began to walk back along the same path by which she had come. Where the path left the river bank she turned. He was motionless, leaning on the bridge, and she could just pick out the black shape at his side which she knew to be Bounce. She raised her hand and waved.

Back in the lower garden, she paced up and down the walks, hesitating to go higher. The rest of the family were still outside and she could hear their voices. She must be alone! Quite alone! At last the others went inside, and she walked up as far as the Oriental Garden. The shadows were thickening there, and the dew was falling.

148

While Ferguson had been sitting drinking he had been dominated by the thought of Rebecca. Ever since her first coming she had thwarted him. Her effortless rise mocked at his laborious upward climb. Her championship of Alice had in his eyes ruined him. The brandy in his mouth tasted like dust and ashes. He slipped out quietly into the garden, and wandered about, keeping behind the hedges, looking for Rebecca.

It was most unwise for her to be out at this hour, at a point in her life when to catch a chill or be unwell would seem like a disaster. High above the house the battlements still caught a gleam of gold from the last rays of light. Sitting in the pavilion she was still and in a reverie for a long time; in such stillness that her ears caught a faint sound, although the footfall was on the sand of the path. She had a moment's warning before a dark shape hurled itself at her, bearing her to the ground. As she fell she shrieked out and, piercing, disembodied, the cry was heard all over the garden, and further.

In the drawing-room of Broxa House the footmen were lighting the lamps and Julia was wondering aloud where Rebecca could be. Sound from outside was muffled by the panes of glass and the many layers of curtains. No one noticed the scream except Giffard.

'What was that?'

'Mmmmm?'

'Did you hear something? Some sort of cry?'

'Bats, probably, papa. They were flitting over the garden before we came in.'

'Louder than that.' For a few minutes he felt uneasy, and then the sound was forgotten.

It had echoed across the valley.

Rebecca's head struck the mosaic floor of the pavilion hard, and she did not give a second shriek, because all the wind was knocked out of her body by the man who crashed down with her. For the first few seconds after her shriek Rebecca could do nothing. Then she tried to struggle, but his weight alone overpowered her.

'Got you,' he said thickly, having been unprepared for

149

her crash to the ground or his fall on top of her. Fuzzily he tried to remember what he had meant to do. 'I'll teach you to meddle in my affairs, you jumped up little nobody,' he finally went on.

Rebecca found that time can stretch, so that each second is an infinity of disgust and agony. It was almost impossible for her to draw breath and she was afraid that she would be smothered, crushed out of existence, die. The weight was quickly becoming the one reality of her world. The effort of continuing to exist under it, to endure it, took up all her mind. She gasped raucously for breath, as he brought down his fist in a blow to the side of her head.

Then the brutal heavy load was dragged from her body and the air rushed into her lungs with a resulting gasp which was much pain as relief. She thought he was only drawing back to deliver another blow and tried to throw up her arm to protect her face, but it had become numb. She realized that a second person must have arrived. Some sort of struggle was going on above her. Even as she realized this and began to make sense of the sounds she was hearing, something wet slapped her cheeks, a hot breath blew into her face, a warm whiskery muzzle was thrust against her, and a paw landed on her chest.

'Bounce!' she whispered, and the dog whimpered excitedly, licking her, then leaving her to dart with excited yelps at the two men who were fighting in the little space of the pavilion. She could see them only as black shapes. It had grown dark and the men were only a greater blackness.

Then one of the men broke away and vanished into the night. The other took a couple of steps after him, then stopped, turned, and came to kneel on the floor beside Rebecca, and tenderly to gather her up into his arms.

Edward lifted Rebecca and took her to the long seat against the back wall, and sat down with her in his arms, pressed close against him, her head on his shoulder and her hands nestled up somehow against the warm tweed of his jacket. His voice had been murmuring her name, and endearments, and insistently asking if she was all right.

'Oh,' she said. It was all that she could manage. She could feel the deep breaths he was taking after the struggle, and she herself felt only half conscious. She closed her eyes and sighed deeply, clinging to him and feeling close, warm and safe. Gradually she began to recover a little from the shock and pain of the attack upon her.

'Are you all right, my darling?' he said again.

'I think so,' she said cautiously, taking one of her hands from its resting-place and patting it over her head and body. She discovered that somehow her thin muslin dress had been ripped apart in the fall. In the delight and comfort of Edward's embrace she felt not in the least dismayed.

'I shouldn't have let him get away,' he murmured into her hair. 'I should have chased after him. It was only that I was so concerned about you. Can you forgive me?'

'It doesn't matter,' Rebecca managed to say. He gathered her even closer, rested his cheek on her temple, and one hand of his went up to stroke her hair soothingly. She clung to him, and for both of them time stood still. It did not need words to tell them that they loved one another. It was as though all the year of gradually becoming acquainted, then becoming friends, had been leading up as inevitably as spring leads up into summer, to the moment when, in each other's arms, they tacitly acknowledged their love. Both, as they recovered a little from the distress of the evening, felt that they were for the first time complete. Words would have been impediments, to those whose essential spirits spoke to one another. Sitting still and silent in the little pavilion as bodily pain and distress subsided, they had a profound experience of spiritual union.

At last they stirred, and exchanged lingering, wondering kisses. Later still the thought occurred to both of them that they could not stop there all night; that the Bovilles would be wondering where Rebecca was; that her dress was half torn off, and it was most incorrect, to say the least, for her to be so. The world invaded their more powerful reality. They moved, tried to look at each other's faces in the

151

darkness, and noticed that Bounce was wriggling restlessly at their feet.

'I must take you back to the house,' he said without conviction. 'Then that villain must be found and punished.'

'No,' she said firmly.

'You can't mean that he should not be punished?'

'I do mean that. I would rather you did nothing.'

'So you know who it was?'

'Yes.'

'And you want to protect him?' His voice was incredulous. They drew a little apart.

'Did you recognize him?' she asked.

'No . . . it was too dark. I think I could make a shot at knowing him again. Height, size, that sort of thing.'

'I can't talk about it now. But . . . if I tell you . . . later . . . why I think it best to do nothing, will you listen to me, and try to see what I mean?'

'Of course.'

'Oh! If only everyone did not have to know about this!' she cried, pulling the rags of her muslin up to her shoulders. As they sat, the thought of the tumult, the questions, the hue and cry and its distastefulness to Rebecca was present in both their minds. Then what an appearance it would have, Edward bringing her in, half naked, from the garden. He wanted to ignore such considerations, to go at once to Giffard Boville, and raise a search for Rebecca's attacker, but he could tell that she flinched from this idea. For him it was a conflict between the right thing to do, and the consequent hurt to her feelings and sensibilities.

The more she thought about it, the more determined she was to be as secret as possible. The shame of it all! Even though she was completely innocent, the affair would blacken her. She would be tainted; and she did not want to involve Edward . . .

There was a way into the south wing, without going up the main grand staircase. Julia or Eliza Ann in such a position would most likely not have thought of it, because they were not aware to the extent Rebecca was aware of the other worlds surrounding them. Somewhere in their knowledge was the fact that there was a back stair for the servants, but the notion of using it even in an emergency would have been so foreign that they would probably not have been able to remember where it was. To Rebecca, that narrow spiral stair in the thickness of the wall, which Alice hated so much when she had to go up and down so often every day with the hot water cans, was familiar. It was the ancient stairway of the tower and there was access to it at the bottom. There was a secluded door shielded from the garden by a little yew hedge, because apart from gardeners, servants were not supposed to be seen in the gardens.

Rebecca knew that the little outside door was the last to be locked every night, and it should still be open. She got up and together, arms round one another, she and Edward walked up the garden and found it; Rebecca tried the handle, and it was open.

'I shall be all right,' she said softly to Edward.

'You might have a bruise or something tomorrow; how will you explain that?'

'I will think of something. Please keep silence, for my sake.'

'Only if I am satisfied with your reason.'

'I will let you know it.' She turned to face him, and by so doing, was in his arms again. 'How can I thank you for saving me?'

They kissed passionately, and clung together; Rebecca was trembling. Then she pulled away, and took his head between her hands, kissing his eyelids as though in blessing, bending his head so that she could do it, and standing on tip-toe. Without waiting any longer, she then stepped out of his arms and went through the door, clutching her tattered dress about her. Slipping silently up the spiral stair she gained the main landing near the entrance to the south wing. High up the stair-well the last footman on duty that night was putting out the lamps as he worked down the house.

And so Edward and Rebecca parted.

CHAPTER TEN

When Alice came into the room next morning, with the hot water, Rebecca was sitting up in bed with her writing desk on her knee and writing a letter.

'Miss! Whatever has happened?' cried Alice, noticing a bruise on Rebecca's cheek.

'Hush! Don't shout out like that . . . it's nothing . . . I was attacked last night, Alice.'

'Who? Who was it? Not . . .'

'Yes, I'm afraid so.'

'He said . . .'

'He said, 'Just you wait' . . .'

'Oh, Miss Redfearn!' Alice covered her face with her hands and sank onto the bed. 'This is the end of me!'

'Nonsense, Alice. Look, I'm not going to say anything about it.'

But you must! Your poor face!'

'Oh, it isn't as bad as all that. I can say I fell against something. Only you and I and Ferguson and one other will know the truth; Mr Gilbank came and stopped him hitting me. So, when I'm not here, if Ferguson does not behave himself – if he knocks you about, or anything – you will be able to go to Mr Gilbank.'

Alice was silent. She did not know how to take this. The thought of her husband knocking her about was a new one, although of course husbands did; they had a right to, after all – but she feared it. Yet not to marry! To have a bastard child and be an outcast, that would be worse; girls had starved to death before, who had tried that, or thrown themselves in a river . . . If Mr Gilbank was on her side she would have a hold over her husband that would keep him in check. At least he didn't often drink. It was always worse if they drank.

'What can I do for you, miss?' she asked.

'Give them a message downstairs that I woke up with a headache and am staying in bed, and please would they not disturb me as I need to be quiet and rest. Bring me a tray up here. Then I will want you to come back later. This letter is urgent, and you must see it gets posted.'

The die was cast; the indecision of the previous day was over. She knew now that the best thing for everyone was for her to marry Simon Lloyd and go away. By staying, she would bring ruin to those she most loved.

Her father's dreams of uniting the estates, the dearest wish of his heart, would come to nothing if she stayed on, for she knew that if she remained unmarried Edward would not marry either Julia or Eliza Ann. Her own father – how she had grown to love him! – how good he had been to her! She thought of a thousand instances of his thoughtfulness and kindness, a thousand times when his pleasure in her company had been obvious. His was a strange character, but she had grown to love it. Even his faults, his hot temper, his touchy pride, were dear to her. Was she to wreck his hopes?

Old Sir Charles, too, would have the ambition of his life unfulfilled.

Julia . . . her dear sister . . . and sisters they had become to one another . . . how tenderly she had revealed her love for Edward! Rebecca did not feel she could be the means of blighting those hopes.

Then, if she stayed, and had to meet Ferguson, she would not be able to keep silent about his behaviour. What would happen then to Alice?

Simon Lloyd, too; it appeared that the only reparation she could make for the crime of unwittingly arousing his love, and so causing his tragedy, was to marry him.

At a stroke, she would remedy all ills . . . She would make the life of everyone in Broxa House happier, by leaving and marrying Simon Lloyd. Mrs Boville would be relieved to be rid of her, so would Ferguson. Alice would miss her, but be more comfortable in her marriage with Rebecca away; Julia would miss her, and never know that, had she remained, Rebecca would have been a bar to her married happiness.

For Rebecca was in no doubt about the way she felt for Edward, or his feeling for her. They loved each other; and because she loved him, Rebecca prepared to sacrifice herself, without thinking that she was also sacrificing him. She was still uplifted by their ecstasy of the previous night, and thought that the high emotion would carry her through the rest of life, with him always in her heart.

Rebecca selected a second sheet of writing paper and went on with her letter, accepting Simon Lloyd in marriage, and arranging to meet him in Liverpool.

It was not, after all, so difficult. Lady Gilbank had suffered a slight stroke a month before, and a message was sent over to Broxa House that morning that she had had a second, and that Sir Charles and Edward were sorry, but they would have to cancel a proposed shooting expedition arranged with Giffard Boville. Ferguson did not appear all day; his place was taken by the upper footman. Rebecca rubbed her face well with rice powder, and not only disguised her bruise but gave substance to her story of a headache.

In the library, she gave Giffard her letter from Simon to read, and told him that her letter of acceptance had already gone. He looked at her, distressed.

'Are you sure, Rebecca? Are you doing the right thing?'

'Quite sure, Mr Boville.'

'I shall miss you.' He stood holding that fateful letter, and for a while they did not speak as Giffard thought about the situation. At last he went on: 'Of course I realized that you were thinking about taking a post somewhere, and I have not been idle. Mr Machereth wanted to benefit you financially, and I was anxious to safeguard your future;

156

together we have put together a small trust fund, enough to ensure that you are not actually in need at any time. It was to be a surprise for your birthday, but if you are leaving the country . . .' he looked down at the letter again, and she could see that he was very much moved at the idea of her going so far away. Tears stood in her own eyes.

'I'd rather Julia and Eliza Ann didn't know about all this business of Mr Lloyd throwing over Miss Marwood,' she said.

'No doubt you're right. Unpleasant business. We won't tell them.'

'They might think I'd gone out under a scheme to provide helpmates,' she suggested.

He shrugged, then asked, 'When are you going?'

'The sooner the better. I have packed my things; it would be ideal if I could go today.'

'You will have to travel by Leeds and Manchester. There is a good train this afternoon; I will come with you.'

There's no need!'

'You will have to put up in Manchester for the night. There is every need for you to be escorted.'

When Eliza Ann and Julia heard the news, Julia burst into tears, and could only be pacified by being allowed to travel part of the way with Rebecca as well, so in a great rush and hurry the three of them caught the afternoon train and were in Manchester by nightfall.

Rebecca would infinitely rather have been alone with her father, in spite of her love for Julia. Her feelings were overwhelming enough without the other girl's emotional reactions. But she was gentle and loving to Julia and put up, the next morning, with Julia's rushing her round the Manchester shops and warehouses and heaping her with presents, with a good grace. Sheets, valances, lace and damask tablecloths were pressed upon her, although she protested they were not the right things for a missionary's wife. What use two dozen dinner napkins would be among savage tribes she could not think.

She had telegraphed to Simon that she was on her way to Liverpool, and given him the address of her hotel in Manchester, so that he was able to reply with instructions. They would marry just before sailing. There were many things for him to arrange, but he would meet her there as soon as he could.

Giffard would have liked to go on with her to Liverpool, but for many reasons he contented himself with seeing her on to the train. Rebecca and he had been alone for a few minutes while Julia went in search of some last present, and had said their goodbyes, so that on the platform itself they said farewell with a look, and a formal handshake. Julia was the only one who could give rein to her feelings, but for Rebecca's sake she tried to smile. 'Let my last sight of you be a happy one,' Rebecca had whispered. As Giffard parted from Rebecca, he handed her a purse with twenty sovereigns in it. They waved, until her train was out of sight.

Rebecca took a room and settled down to wait for Simon. While hating sewing, she loved knitting; so she sat in her window and knitted, and read the books she had brought with her, and gazed out of the window and thought. She went out very little, and then wearing a veil. Her bruise was fading, but she felt self-conscious about it. It was a strange time for Rebecca: a limbo; a nothing time. As she sat in the window she could not help, very often, feeling Edward's arms about her, his cheek against hers. It was something so real, if she shut her eyes, she thought she would open them to see his dear face, with those loving eyes, and his eyelashes . . . she could feel his hand on hers, and longed to lift it up to her lips, and to almost worship every fingertip . . . he seemed so real that it was hard to accept that he was not there, that she would never see him again . . .

His embrace had wiped out the memory of the attack upon her. She never thought of Ferguson except when she wondered how Alice was going on, and sent up a little

158

prayer that the girl might not be too unhappy. But Edward . . .

She had written to him, of course, to explain why she judged it best not to denounce the butler. How difficult that letter had been! He deserved a proper explanation of her sudden departure and marriage. After that night, after the emotion they had felt in one another's arms, the mystical sense of union which had transcended human existence, how could she explain her marriage to another man? A man who had recently been a guest in Edward's own home, and engaged to one of his cousins? All the reasons which had seemed so strong to her in her bedroom at Broxa House evaporated when she had to write that letter. When it was finished – with short, unreal sentences – she had not mentioned her marriage at all. He would know almost at once that she had left Kirkby and it would only be a short time before he discovered that she was married, a little longer before he found out to whom. This must be enough. When she was married and across the seas, there would be no impediment to his marriage with Julia. If only he would think of her, Rebecca, sometimes, with kindness! Yet it would be as though she had never existed, never taken the Parliamentary train from Cross in the spring of 1860, never entered his peaceful existence at all . . .

The extraordinary week went by thus in waiting, knitting, musing, weeping, in the ugly rented room, while Simon, in a torment of longing to see her again and make her his own, rushed about making all the preparations. He did not approach her to help him in those matters, or think that she might wish for a say in their future lives. He simply went ahead, arranged the marriage, was interviewed by the church organizers in charge of the missions, agreed on a post, bought the necessary medicine chest and tropical kit, and booked their berths on a ship, all without telling Rebecca or asking for her aid. He had accepted a posting to the South Pacific.

She in her turn did not realize what was involved. He

had told her to wait for him, and she waited . . .

In Kirkby, Edward received her letter. His mother's second stroke was so worrying for his father and himself that they hardly liked to leave the house. On the day after Giffard, Rebecca and Julia had gone to Manchester, he had sent over a messenger, but on hearing that only Mrs Boville and Eliza Ann were at home, he had shelved the problem of Rebecca's attacker until her return. He was determined to take up the matter with her again and insist that the man must be punished. Giffard and Julia were back home again and Mrs Boville was forgetting that Rebecca had ever existed, before Edward received that stiffly worded little letter from Liverpool, which sent him over the fields to Broxa House at a half run, Bounce at his heels.

He met Giffard Boville outside the door into the garden. It was obvious that Edward was distraught. He burst out, 'Miss Redfearn has left Kirkby, I hear, sir?'

'Yes.' Giffard looked surprised. 'She left suddenly. Did you want to see her?'

'I did. I do.' Edward had turned and the two men stood irresolute among the flowerbeds. 'Perhaps we could talk away from the house,' went on Edward.

They walked slowly together, and Edward spoke nervously.

'Mr Boville, it has been an understood thing for some years that you and my father both wish for a marriage between myself and one of your daughters. I too wish for that. There has only remained the decision as to which daughter would care enough for me, and I for her. That decision is now made; I wish to marry your daughter, Rebecca Redfearn.'

If Edward's face had been white, Giffard's was now whiter.

'What do you mean?' he said.

Edward was hard and determined.

'I am asking you, sir, for your daughter's hand in marriage. Your eldest daughter, Rebecca Redfearn.'

'What has Rebecca told you? What do you mean by this?'

'She has told me nothing. It was obvious to me . . . If you recall, one day last November, I came into the library unexpectedly when you and Miss Redfearn were sitting talking one on either side of the fire. You both turned your heads and looked at me, together.' His hands moved, as though words were not enough to convey that instant of illumination. 'You will forgive me, sir, if I say it was obvious. You could have been nothing other than father and daughter. It flashed upon me then, and every day since has only served to confirm it. Your intellects, as much as your looks; your characters, your gestures – she could be no other than a daughter and, because older than either Julia or Eliza Ann, your eldest daughter.'

'You cannot marry her,' Giffard Boville said stiffly.

'She is of full age, Mr Boville. Your consent will not be necessary, although I would rather have it.'

'You do not know what you are saying. Rebecca is already married.'

'What!'

'She has married someone else. He was getting a special licence. They would have been married yesterday.'

'It is impossible!' Edward did not cry out that she was already married to him; but he felt that on the night she had been attacked, he had committed himself to Rebecca body and soul, and that either of them should marry someone else was unthinkable.

Giffard did not reply. He was missing Rebecca badly, and this scene was painful to him. He loved Edward, for himself and as his future son-in-law; did not like to see him suffer; and could show his feelings no more now than he could a year ago. He walked slowly down the path with the young man without a glance in his direction, but that cry was wringing his heart – 'It is impossible!'

'Who?' asked Edward at last, and, in short, brusque sentences, Giffard had to tell him. The boy would get over it; it was a passing fancy with him; he would forget

161

Rebecca, settle down with Julia, and all would be well . . .

'I would have stopped it,' said Edward, and the iron in his voice – so unlike his usual gentle tones – brought the first cold breath of fear to Giffard. 'I see it all,' went on Edward. 'She is thinking of you, she is thinking of Julia and Eliza Ann; but I tell you now, sir, that if I do not marry Rebecca, I do not marry any of your daughters. I have made my choice: it was her, or none.'

'You must make up your mind to it, Edward. Let me talk to you like a father. She is gone . . . yes, she is my daughter, I will admit it to you. But we could not have united the estates through her, you must see that. I cannot acknowledge her. It would have served no purpose. She is gone, Edward. You must forget her. She is another man's wife.'

'No.' Edward turned and faced him. They were across the fields by now, and standing near the river. 'While she lives, in her heart she is no one's wife but mine. This is self-sacrifice on her part. He is a villain. She is mine.'

'Edward!' cried Giffard, his control almost breaking, all his emotion flowing out to the young man. But it was doubtful if he heard, for already he was starting away up the path towards the footbridge where a few days before he had stood beside Rebecca and thrown twigs into the river. 'Edward!'

Edward turned, but his face was so altered by emotion that he no longer looked like the well-loved Edward Gilbank. Giffard felt that he was seeing a stranger.

'I have made my choice,' Edward said again. 'It is her or none.'

'She is married!' Giffard cried out to him. Edward gave him a strange, distraught stare, and Giffard wondered if the shock had turned the young man's brain. He had told him abruptly, of course – he should have broken it more gently – and when the Gilbanks were in such a state of worry over Lady Gilbank; in the ruin of his hopes, Giffard could feel only concern for Edward, only fear for the future of the young man who now turned and walked

162

away from him. Giffard stood helplessly there in the meadow beside the river, and there was no one he could tell of the event, nothing he could do, no help for it . . .

Giffard was wrong in supposing Rebecca to be already married. At that moment she was still sitting in her window, knitting, and gazing at the clouds.

Edward entered Gilbank Hall in a state of hardly knowing what he did. He had completely forgotten Bounce, who had run at his heels across to Broxa House, and who was still faithfully following him. When Edward stood still for a space Bounce pushed his nose into his hand, and Edward, becoming aware of him, took him out to the kennels and shut him in, oblivious of the reproachful gaze of Bounce's brown eyes. Edward could not bear the distraction of the dog's presence. He could only think of Rebecca, and could think of her only disjointedly, fragmentarily, his thoughts glancing round her like the play of summer lightning.

'What are you doing, Edward?' It was his father, in the doorway, and Edward had difficulty in focusing on him and hearing what he was saying. He almost wondered who this little, white-haired man was. 'Edward!' his father said again. 'I have been searching for you. Your mother is no better. I think she is worse, and we ought to send for the doctor again. Edward! What is the matter with you? Don't you hear what I say?'

The characteristic of Edward's which drew everyone to him was his quiet strength and reliability. He was a rock of shelter to lighter beings. His own needs must, with what effort and cost Edward alone knew, be set aside for theirs. He looked directly at his father. It took a while, endless, to regain command of himself, before he could say calmly and in a way that brought reassurance to Sir Charles, 'It is all right, father. I am here. You had better send Joshua down to Kirkby.'

Simon's first sight of Rebecca was in that ugly rented room, the night before their wedding. All was in readiness. He sent up his name, then climbed the stairs after the housemaid and stood in the doorway, looking over at the girl who faced him.

'Mr Lloyd,' she said. She had never called him anything else, and did not think of doing so now. She stretched out her hands to him. After the dragging hours she had spent, any well-known face would have been a friendly sight, and his, which she had known and loved in those old, simple village days which now seemed so far away, was welcome as it had been when he called during her foster-father's illness. There had been times during that week when she had felt as though reality was losing its hold on her; when she had not wanted to live, and it had almost seemed as though the hired room was an afterlife, in which nightmare had reality.

'You must call me Simon now,' he answered and, walking over, took her hands.

He looked at her face, then looked away, then looked again, forgetting the shape of her face, needing to be instantly reminded of it, yet burning it into his brain. She was as lovely, as gentle, as refined, as he had imagined; on the following day she would become his wife. At that time, in that room in Liverpool, all his denial of worldly ambition seemed nothing, a straw in the furnace of his desire.

After that first few minutes, when he stood inarticulate holding her hands, they both sat down and he began to talk, quickly, telling her all in a rush of words of his preparations. She answered in single words, in monosyllables, shyly. Tropical kit, medicine chests, mosquito nets, notes from former missionaries of the words used by these strange people for whom as yet there was no dictionary, and no bible in their own language.

It would be strange to go out of England into those far-off countries. It would be strange to be married, and to Simon. But all the world was strange.

When she left Cross she had moved into a new world, but she had been moved by a powerful impulsion of her

164

own. She had found a world which she was part of, flesh and bone of hers. She had found Edward, whose heartbeat she had felt when her head rested against him, whose thoughts could enter her brain as though there were no barriers between them; whose impulses she could understand as though they were her own. Edward, whose presence wrapped her in protection. She had been one with him as though they had been meant to come together under the moorland sky.

The next morning she married Simon Lloyd, and began to wonder what she had done . . .

CHAPTER ELEVEN

They had seemed to be on the journey for a lifetime, in the close confinement of the ship, but it had only, so Rebecca was told, been eleven weeks, and the journey was expected to end in another week. Then they would see the islands of New Zealand, and would part from the rest of the ship's passengers. They would travel to the school to which native children from the Melanesian islands were brought, and there join the mission ship on its annual cruise to return scholars, collect new ones and spread the word of the Lord. This year it was to take a teacher to an established mission on an island nearer the main centre of the Melanesian groups, and to take themselves to an island where already one old scholar of the school was living. This island had long been asking for a missionary; the people had pleaded for one. That Simon was married was a bonus, it appeared; Rebecca was to teach the girls, and show then the institution of a Christian marriage in action. She was surprised, on hearing of the extent of her future duties, having only envisaged a life similar to that of a curate's wife in England.

'How can I teach anyone, Simon?' she had asked doubtfully; he was the teacher, in her eyes.

'You have much to teach them,' he answered. 'Why, they do not even wear clothes,' and he looked at her, and touched her light shawl.

Rebecca had had full time to realize the consequences of her actions, in doing evil that good may come. For to marry a man she did not love was an evil, and who was she to say that those consequences she had intended to come of

166

it would be good ones?

A year ago, when she had left Cross, Simon had been her idol, and she had loved him as the novice does her teacher; now her feeling had long since turned to friendship, and he had hurled his career at her feet as the moth gives his wings to the candle. So far he did not regret it, for his passion had not yet run its course; but that passion frightened her in its strange intensity. She gave herself and her proud creamy body to him, and felt pleasure in giving, in fulfilling his need, in holding his restless head in her arms. Was it her, herself, she sometimes wondered, that he loved, or some strange idea of her? He asked her again and again, on that crowded ship, to wear her damask-rose red tabinet dress in the hot tropical evening, and she did so, however incongruous it seemed, to oblige him; then he would stare at her with that intensity which she could neither understand nor return. She would step about on deck, or sit, in the brief tropical sunset, and later be illuminated by the uncertain flicker of lantern light, or the radiance of the tropical moon, and be devoured by his gaze.

Once, entering their cabin unexpectedly, she had seen him with a pair of her stockings in his hands, rubbing them to his cheek, and she had stood stock still half-way through the door, almost horrified at his white, twisted features, then gone away quietly before he had realized that she was there.

Determinedly she had shut Edward from her thoughts. The almost spiritual ecstasy she had known in his arms did not come to her in Simon's, and seemed to be remaining in her heart, in some secret place, a kind of shrine of ideal love, which comforted her by its existence. The scenes she had known with him, of meadowland and moor, she never expected to see again. Her life in future would be led among silver seas on the singing coral and between the swaying palms. Yorkshire, Gilbank Hall, must all fade into memory.

From her upbringing Rebecca had not been led to expect

much of anything so little spoken of as the physical side of marriage. Simon's attentions were, she assumed, very much those of every husband. When he caressed her and made love to her in the privacy of their cabin the proceedings had a curiously impersonal quality. The depths of passion which she possessed, were not stirred, though she met him with affection and welcome.

There was no doubt of the burning longing he had to possess her, yet she felt it was not her – Rebecca – but some image of her which excited him. He caressed not her but a dream. It was as though for him physical love was not a natural part of life but a forbidden thing, almost a thing of shame, and although he had succumbed to it, sacrificed everything for it, and now revelled in it, it was a Dead Sea fruit, a Goblin Market fruit, a Durian fruit, a compound of repulsion and attraction.

Rebecca wondered where the feeling which had existed between them in Cross had vanished to. Where was their friendship, their easy mental companionship, the budding tenderness? It seemed that with the incursion of the new scorching element, what they had once had had vanished away. It puzzled her, as she sat knitting on the deck of the ship at a long lacy border, of which she had made enough to trim all her household linen before the voyage ended. There was not much else to do on board, though their journey was enlivened by the creatures of the sea. The ship was several times surrounded by flying fish, and once by a school of porpoises; a whale was seen blowing in the distance; sometimes an albatross flew overhead, and gradually they approached the shore of the North Island of New Zealand.

Farewells were said to their fellow passengers; how close the knowledge of them seemed, after so long at sea together! Even though Simon had been so much absorbed by Rebecca, and she by the strangeness of their relationship, they had come to feel that the other passengers were as well known as relatives; yet in the bustle of disembarking the feeling was fading already, and within weeks it would have been difficult to remember their faces.

They travelled to the mission school, and had their first glimpse of the people among whom their ministry was to be. From many different islands, the youngsters were alike in having dark skins, more glowing brown than black; shining well-formed teeth, always showing in happy smiles; and very beautiful brown eyes. Their hair was frizzy, thick and black. Brought here for part of the year to become Christians, they learned to read and write in their own languages, to wear clothes, to sit and eat at tables, and to conduct themselves as seemed desirable to the representatives of the English church. Rebecca and Simon admired the love and devotion shown by the missionaries. They also liked the sweetness of the natures of these native children and found it hard to believe the many stories of barbarity which they had heard during the voyage. It was hard to believe, when greeted by broad shining white smiles, that the islanders had been guilty of the murder of earlier missionaries, and of cannibalism, or that whole tribes engaged as a pastime in bloody wars.

In some ways, however, Simon's attitude gave the bishop cause for concern. He was full of zeal; but it was the zeal of the general for his soldiery, or at best the shepherd for his sheep – real, not metaphorical sheep – as one immeasurably superior he spoke to the children.

'They must be treated as equals,' the bishop said to him. 'You must ask them to do nothing which you will not share with them. Have you noticed how, in the compound, the teachers take part in the cleaning and general work? This is to ensure that the boys accept it as dignified, and do not learn to despise this most necessary part of their education. We must always share and share alike, and habits of diligence, cleanliness and order are almost as essential for their salvation as learning of the love of God. The people of the islands are coming into contact with traders of the worst sort, who for the sake of the sandalwood will trade them guns and whisky, who will rob and debauch them unmercifully. We hope that these boys we

169

train here – together with their wives-to-be, the little girls who are also here – will set an example in many ways in the islands, when they return to their homes. Once we have native deacons, the church will grow amongst them as their own self-organized native church.'

'Treat them as equals?' exclaimed Simon. That one phrase had stuck in his mind.

'In every way, or you will do more harm than good.'

'Surely they are naturally inferior!'

Rebecca, listening, shuddered slightly. She was beginning to know Simon, and to realize on how fragile a base their marriage rested. When she was a poor village girl he had thought her inferior, and had been able to keep his passion under strict control. Physical passion only, it had been, and was, for she had many assurances that he undervalued her intellect, as surely as he was undervaluing the natives. She had more discernment and, by growing to know Edward, had now a perception of Simon's limitations, his narrownesses, which of old she had been too dazzled to see. If his success in this new sphere was to rest on an assumption of equality with those he felt were inferior, it would be as obvious to those untutored minds as it was to her.

'Forget your ideas from England,' said the bishop. Then he went on, almost dreamily, 'Bishop Selwyn said, some years ago, that the soul of the church must not be confused with such beggarly elements as thousands a year, and parks and palaces . . .'

'Of course,' said Simon hastily, 'of course.' But his face had a strained look, and his lips were gathered together, as though to prevent words escaping.

'They are God's children, as much as the bluest of English blood, and unless you can deal with them so, your aim cannot be achieved.' The bishop was silent, looking at Simon with eyes in which the love of his fellow creatures produced a saint-like strength of soulful expression. 'When you are at your post, I would wish you to conduct yourself with humility towards the native chiefs, never forgetting that you are in their country, and the temporal authority is theirs. How can you teach respect for authority if you are seen to flout it?'

Rebecca's knitting needles flashed as she sat in her corner, modestly not speaking. He had humbled himself in his passion for her; could he make this further submission? Bring himself down to the level of the Lord's apostles, who, with 'only tattered nets and leaky boats, had yet lacked nothing'? Down to their level? Up to it, she thought, in spite of Cross, and the deference accorded there to the Church and the landowners, of which Simon had been one and had intended to ally himself with the other. She saw him bow his head before the bishop's gaze, and allowed herself to hope.

They had hardly had time to accustom themselves to the life of the mission school, before the time for the annual cruise among the islands came round. The ship was a stout little vessel; the returning scholars were crazy with excitement, half glad and half sorry to be leaving the school and returning to their islands. Over forty gleaming, excited faces and chattering voices made the little ship a joyous sight. 'It's a very little boat,' thought Rebecca as she stood and looked at it.

'You're not afraid?' Simon asked, looking across at her one evening, as they finished superintending the loading of their baggage on to the craft. Rebecca looked down at the boxes, remembering their contents – broadcloth cloaks, cashmere gowns, fur tippets, lace curtains, chintzes, damask tablecloths . . .

She was dressed in the lightest of the muslin gowns made for that summer, the one in which Simon had seen her on the day of the croquet party – little lavender sprigs; and she could feel the trickles of sweat down her back between her shoulder blades. They were going much nearer the Equator, to their post . . .

'No,' she replied, smiling bravely. After all, it was an adventure, was it not? A great adventure. The spread of sea lapping quietly before them, so warm to touch, had a grandeur about it very different to the icy North Sea, a suggestion of illimitability.

'No, I'm not afraid, Simon. We will be doing good together. If only all the people are as tractable as Summa here.' On first seeing the returning student who was to be their helper and interpreter, she had felt fear, fear of the unknown, for his aspect was very strange to her, but now she was used to the great aureoles of black hair, the simple single garment, which showed most of Summa's legs and the whole of his chest and arms, his broad feet which pointed out to right and left as he walked. He was always cheerful, never worried, and she had grown to like him.

It was only when she thought of cannibals, and remembered that Summa would be the only person on the island whom they had already met, that she had fears.

It was the first time since their marriage that Simon had seemed truly to care about her feelings, the first time she had heard genuine concern in his voice. Before, he had carried her before him like a captive, a prize fallen to his bow. It was heartening that he should now speak like this.

Before they came in sight of the island which was to be their home, after weeks of cruising a silken blue sea in the creaking boat, before ever its soft grey outlines became tangible on the horizon, Rebecca, living on the boiled yams and freshly caught fish which were the staple diet on board, sleeping on a narrow berth and washing in a bucket of salt water, had become aware that Simon's passion was to have still another tangible result. She realized that she was to have his baby.

'Simon,' whispered Rebecca, reaching down in the darkness from her upper bunk to touch him in the lower one. 'Simon, we are going to have a child . . .'

He took her hand, and did not speak for a minute, while she wondered what he was feeling. 'So soon?' he said at last. 'I was hoping such a thing would not happen for a long time. It will be difficult enough at first, carrying out our new duties.'

She experienced a slight chill of disappointment at his response to her news. Rubbing his fingers with hers, she asked, 'Are you not pleased? It will make no difference to our work. I will see that it does not.'

'Go forth and multiply,' he said quietly. 'We have gone forth, and our marriage is to be blessed. Of course I am pleased, Rebecca. I would not have wished for an unfruitful union, and the possibility of children so soon should have occurred to me.' He returned the pressure of her fingers, then released her hand as he prepared for sleep. Soon his quiet breathing told her that it had come. She lay awake and tried to persuade herself that he had greeted the news with joy. She felt joy, and completeness, as though her body had a need for motherhood.

On the following morning the island gradually became nearer. It was a distant mass, green over with trees, though they could not yet be distinguished. Volcanic mountains rose clear of the rain forest, their peaks hidden by caps of cloud. All around the island the sea broke over the reef and from the ship they could hear the sound that it made. As the distance lessened between the boat and Mutu they could see bays of gleaming white sand.

They anchored some hundreds of yards off the coast of the island, with a string of other, lesser, islands stretching on either hand to the horizon. Rebecca knew that this would not only be her first married home, but the birthplace of her child, with all the risks and dangers to her own life. From her memories of Cross she knew something of these risks, which she would have to face far from her own kind.

Often, she had found, the sea was not blue, but grey; for it reflected the skies, as much here as at home, and when the sky was muffled in grey clouds and the humidity was more than usually oppressive, the sea too, for all its warmth, was dull and softly grey; but on the day they dropped anchor at Mutu it was the blue of the sapphire, and drifting across it were shoals of narrow shapes of burnished gold and gleaming copper – at first they seemed to be fish. She exclaimed at them, and Simon came to her side, and together they leaned over the gunwale and looked into the water; then she could see that they were leaves, fallen from some tree on the shore and drifting in the current, spreading across the sapphire blue like leaf-shaped golden sequins. They must have come from inland trees, for the edge of the island was fringed with palms, bending their slender trunks in the wind, the mop-like heads bowed, and long fronds of leaves showing silver, then green, varying as their movement.

These were not palm leaves floating on the satin water; but there were many different kinds of trees on the island: green wooded ridges of hills rose up, with here and there rocky crests, and behind them all great mountains, superb in their stateliness and dignity.

'There are our people,' said Simon, and there was wonder and awe in his voice, as though the truth of it had just come to him. Looking where he pointed, she saw a group of dark figures, almost naked, some with their black bushy mops of hair whitened by coral sand, gesticulating on the shore. 'Let us pray,' and he dropped on to his knees; 'let us pray for the success of our work here; that we bring to these poor heathens the blessing of the love of God.' She knelt beside him, and with all her heart joined in the prayer. Their future, uncertain, hard, perhaps brief, seemed at that moment to be wrapped in glory – she was often to remember their exaltation, as they knelt in the stern of the ship, gazing across the water, sapphire and gold, to their new-found shore.

A canoe was being pushed out from the bank. A sound could be heard, of many voices, but faint because distant. The long craft coming towards them moved slowly, poled along by two men, one standing up in it at either end. Simon said they were using the same actions as the undergraduates did at Oxford, when they punted on the river.

One of the natives who clambered aboard was another old scholar of the mission school, and he had a happy reunion with the bishop and with Summa. The day had already reached afternoon and the bishop decided that, as the village where a house had been prepared for the Lloyds was some way off, and there was all their luggage to be seen to, it would be wiser to put off a start until next morning at dawn. Simon asked what the people on shore would do, during the rest of the day and the night, but Summa and the other ex-scholar, George Sulu, waved their hands airily and smiled, and it did not seem to matter. Long into the darkness the bishop, Simon, Summa and George Sulu sat and talked, and it seemed a short night before they were woken by the sudden daybreak at six o'clock.

Among a babble of excitement, the canoe was loaded, Simon said goodbye to the children who had not yet been returned to their own islands, and Summa checked the trunks and boxes. There was quite a little ceremony of leavetaking. Rebecca was seized with sudden fright; she was sure that she would never learn to distinguish one dark face from another on the island, or understand the bubbling voices. Among the noise she found herself handed down into the narrow boat, seated on one of the trunks, opposite the bishop. There was not room for everything, and the canoe would have to make a second journey. Anxiously she asked Simon if everything was all right, until he became impatient, and told her to stop fussing. Still nervous, she subsided, still certain that something would be left behind, that the canoe with its high prow inlaid with mother-of-pearl would overturn, that Summa, still on the ship, would fail to join them on the island, something . . . she had not yet learned the sense of time which operates in the Pacific, where nothing ever hurries, where there will be tomorrow after today, where in their own good time events take place, and if they do not, well then, they do not, and it does not seem to matter . . .

They poled away from the ship, and silently, slowly, moved over the ocean. Rebecca realized why they had not gone further on the larger ship; the coral reef did not permit it. Once inside the barrier, the sea was very calm; looking back when they had been under way for a few minutes, Rebecca could tell that the long billows of the ocean did not reach within the reef; here the surface of the sea was absolutely still, and just under the surface she could see the rocks, a few inches down, it seemed, so that the keel of the narrow craft at times scraped over them. The tall figure of a naked man in the bows of the canoe stood with authority, choosing a path through the submerged rocks, placing the long pole now here, now there, un-erring, his body outlined against the sky which was just beginning to show hints of blue cloudlessness after the early trace of grey.

It was a silent voyage; the journey needed skill and judgement, and everyone was following with their eyes the slow ballet-like movements of the pole, now dipping, now slowly rising, so that the canoe wound its way over the glassy surface and the fringe of palm trees, the groups of waiting islanders, became gradually nearer. The canoe was moving at an angle of forty-five degrees to the shore, so they would make contact with the silver-gleaming sand at a suitable landing place, and the islanders ran alongside, keeping pace with their dreamlike progress. Rebecca could see that there were men, women and children, and that they wore flowers in their hair.

The canoe came to a gentle halt, grounded on the sand, and the men jumped over the side and began to haul out the boxes and trunks. Simon, looking brisk and capable, was in charge and, taking off his shoes and socks and hanging them round his neck, stepped over board. Look-ing over the side, Rebecca realized that she too was going to have to step into a foot of water. The bishop had also removed his shoes and socks so hastily – though there was no need for haste except that she felt she must not hold up the party – she stripped off her shoes and stockings as modestly as she could and, holding up her long muslin skirts, stepped out and found herself standing in water as warm as her skin. The island people stared at her feet and ankles with undisguised curiosity, but she did not take offence. It was natural enough. She had, she thought, looked at Summa's feet with equal curiosity when she first saw them. The difference between human beings must always seem strange and marvellous to them on first contact. White skins as opposed to brown. She felt a little self-conscious, on realizing that not only the crew of the boat, but also the people on shore, who had now reached the sand level with them, were staring with fascination; but she had a part to play, the wife of a missionary. She held up her head and carefully waded to shore, clutching stockings, shoes and skirt hem in her hands, putting one foot carefully down in front of another, flinching a little when she felt a sharp shell or piece of coral, but relishing the sand in between.

Once on shore she was surrounded by curious people; their velvety voices chorused, exclaiming, speaking to each other about her, remarking on her clothes – they wore next to nothing themsleves – her features, height, and shape. It was obvious that this was the meaning of their talk, though she could not understand it. George Sulu noticed what was happening, and with a few short sentences scattered the throng, making them leave her enough space to breathe. Rebecca could guess the gist of his words, and sensed that he was proud of his position as an interpreter, regarding himself as superior to the other islanders because of his travels and command of languages, and was taking up something of a proprietorial position in regard to herself, Simon and the bishop, much as the owner of an elephant might do when travelling the country roads of England. The bishop turned and smiled at Rebecca with a twinkle in his eye. Never had she seen such a kindly and benevolent look as was on his face at this moment.

Soon the canoe was empty, and without fuss its crew turned again to the sea and began to pole back towards the ship lying at anchor off shore. They were returning for the rest of the trunks and packages, and Summa.

'I will go with you to the village, and meet the chiefs,' said the bishop. 'I know them well. We have persuaded them to live at peace, and leave off that tribal warfare which used to split the island. They haven't yet accepted the Christian religion, or been baptized, but I think you will find that they will attend the services, and you will convert them in time.'

'How long will you be able to stay?' asked Rebecca.

'A few hours only; I return to the ship tonight.'

'Such a short time!'

He smiled at her, and in that smile was a full comprehension of her fears and trepidations, and at the same time he seemed to make her a gift of comfort and courage. He was a man of rare quality. Yet he spoke no word, and when George Sulu suggested that they make a start on the walk to the village he agreed and turned from Rebecca without another look; yet she felt that her faith and courage had been restored.

They had been walking for some time along the margin of the sea, partly on the silver coral sand and partly across the mudflats filling a bay, for the tide was out. A pretty creek of clear water flowed into the sea at this point, and higher up Rebecca could see how it deepened, cutting into the green trees, and was crossed by the single trunk of a palm tree. Their party did not turn up to cross by this simple bridge, because they were going across the bay from point to point, walking across soft grey mudflats which filled it. Further out towards the sea was the coral, and further still the white line of the reef, but the ship was out of sight. They were silent, beginning to feel the sun's heat, and were all barefoot on the silky mud. Tiny grey and bright yellow crabs, varying in size from ones no bigger than Rebecca's little fingernail, peeped out from the mud, and here and there scuttled from one hole in it to another; but the vibration of footsteps frightened them and they shot into hiding. The European shoes and stockings were being carried in triumphal procession by the children of the party, naked as the day they were born, as were the women. The men were more decorated with ornaments, and a few had pieces of calico as garments.

The mud, oozing moisture between Rebecca's toes, was deliciously cool, and when they crossed the creek itself, here grown wide and shallow as it flowed towards the sea, she relished the water and was sorry to leave it. A few hundred yards more, though, and they were climbing the sea bank again, and then they struck inland into the bush. What, she wondered, was Simon thinking, and feeling? He was ahead of her, separated by several of the island natives and by the bishop, but at that moment he turned and looked back, so that their eyes met, and he smiled. It was the first time since their marriage that she had felt glad with the old gladness, the pleasure in his company which she used to feel in Cross. In a strange world, and far from home, she had his company, and he hers.

The trees of the island rose high on either side of them, and almost met overhead. The path was narrow, and Rebecca realized that they always walked in single file. Never, in her residence on the island, was she to see two people walking and talking, alongside one another, as would be natural in England. Automatically, they fell in one behind the other, and the paths reflected this, for they were only a foot wide. Made by bare feet, they were kept clear of vegetation by the constant passage; and to walk the footpath through the forest was to walk in some green-aisled cathedral, dim and mysterious, with a sort of holy beauty. Around them the people of the island had broken out again into gurgling chatter among themselves, and Rebecca, finding the path smooth and welcome to her feet, had not resumed her shoes.

The forest trail wound ahead, and after the first few yards they had lost sight of the sea; that illimitable expanse of water, the boundless sky, the tossing heads of the coconut palms, might never have been, in the green world they were traversing. Twisting tree roots crossed the path and they had to pick their way across them. They were lucky that it was the drier part of the year. Often these paths were thick with mud, slippery and difficult to travel. The rain forest was tangled and chaotic. Here and there a tree had half fallen, yet was still held by the luxuriant, rampant undergrowth. There were many different trees and among them the bishop pointed out the fern trees with their straight stems and the leaves sprouting like a bouquet from the top.

The whole place pulsed with thrusting life.

They came out into a glade in the forest, where the sun shone down lighting up a patch of scarlet flowers borne on long stems, as high as Rebecca's waist. As they passed into the pool of sunlight Rebecca felt as though she had been struck a blow by its heat, and looked forward to regaining the cooler shadows of the forest. Before they did so, raucous cries echoed from one wooded ridge to another, and a couple of parrots ricocheted across into the clearing from the other side of the valley, with great impact and commotion.

After their long journeying on board ship, Simon and Rebecca found their muscles were out of practice, and on this dreamlike progress they were rapidly growing tired. Rebecca felt the nausea of pregnancy and longed to rest, but she urged herself forward, her face white, and half stumbling where the path lay over rocks. It was, really, not so difficult a task to keep walking, she thought, compared to many which must be awaiting her. The regained shade of the trees was a help; the startling beauty of the aisle-like route; the amusement of watching the child ahead of her, who had proudly kept possession of one of her stockings and was carrying it on top of his head.

It was not so much longer before they came into an area which had the feeling of a human presence. The tall trees were fewer, and small young trees bearing fruit appeared near the sides of the path; here and there were small clearings, which had the air of cultivation, a mat of identical leaves growing as though from a crop planted there. They met a side path, joining theirs, and trotting along it were two glowing, golden-skinned men, bearing a

180

pole on their shoulders and on it a great bundle of some plant which they had evidently been gathering. As they came abreast of the bishop, the man in front looked at him and smiled in greeting, but trotted on with his companion behind him, so wrapped up in their task that nothing could deflect them from it.

The group of travellers was now approaching the village which was to be the Lloyds' home; a thatched hut appeared, the native type of house, and then another, and with a turn in the path, they had entered a wide clearing.

In some painting of paradise, this village might have served as a model. It seemed to the two who were seeing it for the first time that it was like a heavenly orchard, with homes set here and there among the trees, on a smooth floor of short grass. By the doors of the dwellings were bushes of flowering plants. The houses seemed to have grown there as naturally as the trees, for they were made of soft golden brown woven panels, on a foundation of stones, and with palm leaf thatch. The air of the clearing was drowsy with heat and sun. Between the houses, connecting them, ran the now familiar paths, streaks of soft brown just wide enough for one pair of feet, and moving in a stately way here and there along the paths were people, upright and dignified, never rushing, it seemed.

In front of the largest house, on the highest plinth of stones, was a gathering of people, and the bishop went forward with his hands stretched out in greeting. A tall, handsome man met him – the chief; a smaller, twisted, evil-looking man was also there, the chief from the next village. The bishop signed Simon and Rebecca forward and introduced them.

'For many years the two villages have been at war,' he said quickly; 'now we have persuaded them to stop fighting. You are their guests; it is necessary for them to accept you. Their order of precedence is stricter than ours, their protocol more rigid, and you must conform to it.' Turning to the chiefs, he spoke in their own language and introduced Simon and Rebecca. It did not need her prior knowledge to tell Rebecca how much inferior in this world a woman's place was to that of a man; she could sense it strongly in the looks of the two chiefs, and the reactions of the others in the crowd, so she spoke little, soon took a step backwards, and stood with a deferential air. As the first European woman they had seen, she had curiosity value and eyes were on her, but there was no doubt that she ranked much lower than the two Englishmen.

When she had the opportunity to speak again to the bishop, Rebecca said, 'What a fierce look that chief has! What a contrast to the other! He looks truly a noble savage; but the one-eyed, twisted one . . .'

'Are you judging by appearances, my daughter?' asked the bishop, much amused. 'The chief – Ratu Vussi – without the eye, had it knocked out by the chief you so much admire – that noble savage, Ratu Naka; and no doubt some of his twistedness is due to injuries from the same source.'

'Oh!' and Rebecca looked abashed; the bishop smiled as he turned back to bless and greet all the many people thronging up to him. Women came to Rebecca, smiling and talking, but she had to shake her head in non-comprehension.

'They want to take you to show you your house,' explained the bishop, noticing, and, surrounded by the women, patted by their soft hands, Rebecca was led away.

182

CHAPTER TWELVE

When Rebecca had left England, she had vanished from the sight of those she had known in Yorkshire as thoroughly as though she had been spirited into another world. Mrs Boville had forgotten her in a week. Julia and Eliza Ann, finding that to mention her was unwelcome, only spoke of her when they were alone together, and in the flurry of the family's removal to London they were kept very busy. Giffard Boville never spoke of her at all. Her old neighbours in Cross had grown used to her absence, and were busy with their daily lives. There had been a great deal of talk about how the curate had jilted Miss Marwood – it had been a nine days' wonder; but as he had never told Maria whom it was he preferred to her, the 'other woman' remained a nameless, unknown hussy, in Cross, and wild rumours gathered about her. There would have been much surprise if they had known that this scarlet woman, this Jezebel, was their own Becky Redfearn, who would have had everyone's good word.

Alice, the maid at Broxa House, missed Rebecca very much, and felt very alone as she prepared for her hasty wedding. Edward Gilbank made a point of coming over, one afternoon when his mother was sleeping peacefully, and seeking her out, speaking gently and giving her a sovereign, and she went to London with the Boville family, as Ferguson's wife. He was, at this stage, not unkind to her.

There were two hearts, though, in Kirkby, in which Rebecca's absence was felt, during every hour of every day.

Giffard Boville might not mention her; but he had grown to love and rely on her, and felt more alone than before she had come. Once again there was no one with whom to share his thoughts. His relationship with his other daughters had improved enough during Rebecca's stay for them to have been some comfort to him, if they had been free; but their mother organized every minute of their time, and if Julia sometimes crept into the library for an hour in the twilight, it was as much as she could do. Then, he was soothed and happy, but there was a lurking shadow – the feeling that he ought to tell her to stop thinking of Edward Gilbank as a possible husband; that the match between the families was off. He could not bring himself to do so, he who had never before lacked courage. He dropped hints, and shifted uneasily in his chair. Julia, who knew how occupied Edward was with his mother's illness and the care of his father, who was nearly distracted, did not say anything openly about the matter. Eliza Ann's growing preoccupation with Henry Camm, and his with her, meant that she had little time to think of her father's needs and possible loneliness; but she, too, sometimes came into the library and sat by him as Rebecca had done, until her mother's voice was heard.

The other heart which was missing Rebecca was that of Edward Gilbank. Her absence, and his need of her, could never be forgotten. It was fortunate for him that in those first days, after he had been prevented from following her, he was kept so busy at home; for the first sharp anguish could not be given way to, had somehow to be put aside. When his mother had lapsed, after a second stroke, into a coma, and the active care became more passive, he had survived. He lived, though she could not be with him. He breathed the air, though she did not share it. At first her departure had seemed like a betrayal of the love which had been tacitly accepted as supreme, when they were in each other's arms. There was this to cope with. They had loved each other, and she had gone off without a word and married another man – one for whom he felt she could

184

have no respect. The sharpness of that was enough to kill a man. Edward, sitting in the gloom of his mother's bedroom and listening to her irregular breathing, had not been killed, though he wondered at it. How was it that he was still alive? That was the theme of his blackest thoughts. Life, though, was strong within him.

Her letter, carried always in his breast pocket, had been read through until it was likely to fall apart at the creases. It had been hard to accept that she had believed herself to be acting for the best, for his welfare, for Julia's welfare. Did she really think, that, loving her, he could marry Julia? Had she not realized, in the oriental summerhouse, what she meant to him? He knew that she had realized, that they had shared the experience, that she loved him.

Stupid self-sacrifice! Yet – did she care for this Simon Lloyd, then, after all? Had he been deceiving himself? She did not love him! He had imagined it all! Imagined their gradually growing relationship, the pleasure which gleamed in her eyes when she saw him, the quiet strolls through the woods and by the river, as they had come to realize that they were everything to each other! He had imagined this, had he? No . . . his temporary anger evaporated. Those times together were too real, too present in his heart, to have been imagined. Worst of all, they had left their imprint on the landscape. His impressions of her were so vivid that a hundred times a day he thought he saw her, as though she had that instant just turned the corner out of sight, just paused, then when he looked, vanished . . . and because, gentle and gentlemanly though he was, Edward Gilbank was a man, and desired Rebecca with his body as well as his heart, he could not help being tormented with the idea that she was another's; in his blackest moments he could hardly keep out of his mind images of her, belonging to Simon Lloyd . . . it was a bitter cup to drink, and he writhed with the pain of it.

It was said after, of Edward Gilbank, that he must have thought the world of his mother; just look how the lad had lost weight, and his hair was showing grey. The Gilbanks didn't show grey early as a rule, said the old wives in the neighbourhood, raking back and comparing Edward with many a one of his family on both his father's and his mother's side; they felt concern for the lad, he looked that upset. Quite grey he was going, and thin. Poor Lady Gilbank, and poor Sir Charles! Well, it must come to us all. Look how the Bovilles had gone off to London, just when the Gilbanks were in the midst of their trouble. Fine friends, they turned out to be, to poor Mester Gilbank. What were friends for, if they weren't there when you wanted them? Miss Redfearn, as well. He had been sweet on her, anyone could see that. Then she'd gone off, and married someone else, so they said. Very fishy, all of it. She'd seemed such a nice lass, better than that Julia and Eliza Ann, and everyone had hoped they'd be happy, and that Sir and Lady would have their grandchildren about them, and now look at the state of things.

This was the old wives' talk of the neighbourhood; and while the men pooh-poohed it – mere women's talk – Edward was given their gruff sympathy, without more than a handclasp with extra meaning in it, or the passing glance as they said 'goodday' with a little more depth – a little longer meeting of the eyes – a mere fraction, but it was enough. Edward was surrounded by the sympathy of those among whom he lived, closed round him like a protective mesh, a hammock which somehow kept him above the flood.

Across on the other hilltop, Broxa House lay empty. He could no longer watch at night for her candle, as he had grown into the habit of doing, picking out that one corner window in the massive pile. With Bounce, when he was able to get out for an hour, he sometimes went over to Broxa House, and walked up through the garden, and looked in at the summerhouse, but soon found that it was too painful, and tried to walk always in the other direction, on to the open moors. His feet drew him back, from time to time, and he would go down to the river, and stand on the bank, and feel he could see her turn, just as she left him on that day when they had last stood there together, to wave, at the bend . . .

It was a blessing, folk said, when Lady Gilbank, after lying senseless for some weeks, died quietly. All her life she had been a sweet and gentle soul, and it was not like her to give trouble to anybody; she had had to give trouble enough, in these last few weeks, while she lay first partially and then wholly helpless. It had been a labour of love to her husband and son to tend her. Fierce little Sir Charles had forgotten himself, for he truly loved the wife he had so dominated and ruled over, and at the last he had thought of nothing but doing his best for her. He was at her bedside night and day, and it was all Edward could do to make him go and get some sleep. By the time she died, and he sat stunned and unbelieving, he was reaching such a state of exhaustion himself that if she had been ill much longer she would have taken her husband with her to lie in the quiet churchyard of Kirkby.

When all was over and they had returned from the funeral, Edward and his father sat together in the Great Hall of Gilbank, where the fireplace was once more filled with fragrant boughs of larch and pine, and the doors stood open to let in any breath of air. Harvest was still going on in the fields, small upland fields; up here the grain ripened late, and the hot weather was a boon at this time of year.

The two men sat in silent companionship, each grateful for the other's presence, but not needing to speak. The rough, antique furniture of the room, the rugged tables and chests and aumbries, the ragged carpets where their forefathers had strewn rushes, the hammerbeam roof over their heads, the dogs stretched at their feet, spoke of the continuity of life. The Hall had seen Gilbanks come, and Gilbanks go, for centuries. Death was no stranger to it, nor mating, nor birth.

'Life goes on,' said Sir Charles at last, with a sigh. He looked over at his son. 'But after you, Edward, there is no one. Unless you marry, you are the last of the Gilbanks.'

'I shall not marry, father,' replied Edward.

'It's come to nothing, then. Giffard Boville and I could have saved our breath to cool our porridge.' The old man sounded bitter, and tired. 'What is wrong with you, lad? Don't you want to see your children here? Hand it on to them when you are gone? With Boville's eldest daughter you would have had all the land from here to Broxa Moss.'

'I'm sorry, father.'

'I shan't last long, you know. Not with your mother gone.'

'Of course you will.' Edward put his hand over that of the old man, and pressed it. His parents had been in their thirties when they married, and he had been born when they had given up hope of a child. Sir Charles's hand was that of an aged man.

'Don't speak so.' Edward determined that he would devote his life to his father, and make his last years as happy as it was possible for them to be. At least he could do that much. He did not realize that for him, too, the thought was a lifeline. Without it, once the illness and death of his mother was over, he might have lapsed into indifference; have sat eating his heart out for Rebecca, daydreaming until he grew away from the world and its concerns and could no longer take part in it. He could have grown into an eccentric recluse, brooding alone on his sorrow.

'I can't face life without her,' said Sir Charles, brokenly.

'Perhaps we will be best going away from here for a while.' Edward looked at his father with concern. 'Would you like to travel on the continent? We often thought that if mother had been willing to come with us, we would have done that. She would like to think you had gone at last.'

'Do you think she would, Edward?' The old man brightened a little.

'I'm sure of it.'

The brightening had not lasted long.

'I don't know. It would be such a trouble.'

'Not the least trouble in the world. You know you like to travel.'

'I don't want to leave home now.'

'Suppose we were to go abroad for the winter? You felt the cold cruelly last time. Don't you remember how you wished for a warmer climate, when you had that cough?'

'Aye, and so I did. I was really very ill with that cough, wasn't I, Edward?'

'Very ill, father.'

'Your mother said, I remember, that the Yorkshire winters were too much for me.'

Edward remembered; he could still see in his mind's eye his mother's gentle fussing, hear his father's tearing cough, and his irritable voice – 'I was born and bred in Yorkshire, Martha, and the winter hasn't killed me yet!'

'The south of France might suit you better, father.'

Sir Charles's interest had been aroused. It was not many days before he was prepared to agree that it might be a good idea to winter abroad. A fortnight, and he got out a map; a month, and he had extended the plan to include a visit to Rome; six weeks, and they were not to stop short of seeing the pyramids in Egypt.

Lady Gilbank was not forgotten; but in travel, her husband found some sort of anodyne; in looking after his father, her son found a reason for life.

By the time that Rebecca was settling into her first married home in a village on a tropical island, the Gilbanks' plans were under discussion, and by the time she was experiencing for the first time a southern Pacific summer, Gilbank Hall was shut up.

On either side of the valley, the two houses stood dark and empty, with the winter winds curling round them, the last of the autumn leaves blown against their fastened shutters and lodging in the crevices. The two green dragons, gazing out of their ornamental garden towards the Hangman's Brook, Gibbet Moor and Black Crag, on the other side of the valley, had their blank green gaze filmed over with a sheath of ice, and the little pavilion was

189

filled with a snowdrift, blown in through the cracks round the closed doors, resting on the seat where Edward and Rebecca had been clasped in each other's arms, and had forgotten everything but their love. The winter skies were black, and the months were long; the upland people crouched over their fires, told long tales of the boggarts of the moors, and knitted, watched the firelight, and endured, while under the stone slated roof of Gilbank Hall, and the battlements of Broxa House, the hearths lay cold and empty.

The work which lay ahead for her became obvious to Rebecca in those first few hours in the village of Lalotu. The women who surrounded her as she stood for a few seconds in the doorway of her new home, before entering, were naked, and she knew that she must teach them to be ashamed of their nakedness and cover their gleaming bodies with calico. They were fragrant, sweet-smelling bodies, and she wondered at it, when she herself felt so hot and sticky, so far from being fragrant. She must first learn the language. Then she must learn how one lived, out here; what there was to eat, how it was cooked, where she could do the washing. By the time the coming baby arrived, she must have made all preparations, must be well organized. Simon's needs would have to be met, in this place where nothing was as they had known it in their lives before. Men always expected to be looked after. The house stood, like others in the village, on a plinth of stones. She did not know then that the height of the plinth indicated the social position of the owner, but she noticed that the Lloyd plinth was not as high as the chief's, but higher than most of the other homes. The single room beneath the high roof – the ridge pole a palm tree trunk – was large, some forty feet long by twenty wide; and she knew that it was to be used as a school as well as a home, and that until a church was built, small prayer meetings too might take place here. Part of the end was partitioned off by a strange curtain. Going over to it, she could see that it was unlike any cloth she knew of – stiff, like thick paper, or a kind of papery felt, of an ivory white background printed with a simple but lively pattern in brown and black. Behind this hanging a pile of mats lay on the floor, and she guessed it to be the bedroom. The whole floor of the house was covered with similar mats, beautifully woven, with a flat, finely plaited surface, decorated here and there with patterns in dark brown. In the bedchamber section, the mats were more elaborate, fringed with gaily coloured feathers.

The women gestured to her and she decided that, for whatever reason, they wanted her to lie down. There was nothing she wanted more, herself; so when one of them fetched a fringed mat from the inner room, spread it on the floor, and patted it, she lay down gratefully. The day had now reached a peak of heat. Around her the women settled down, cross-legged on the floor, or lay as if to sleep; children lay, or sat; talk became quiet and murmuring, and Rebecca slept.

When she awoke, she was greeted by smiles; it seemed to have delighted the women that she could sleep among them. They were eager to take her somewhere else, to show her more; going out of a second door in the house, they took her a few yards to where a much smaller building stood on its own, and on entering she found that this must be the kitchen. Two large black earthenware pots, shaped like tall wide bottles, lay on the floor near what was obviously a hearth, and in palm-leaf baskets hanging from the roof were yams, which she had recently learned to know, and dalo, both root crops she had tasted for the first time not long before, but found to be good. The yams tasted as much as anything like potato, and the dalo had the look and something of the texture of turnip, but did not taste like turnip; she liked it better. There were a few coconuts, and a number of half coconut shells, polished and gleaming dark brown, like cups, she thought. This was where she would be cooking, then . . . she wanted to express her gratitude, and one of the words the bishop had tried to teach her came into her mind.

'*Venaka,*' she said, and opened her hands and arms towards the women in a gesture of friendship. '*Venaka, venaka.*'

Around her the smiles grew broader, and they took up her word delightedly.

'*Venaka, venaka,*' they echoed.

There was so much to learn during those first days and weeks that every second was occupied, and Simon and Rebecca did not have time for reflection, or for homesickness. The bishop had only stayed for a few hours, and during that time they had all shared a ceremonial meal, sitting round on the floor of the chief's house, and eating from leaves instead of plates, and with their fingers. The food was delicious. Rebecca felt a little self-conscious, because in this society the men always ate first, the women serving humbly and then eating afterwards; but the bishop insisted that Englishwomen did not behave like that, and because she was hardly regarded as a woman, being white and a stranger guest, Rebecca joined the men at their meal. It was not easy to eat neatly with her fingers, but she found it quite possible, and sat with her legs tucked modestly to one side and her feet well concealed under her skirt.

Afterwards, when she dipped her fingers in a shell of water handed by one of the women, she decided that this was really a very sensible way to eat. Later, sitting in the shade of a frangipani tree and enjoying the fragrance of its beautiful blossoms, she could hear the women eating their meal by themselves, and quite envied the chatter and giggling that she could hear going on.

When the bishop left, they did not feel so very alone; after all, he had only gone as far as the steamer, to sleep at anchor for the night. The next day they had all retraced their steps along the forest paths, and gone to the beach of silver coral near the boat, shouted over a few last words, and waved as long as they could distinguish the figures on board.

The return journey to the village of Lalotu had seemed shorter than on the previous day, as a familiar path always seems shorter than an unknown one. The bishop and the ship had gone, but they were still in the vicinity, cruising on the last of their visits to other islands, dropping off the last of the returning scholars and picking up new ones. The air thickened towards summer and time passed; the bishop would by now have returned to New Zealand; it was then that the isolation of their situation, on the island with no hope of seeing a white face until the following year, when the bishop would return, came home to them. The only link they had was the two ex-scholars, Summa and George Sulu. The heat was wearying and oppressive. The air was warm and heavy, surrounding them like an ethereal blanket.

The island of Mutu had several villages scattered among its mountains and valleys, usually hidden among the tall growth of the bush. One village, which had of old had a particularly warlike reputation, was built high up on a rocky outcrop like the eyrie of an eagle. It was an inconvenient situation, and Simon had been asked by the bishop to see if he could gain enough influence with the people to persuade them to build another village in a healthier place near the shore, where there were fewer mosquitoes, and there was a more plentiful supply of fresh water. It was surprising how much had been accomplished already by a relatively recent contact with Christianity. The bishop called at the island and he tried to explain to them that fighting, thieving, cruelty and immorality were incompatible with the teaching of Christ and the love of God, and he had to hope that they would not make too much contact with the white traders of the area, until their faith was secure enough to armour them against their evil influence.

He had reasoned earnestly with the people, picking up their language very quickly and writing down some guidance on it; he had taken away George Sulu as his first pupil, and later Summa, both of whom returned full of the wonders of the community in which they had lived in New Zealand; now, as a consequence, he had ten pupils who had gone off with him this time in the boat, and the people had asked for a missionary, and Simon had been appointed.

The most startling effect of the bishops's contact with the island was that these people, who before had fought bitterly among themselves, were now at peace; they had been cannibals, but now had given up the practice.

The awe which they had felt on meeting these strange white-skinned people, with a boat which moved apparently by itself, and who were draped in mystic clothes, must have influenced them strongly. Demi-gods had come, to walk and talk with them, and wonders to perform. Their old gods must have lost their power, and the spirit temples were deserted, while they thronged by the hundred to listen to Simon conducting services in the open air, in front of the enormous banyan tree.

But when those first few weeks were over, there came a time for both the Lloyds, when the ocean did indeed seem illimitable, and their isolation difficult to bear.

Rebecca had discovered very quickly how it was that the people of the island were so sweet-smelling and clean. On the second day the women had come to her in the late afternoon and by many gestures shown that they wished her to go with them. They headed off along one of the forest trails, and soon were walking by the river which ran down from the mountains, near the village. A great shouting and talking could be heard, and Rebecca was astonished, as they came on a deep pool, to see all the men and boys of the village, quite naked, splashing about in the water, merry as a troop of schoolchildren. They shouted out to the procession of women as they walked past, and peals of laughter echoed up into the trees.

Rebecca felt acutely embarrassed, and did not know which way to look; so she looked straight in front of her, while her cheeks burned. They went on, deeper into the bush, and the sound of the men faded behind them. Then they came to another pool, very secret and beautiful, where among the tall trees the water widened and was still deep. The women walking ahead plunged straight into the pool, some of them submerged themselves in the water then surfacing and shaking the water free from their fuzzy heads of hair. Others stood about rubbing themselves all over with water. Rebecca realized that they expected her to join them. Downstream she could still hear the faint shouting of the men. If only she felt sure what to do! Simon was still in the village, working on his next sermon. He was going to try to give it in the native language. Not that he would have come here, to this pool . . .

At last the look of the cool water, and her longing for a bathe, decided her. If only she had brought her soap. Shyly, she stripped off her clothes, until she stood naked as the others in the warm air. They had consideration for her shyness, and did not stare at her. They looked the other way, but she knew they were curious, and it was natural good manners which restrained them. Gingerly she picked her way into the pool; the bank was muddy, and she finished with an undignified slip, but it was worth it, to feel the water on her limbs. She did not stay in the pool as long as the others. Quite soon she felt her shyness returning, and was anxious to put on her clothes once more. There was no way of drying herself but she realized that by the time she had been out of the water a few minutes, she would be dry. It was a very hot day, though then she had hardly begun to learn the meaning of heat.

When she told Simon of this experience, he was horrified; but she was firm against him.

'You should go to bathe with the men, Simon,' she told him. 'They would appreciate it; you remember what the bishop said.'

'Certainly not.'

'You would feel so much better for it.'

'I have been washing, of course. Are you suggesting that I have not?'

'After bathing, Simon, they rub on scented oil; can you smell it on me? Oh, it is so soothing to the skin! Mine was ready to crack before, it was so dry. Now it is quite comfortable.'

'You must not adopt heathen ways, Rebecca! Do not forget who you are. Behaving like a native woman! And why aren't you wearing your shoes?'

'When in Rome,' answered Rebecca. She was annoyed, and it was an expression she had heard him use. He looked uncomfortable, and his socks and shoes must be so hot. At first the soles of her feet had been tender, and every twig had hurt her, but with the heat and her pregnancy, her ankles were swelling, and she could not put on her shoes. Gradually she was finding it less painful to walk without them, as her feet became hardened. She had tried to make some sandals out of cloth and the laces from her boots, but they were not very satisfactory and as her feet were hardly to be seen under her long skirts, she could not see that it mattered.

'Rome!' exclaimed Simon. He looked thoughtful. 'They rubbed on oil after their baths in Rome.'

'Our Lord was anointed,' added Rebecca. 'I don't see anything wrong in it.'

'In hot countries it may be the right, the proper thing to do,' decided Simon. 'I'll try the oil – can you get me some, Rebecca? I will bathe, but by myself, and I'll try some oil.' Her apparently easy victory surprised her, but she said nothing, guessing that he had been in great discomfort to be persuaded so quickly.

The next day, after an earnest conversation with George Sulu and Summa, Simon did some exploring and decided on a small pool, neither the pool of the men nor the pool of the women, and here he had his bathe, and admitted that he found himself refreshed.

Rebecca had bartered for some of the scented oil – she was discovering how much she could get for a fish-hook – but she was determined to learn how to make it for herself. The oil itself was from coconuts, but the perfume was from flowers and sandalwood. Inside one of the other houses in the village she sat opposite to a fat old woman, and tried to understand her instructions. There was a

196

biggish log of sandalwood; this was flaked off by degrees, as much as was required, and soaked in the oil. Then there were the flowers, which could be gathered at will from the bush, or from the plants which grew in the village. By her own door Rebecca had a small tree of the fragrant frangipani, but the other flowers she could only name by the strange names given them by the islanders.

She began to understand how big a wonder iron was to these people. Flaking off sandalwood with a sharp shell was laborious; with a chisel from Simon's little kit of carpentry tools, she herself could do it in a fraction of the time.

In this society, personal property was an unknown concept; the community shared their goods to a large extent, and after Rebecca had demonstrated her proficiency on a log of sandalwood with a chisel, all the women in the village came to ask if they could borrow it, and the folk of the area smelled for a time overpoweringly of sandalwood, to the neglect of the flower scents.

It might have seemed difficult to persuade these children of nature, in their warm air and naked freedom, to accept the constrictions and unnecessary heat of clothes, but it was not. The demi-gods wore clothes, and to do so was to take part in their magic. Woven cloths had no part in their culture, but the tapa – the beaten-out cloth, like papery felt, from the bark of the mulberry tree, printed with earth colours – was ceremonial dress, worn on marriage and high festivals.

Simon had been supplied with bolts of calico, some of it plain, some of it printed in gaudy colours, and it had a great attraction for the women and for the men. They could hardly wait for Rebecca to portion it out and explain what to do with it. The simplest thing, much adopted in the Melanesian islands, was to take a length of about two yards, a narrow width for the men and a wider one for the women, and drape it round from the waist downwards, wrapping it over in front and tucking the free end into the waist to secure this. This did not cover the women's breasts; but at least the more embarrassing part of them – to Simon's and Rebecca's ideas – was decently clad, and in time the other might follow.

It had been a time of unpleasantness to Simon until the women started wearing their skirts. Sex and clothes went together in his mind, and Rebecca's stays and stockings meant almost as much to him as her body. The attitudes of the native peoples shocked him. He had been warned that the most difficult thing for them to accept was the concept of Christian marriage. Promiscuity and several wives had been their custom from time immemorial. When the women were wearing skirts he could at least raise his eyes from the ground when he was talking to them.

But with clothes came other problems, such as the washing of them, and Rebecca had to teach the women how to wash clothes. They found a shallow, sparkling river with plenty of stones to sit on while working, and she showed them how to wash their garments. It was a delightful occupation! They went along together in groups and, after filing through the bush, settled on various stones in the river and rubbed away, coming back with their long skirts trailing wet around them, and the newly washed clothes in palm-leaf baskets.

It was difficult to get used to the heat, particularly in this matter of wet clothes. Rebecca saw women out fishing in the sea, and wading ashore wet to mid-thigh – but no thought of taking off their skirts to dry them. In half an hour they would be bone dry again, unless it rained, and if the warm rain came, then the skirts would dry when the sun came back. . . .

The heat was increasing. Neither Simon nor Rebecca realized how lucky they were to be on this particular island, where the breezes from the sea kept a little air moving; on some of the bigger islands the airlessness and humidity were almost unbearable. As it was, they suffered from all manner of minor discomforts from sweat rashes to prickly heat, particularly Rebecca, and still the weather got warmer.

CHAPTER THIRTEEN

Simon was revealing unexpected characteristics, as
Rebecca grew to know him better. He had more determination than she could have realized. The passion which
had swept them both to this speck of land in the boundless
sea had been one manifestation of it; now, day by day and
week by week, he hammered out a timetable for their
lives, and despite heat, unaccustomed food, strange sur-
roundings, he stuck to it in every detail. They rose at the
swift dawn, and went at once to prayers; then a breakfast
of fruit, which Rebecca had collected, or bartered for. It
was all they felt able to eat in the heat. Then school for the
children and young people of the village, with Rebecca
teaching the girls and women diligence in their household
tasks, and her own ideals of Christian life. At noon they
had a little food, and then rested during the heat of the
afternoon, before Rebecca began to cook the evening meal.
After the night had descended in its usual abrupt fashion,
with the brilliant brief sunset which flared for a few
minutes on the horizon, they felt, in the comparative cool
of the evening, that they could eat at last. Then they sat at
their table, with the children from other villages who had
come to learn and who lived with them, to a meal of the
things which grew or could be caught on the island. At
first each day's cooking had been an adventure to Rebecca;
she had to learn which were food plants, how to grow
them, how to harvest them, how to cook them. The
women of the village took her to their hearts, and thought
it a great game to teach her. At first, when her feet were
tender, and she flinched as she walked the bush, they

turned aside to laugh, but not unkindly. It was impossible to wear shoes on those swollen feet, so at last Simon gave in, though he resolutely went on wearing his socks and light shoes. This was one of the ways in which he showed his resolution; he would not vary by one iota his European ways.

Dalo grew in clearings among the trees of the bush. Its large leaves, glossy and heart-shaped, waved luxuriantly, and Rebecca learned how to cook the leaves in the cream from a coconut, the stems, and, most often of all, the root, swollen to the size and colour of a swede, but different in flavour. They decided they liked it almost better than potatoes. A great dish of dalo roots was served at the evening meal, and each took as much of it as they wanted.

The native families still ate with the men first, and not until they had finished and left the floor where the meal was laid did the women and children eat. The Lloyds set the European example. Husband and wife ate together, neither appearing to be superior to the other, each passing food and serving one another. They ate at a table, and their strange ways were of great interest to the villagers. Chairs were a curiosity, and every man in the island wanted one, so that he too could sit in state, but those which were made were rarely used. They were too much in the habit of sitting on the floor, cross-legged on the mats woven by the women, to change.

Simon held a short meeting every morning, for prayers; and after the evening meal for explaining the Bible. His group sat on the floor of their hut, cross-legged in a circle.

Each Sunday was marked by the strictest observance. Food was prepared the day before, and it had to be such as would keep in the heat and humidity, hung in palm-leaf baskets to keep it safe from the tiny ants. People from all the island villages came to the Sunday services, and Simon felt that he was making real progress against the forces of darkness.

Tempers, they found, were easily frayed in the heat. Both of them had to make constant efforts not to be

200

irritable. They could not give way, when they were surrounded by shining brown faces, innocently looking to them for an example of this good new life.

Simon's passionate love for Rebecca had been, after all, of short duration. It would have lasted longer, if she had not become pregnant, and might, in that case, have subsided gradually into something which, at a lesser level, would have lasted. As it was, denied a time of calm and consolidation, battered by the strains of their new life, it ebbed away. He was frustrated by her pregnancy, because he found her swelling shape not touching, or moving, because it was his child, but abhorrent. He had to turn his eyes from her figure. Her whole appearance, here on the island, irritated him, because it reminded him, not of the delicate lady he had seen in Yorkshire, but more and more of the country girl he had known in Lincolnshire.

Loose dresses had had to be made, or she could not have stood the heat; the crimson tabinet was seen no more. Her stays were set aside, her stockings unworn, her feet bare, and peeping unashamedly from under the hems of her garments. That richness of hair, once dressed high and set with a rose, was now coiled simply at the back of her head, as she had worn it in Cross. If she followed the fashion of the village people, and tucked a flower into it, for the sheer joy of their beauty, it was the flaring hibiscus, or the sweet blossoms of the frangipani.

In spite of Simon's disapproval, in many ways Rebecca revelled in the new life. Learning to fish from the rocks, and then cleaning and cooking her catch, had all the charm of novelty for her. Going into the cool glades of the bush and digging up her dalo, or her yams, or cassava, and taking it to her cooking hut, in company with the other women, gave her a daily interest. She gathered ota fern, and cooked the tips of it. When the children of the village harvested the sea urchins, piled them up on the beach, and lit a fire of palm fronds over them, she took her share – for most things were shared, in the little community – and learned how tasty the slivers of yellow flesh could be.

Simon did not know what he was eating, or he might not have enjoyed it. In her simple shifts, bare feet, and with a flower in her hair, she was like a graceful queen among the shorter, livelier brown-skinned women, dressed only in their skirts, and while she learned from them, taught them.

Simon's attitude to the child growing in her body distressed her, but she had never been able to understand his sexuality. With Edward, how straightforward it had been! Their acceptance of one another, and his protectiveness, had seemed the most natural thing in the world. It was not necessary to speculate on how Edward would have acted, had it been his child – had she been his wife; she could sense, as though they were one creature, how his eyes would have lit with pride, how he would have laid his hand on her belly in reverence and love, and looked at her almost with worship; how his unspoken plans for the baby would have been in the air between them, as they sat either side of the fire in the Great Room of Gilbank Hall. There were moments, when she was sitting on the rocks, fishing, when like a cool mirage thoughts of Edward rose in her mind. She allowed herself to think them, because this secret dream, these daydream thoughts, enabled her to bear the heat of the day and the difficulties of living with Simon. Somewhere on the other side of the world, Edward existed. Oak and ash and thorn grew. Hard cold snow and biting winds blew over the moors, and brought the blood racing to one's cheeks, and there was love, and constancy. She did not try to imagine Edward married to Julia, though that was the whole object of her sacrifice; to do so would have been asking too much. But times they had spent together, paths where they had walked in each other's company, moorland over which Bounce had run while she and Edward walked and talked together, the little town of Kirkby where sometimes they had chanced across each other and continued side by side, the rooms they had sat in, drinking tea or eating with the Gilbanks and the Bovilles, these returned to her strongly in memory.

Far away in the tropics, the wife of another man, she let herself dream secretly of Edward, and it gave her strength to go on day to day. There had been such love, and she had known it. There was such a county as Yorkshire, and she had been at home in it. Like a grail, her thoughts went on before her, and lit the way. She could endure anything, withstand anything, for once she had been loved.

Rebecca's child became due as the heat of the summer at last faded into the more bearable temperatures of autumn. There was very little change in the foliage of the island, but some of the food crops came to an end and they ate the last of the breadfruit and the soursops. Other trees began to bear, and it was time to plant some things, to harvest others. At the doorway of their house Rebecca sat and sewed simple garments for the coming child, and all around she watched the babies of the village, learned how they were reared, and made up her mind what practices she would adopt, and which were bad and must be fought against.

She woke before dawn and knew that her time had come. The cries of the birds echoed. A moth the size of a wren had not yet gone to rest, and was blundering about the sleeping area. The sand wasps were busy in their little nests plastered against the underside of the roof.

All things had been in readiness for some time. Rebecca went and sat on the step at the front of the house. There had been a tiny trace of blood; her inside was squeezing itself up, now and then, strongly enough to be felt distinctly, but not yet strongly enough to be called pain. Parrots crashed through the air over the village, and a litter of little pigs ran squealing by. In the distance dawn was breaking, and the first of the women came out of her house and began to pick up the leaves which had fallen during the previous day on to the narrow paths. By a few minutes after sun up all those little paths, and the wider areas in front of each house, would be immaculate and brushed, the sandy texture of the dried-out soil clean and soft for the passage of many feet. The velvety sound of the voices of the women, speaking to each other as they went about their tasks with graceful movements, was in the air like a groundswell to the birds. One of them sang a hymn which Simon had been teaching them, and the soft lilt of the rich deep voice made the English hymn somehow take on the rhythm of the island. It was too early to say anything, Rebecca decided. From her experience at various times, she knew that a first childbirth was likely to be a long process, and that she might be in labour all day. No need to see that repugnance on Simon's face at her physical function before it was absolutely necessary. In her heart, she felt joy, struggling and bubbling to the surface; wherever she looked, she loved; the world was beautiful, and God was good. Nothing was to matter that day to Rebecca but the child inside her.

There were unusual signs of activity, and Rebecca remembered. The chief of a village on the tiny island which lay at the end of their own larger one had died, and today was his funeral. Most of the menfolk of the village and some of the women would be going, bearing gifts as a mark of respect. For a hundred days the period of mourning would last, and in the bays of the small island no one would be allowed to fish; no singing, no playing on musical instruments, no dancing would be allowed. The men would have to refrain from their drinking of kava, and life on the little island would be in a state of suspended animation until mourning was over.

Simon had woken, and was standing beside her.

'I will be going over to the funeral,' he said. 'It is too good an opportunity to miss. I will tell them of the after-life, and how, had Katufa been a Christian, he would now be entering into it.' His eyes were bright with fervour, and she looked up at him doubtfully. Should she tell him, and keep him by her side? What use would he be? Less use than her friends among the native women. She held her breath as a stronger contraction washed over her and knew that she would be glad if Simon were out of the way for the day, he at one end of life, and she at the other.

'I'll get breakfast,' she said.

'We haven't had prayers yet,' he reminded her.

As she knelt with the native children, on the floor of their house, and they sang a morning hymn, Rebecca was uplifted. Her day had come – her day. The greatest day of her life, she felt. Every moment of it was golden. The fruit, as she served it for breakfast, was gilded by the sun; she was serving the ambrosial fruits of the Garden of Eden to the children of Paradise . . . Simon was hunting for a suitable funeral gift. All the other households in the village would be taking mats, or tapa, or fans, choosing the best they had. Simon chose a length of valance, which on the other side of the world Julia had once pressed upon Rebecca in a Manchester warehouse. It would be prized above the mats and tapa which the islanders produced themselves.

'You don't think it's too much?' queried Rebecca hesitantly. It was not often nowadays that she voiced her opinions to Simon.

'Nonsense.'

The people were leaving the village on the long walk to the tip of the island; they should reach it by the time the tide was out, and they would be able to walk across to Ota. Swift tropical rain was falling, rain which felt warm on the skin, and those of the men who had given themselves elaborate coiffures in honour of the dead chief held palm leaves over their heads for protection. Carrying his rolled-up valance, and in his clerical clothes, Simon joined the people filtering out of the village clearing. Rebecca, holding her arms round her body and watching as a stronger contraction swept over her, knew that they would not be returning until nightfall, and perhaps they would be away until the following day. The children of their school bobbed along behind Simon, in single file as always, and they all disappeared into the bush. With the exception of half a dozen women, the village was deserted.

Rebecca was becoming accustomed to the form her contractions took, and found that she was still able to walk, talk and arrange things in between them. So she explained matters to her friends, and they came to keep her company, and throughout the morning while the warm rain fell they sat on the floor, watching the rain through the open doorway, and talking of the ceremonies which would be taking place at the funeral. They ate a little; Rebecca slept a little; the time passed, slowly. One woman stayed with her while the others went to cook. They brought food to Rebecca, but she waved it away. Sunset had passed, darkness had come, and the time of blackness of soul was upon her; the time when the womb has finished its opening movements, and prepares to change, to those surges which push out the child into the world. Down, she went, in that darkness, from which nothing could save her, and for a little while sadness, death and horror possessed her. Was this what it was like, to give birth? The depth of her depression seemed like a black pit, and she was forced to cling on, mentally, to the little flickering light, and the barely distinguishable faces of her friends, Lala and Vivi. It seemed like an age; it was twenty minutes, that she wallowed in despond, before the mental clouds began to lift, and she sensed the change which had come over her. Life had its demands to make; the life she had been nurturing for nine months in her womb, and her own life, which still had work to fill it. She knew then why childbirth is called labour, for she found that her body was demanding that she work, to expel the child. The way was ready, and it must pass through, to take its place in the world, its chance. She pushed, and rested, and pushed, and rested, and Lala held her hand, and Vivi's soft voice murmured encouragement.

A cry; and she could feel the warm, damp body of her child resting on the inner side of her thigh. So soon after that last heave! She had not dared to hope that that effort – superhuman almost as it had seemed when she made it – could have achieved the object and brought about the birth, but she knew, without Lala's cooing welcome to the baby, that it was so.

'Where is it? Where is it? Let me see,' she panted, struggling to get her head forward and see the newborn creature.

Vivi picked it up, and bit through the cord which held it to Rebecca. Then she handed it to its mother, and the dim glow of the tiny lamp showed the happiness in Rebecca's eyes. The baby was crying, but as soon as Rebecca took it in her arms and nestled it close to her breast, it was quiet, and still, and seemed contented.

'Little one,' she breathed, and looked fondly down at it. 'Little one . . . is it a boy or a child, Lala?' But Lala did not understand, and Rebecca had to ask again in her careful halting Melanesian. Lala's face saddened, as though she were about to give bad news. The baby was a daughter . . . 'I don't mind,' said Rebecca, and the two women looked at her, uncomprehending. A boy baby was what everybody wanted; a girl child was worthless, just born to work and plant crops and look after the men, and then in its turn bear more children. Rebecca, though, was elated, and did not seem to mind that her baby was a girl.

'My baby,' she crooned to it, gentling the fine short hair on its forehead.

It was over, and in a little while, when Lala and Vivi had cleaned everything up and brought her a drink of coconut milk, Rebecca settled down for the night alone with her baby in the house. Fulfilment was hers, and she did not miss Simon, or feel fear at being alone. Nothing could touch her then, for she was in her own world of happiness. Exhausted, though, she was, and slept soundly. Not too soundly; she would have woken if her tiny newborn baby had given any cry, but soundly enough to be refreshing. Baby too must have found her entry into the world wearying, for that first night, cuddled down into the hollow of her mother's arm, she also slept, twitching slightly, and now and then uttering little questioning noises. Before first light Rebecca was awake again, and looking down into the pair of dark eyes raised to hers. The baby was hungry, and had apparently been born knowing exactly what to do about that . . .

By the time Simon returned from Ota, it was late afternoon. He came back cheerfully whistling, and calling out for her. She called back, from the shelter of their sleeping place, and he came in.

'Come and see your daughter,' invited Rebecca. He stood and looked down at her and the baby, without a word. 'Don't you like her?' said the new mother. 'Look, she's looking at you. That's your father, little one.'

'You didn't say,' said Simon. 'I would have stayed with you. Why didn't you say? Was it sudden? Weren't you expecting it to happen yet?' His voice was concerned, but strangely colourless.

'There wasn't anything you could have done,' explained Rebecca. 'I had Lala and Vivi. These things are better managed by women.' She smiled up at him, and wished that he would reach down and kiss her, take her in his arms. He held out a finger towards his daughter, and she grasped it with her tiny fist.

'Have you thought of a name for her?' He still sounded stilted. They had not discussed the coming child, had made no plans. He had seemed not to want to acknowledge the coming event.

'I'm going to call her Margaret,' her voice was firm and decided, and he realized that she was not open to influence from his wishes. Still he showed no sign of caressing the mother of his child.

'Why? Why Margaret?'

'Because,' said Rebecca dreamily, looking down at her baby, 'when she grows up, she will have to fight dragons. Green dragons . . . do you remember the window in the church at Cross? With St Margaret?'

He sighed. 'Then Margaret it is,' he said wearily, and, getting up, left the house. Lala and Vivi came forward hastily to tell him that they were cooking the meal for him and the pupils, and it was nearly ready. He nodded at them, and said that he was just going for a short walk in the bush and would be back soon. He took his way on a

208

narrow path, past the bathing pools, and over the river by the trunk of the felled palm tree which lay across it. Then up a rocky slope, until after a quarter of an hour's steady climbing, he came out on a little crest of rock which commanded a view of the slopes of the island running down to the sea. The sea itself could be seen from here. It seemed to have graded bands of differing blues; the hard blue of the turquoise, the melting blue of the sapphire, the hazy blue in the distance of the amethyst.

Lala and Vivi had not been surprised at his gloomy air. Men were always like that at the birth of a girl baby; they had told Rebecca so, and she had not believed them, but now they were vindicated. Mr Lloyd was not pleased. They looked at each other on their way back to the cooking hut, and were satisfied.

Somewhere over there – many thousands of miles away – was England, and Cross, and the church where he had been curate, with its Marwood window of St Margaret and St Catherine, and Lady Marwood and her two daughters . . . and their uncle who was a bishop . . . it was an hour of agony for Simon. He had thrown all that away; all his prospects of a career, in the green fields of home, a fat complaisant wife, a cosy home, self-consequence among the neighbours, when he had succeeded in gaining his living. In return he had this wilderness, and this wife who was no better than a village girl. He had been deceived . . . but Simon knew, even in his bitterness, that it had been self-deception. He did not in his heart blame Rebecca for their predicament, yet he could not feel charitable towards her. If it had been unwittingly, she had deceived him; if it had been unintentionally, she had taken him in. He had been attacked on the weak side of his nature. He winced at the recollection of how he had felt; and then found it difficult to remember just how he had felt, at the time. By their very intensity, his feelings had burned themselves out, and he could not now recapture them. Imagination had never been strong in Simon. When he had been in love with Rebecca, he had been unable to imagine the results of his actions, and now he was here, on this island which was as close as man could imagine to paradise, and no longer in love with her, he could not send his imagination back and recapture those days when he had been so. Regret was all he could feel: bitter regret. Rebecca was the cause of it; she should be made to rue the day . . . Delilah, deceiving him . . . he could never feel for her again, he decided at that moment. It was half an hour before Simon came down from the rocky outcrop.

Simon's path back to their own house lay past the high bulk of the Spirit House. It was a narrow, tall building, and since his arrival had not, to his knowledge, been in use. The new God had struck awe into the village, and their old ways were discredited so thoroughly that the old religion had been deserted, though the chiefs still refused to accept Christianity – largely because they would have to give up most of their wives. How he hated this visible presence of the old ways! He stopped and looked at it. It was time that something was done. Simon's mood was right for action. On the Spirit House he could let out the violence of his feelings safely, though this wasn't his conscious thought.

'Summa!' he called, running towards the Lloyds' house. 'Summa! George Sulu! Come and help me!' Both the young men came running eagerly. 'Fetch long sticks. We are going to pull down the Spirit House. Something with a hook on the end. Lash my curved sickle to the end of a pole.'

Summa at once went to do as he was told, but George Sulu paused.

'Pull down the Spirit House, Mr Lloyd?'

'Certainly. It has stood long enough.'

'It is a dangerous thing to do.'

'I will be careful it doesn't fall down on my head,' said Simon, deliberately misunderstanding George Sulu's concern. Sulu stood motionless as though he could not decide to join him. 'You have been confirmed, George!' Simon

210

reminded him. 'You do not have any lingering belief in the spirits, surely? Or you can be no Christian!' The strong tone – and perhaps the edge of contempt – in his voice, decided George Sulu. He tried to make up for his obvious fear by bustling about, finding a thin thong of bamboo to wrap round the handle of the sickle, securing it to the long pole Summa had produced. Then the three of them went to the Spirit House, and Simon set the example by digging the point of the sickle into the palm-leaf thatch and pulling. At that, a great lump of the roof came away, and Simon was pleased to realize that the roof was rotten. Palm leaf thatch did not last many years on the island, and this had obviously reached the end of its time. There was a rending, and several of the villagers put their heads out of doors to see what was happening. It was the time when most of them were eating, and Lala and Vivi had already started to feed the school pupils, as Rebecca had told them to when she realized Simon was not back, and the meal was ready. Ratu Naka, the chief, had been alerted by one of the young men of the tribe, and he came out of his house, (the most magnificent in the village, and standing on the highest plinth). He spoke to Simon in the native language, alarmed and frightened at what was happening.

'My God will not allow the Spirit House to stand any longer!' shouted Simon. 'Down with it! Down with superstition and evil practices!' The chief laid his hands on Simon's arm in concern, and explained that anyone who damaged the Spirit House would die; not sometime in the future, but quickly. The vengeance of the spirits was swift! Simon refused to listen. The Spirit House was doomed. He raised his weapon on high again, and pulled a great mass of thatch off the roof. All the villagers shrank back in terror, looking at Simon with frightened eyes. He was not struck dead, and went on with his task, pulling more and more of the thatch until the ribs of the roof began to show. Summa was actively helping but George Sulu was not being very useful.

'Thus perish all the enemies of Christ!' roared Simon,

211

letting go all restraint, and completely possessed by a passion of destruction. He pulled and lunged at the roof, swept about inside, throwing down the ornaments and tearing out the tapa cloth, kicking them contemptuously out of the narrow building and down the plinth. The crowd shrank back in horror, but he ignored them.

Later, having done as much destruction as he could, he took out flint and tinder, and set fire to the ruined building. It was a still night, and there had been a hot afternoon to dry out the rain of the previous day; the whole thing went up like matchwood, and after a short raging fire of half an hour, the House was consumed. The stone plinth was blackened, massed with charred fragments.

'Your spirits have not hurt me!' cried Simon, standing exultant among the smoking ruins. 'They are defeated!'

It seemed to the wondering natives, who had expected to see him struck down at any minute, that Simon's power was very great indeed, and that of his God. If he were still alive by morning, it might be true that his was the real God.

He returned to his own house and to Rebecca in a much better mood than might have augured. He bent and kissed her, and spoke to the baby, forgetting for the time that it was his feelings about Rebecca which had spurred him on to destroy the Spirit House in the first place, and he talked of what he had done, until it was time for sleep.

Rebecca had passed the day in dozing, and gazing at her baby. It was heaven to forget her household cares for a while. Lala and Vivi, with a great deal of giggling and excitement, were managing very well. They remembered the ways she had taught them, and thought it great fun to be looking after their white father, who was bringing a life where goodness and kindness even to women was the rule, and hard cruel things like fighting and desecrating your enemies were not done any more. They were enthusiastic for these alterations in life, and setting out the food on the Lloyds' table made them feel tremendously important.

212

They had been in the middle of feeding the school pupils when Simon made his assault on the Spirit House, and Rebecca would not let them go to see what the commotion was about; but by the time the ruin was burning the meal was over, and Rebecca could restrain them no longer.

Soon after, Simon, blackened and exhausted, had come in; and she was delighted to hear what he had done.

'That nasty old Spirit House!' she said. 'I'm so glad it's gone, Simon. It seemed to cast a shadow over us.'

He sat for a while beside her, and she asked him about the funeral; he had to cast his mind back, for it seemed an age since the previous day. For the time being his exhilaration, as a result of the overthrow of the Spirit House, was sufficient to make him forget his grudge against Rebecca, and he sat quite calmly and told her of the funeral ceremonies of the chief. All visits among the island people were attended with great ceremony, and there was always a scrupulous interchange of presents. How much more so on this occasion! The visiting mourners had been wearing all their ornaments in honour of the dead chief, large tortoiseshell earrings and nose ornaments, armlets, anklets and necklaces, and on their arrival everyone had jumped up, and shown them to the place of honour, to be seated on their best mats. In return the visitors had offered their gifts, and taken part in the bewailing. Trees had been felled as a sign of respect; and the chief's house burnt. Simon remembered this as he was firing the Spirit House; that too was dead, had served its purpose. He had been too late to stop the killing of two men, in order that their spirits might attend the chief in the other world; but he had, he told Rebecca, spoken out powerfully against such things, and succeeded in stopping a headhunting expedition in the late chief's honour, which had been in contemplation. The missionary influence was in nothing more effective than in stopping headhunting and other inter-tribal killings. He had told the assembled people how, if only the dead chief had been a Christian, he would now be assured of eternal life in the arms of a loving Saviour. During that hour,

Rebecca had no inkling of Simon's change of heart towards her, although she had been gradually coming to realize that things were not as they had been. Her first reaction was that it was natural for a strangeness to be between them when all around was strange. On the day after his return from the funeral and his destruction of the Spirit House, she saw nothing of him until towards evening; and then she pleaded with him, 'Stay with me a little; I have hardly seen you since you came back.' The baby was delightful; but she had been lying, alone with her, all day in the sleeping area, with only the occasional company of Lala and Vivi.

'There is nothing to talk about,' said Simon curtly.

'Read to me, then, Simon. We used to read Wordsworth together, long ago. We have not done that since we were married. We brought a volume of his poems, they are in the large trunk, near the top. I often read one of my favourites, if I have a minute.'

'We cannot spare time for such frivolity.' Simon was stern. 'What good would we be doing, if instead of the Bible we were seen to be frivolling with such light reading?'

She was silent, and he looked down at her pensive face, and the downy head nestling on the pillow beside her, and felt a twinge of conscience.

'I will read to you from the Bible if you like,' he volunteered. 'That would have a good appearance to the natives.'

'Oh! Appearance!' she exclaimed shortly. Then: 'Yes, Simon, I would like that.'

Rebecca should have been thankful for Simon's concern for appearance, for it saved her from feeling the full brunt of his disappointment and regret, in the weeks and months which followed. Her strength came back only slowly in the sapping heat of the island climate. Winter – if it could be called so – was a relief, but it was still very hot, and Rebecca was finding it very difficult to acclimatize. Simon did not seem to be nearly as affected as she was. While she was tormented by the insects, prickly heat and mysterious rashes and bumps, he looked much as he had ever done, and seemed to be able to stay cool even in shirt, trousers, coat, socks and shoes. His ascetic, pale face, with the fair lick of hair still falling over his forehead, the cool grey eyes, were unchanged while she felt as though she was shining with the heat, and wished she could wear just two yards of cloth wrapped in a skirt around her waist.

Little Margaret was a contented, thriving baby. Life had not yet shown her its green dragons, and she cooed when she was picked up, gurgled with happiness when she was fed, and waved her hands happily at the leaves when she lay in the shade of a tree. She slept at her mother's side, and Simon had not resumed his privilege of doing so. 'You need to rest' he had said to Rebecca, and she tried to think that it was his love for her that made him considerate, instead of a lack of love. There were often times when she longed for a friendly touch, an arm round her shoulders, a body holding her close in tenderness, but she soon learned not to expect it. If she ran her hand over Simon's hair, he jerked his head impatiently, and if she touched him, he drew away, exclaiming, 'It is too hot for that sort of thing, Rebecca.' She had not had in mind 'that sort of thing', only the pleasure of affectionate contact; but it was denied her. For a naturally loving girl, this was a kind of slow starvation, and she began to lose her bloom, and look thin and worn.

The time for the bishop to return, on his annual cruise round the islands, was approaching. They could decide to return with him to New Zealand, or choose to remain on the island for another year.

The arrival of the mission ship was announced by a breathless runner and the village, with the Lloyds, as one person, decided to go to welcome him. The canoes were loaded with people and there was a tremendous noise of welcome, a great deal of clattering and of scrambling up the ship's side, before the canoe journey with the bishop back to the mainland. He looked just as he had the year

215

before; just as stately, as saintly, as kind and loving, as ever. His keen eyes rested on all of them, white missionaries, black natives, with the same gentle, loving perception. He was to sleep one night at the chief Ratu Naka's house and one at the Lloyds', so they looked forward to time for talk with him. The ten returning island boys, all from other villages, not the one which the Lloyds had made their home, would prove valuable allies in the work, they were sure, in the coming year; for now, they had all vanished into the bush with their welcoming relatives, towards their own villages.

The bishop was delighted with the destruction of the Spirit House. Simon showed him the chief's staff, which he had ignominiously kicked out of its place of honour in the Spirit House, and which Ratu Naka had rescued and presented to him to keep, and they told the bishop that the sacred canoe, which formerly no woman had been allowed to touch, had now been given over to the women to use in their fishing expeditions. He praised all this, and the work Simon had begun in translating the New Testament into the island dialect. This he promised to have printed back in the mission school so that in future copies could be distributed on the island.

The scholars were all examined in their studies, and the bishop said that he was more than satisfied; he looked round the village and saw the soft, shy girls in their pretty patterned skirts, and praised Rebecca. At any appearance of the bishop outside, he was at once followed by about fifty of the local people; and when he went to bathe, they followed him still, just as curious to discover if he too were white all over as they had been in the case of Simon and Rebecca.

The bishop's stay extended over Sunday, and he took the service himself, in the open air. With her baby in her arms, Rebecca sat down on the grass to await him, among a great crowd of natives. She was hoping that little Margaret would not take it into her head to cry. Ahead of them lay the magnificent forest trees which bordered the clearing, their great gnarled trunks bearing spreading branches, each tree itself a miniature forest, for it supported orchids and ferns growing upon it. The banyan tree where Simon usually preached was in another direction; this had been selected today because there were even more people than usual; they had come from far and wide to hear the bishop.

As she sat waiting for that august figure to appear in front of the noble backcloth, Rebecca was reflecting that it had somehow been settled, without any overt discussion, that they were to stay another year on the island. There had been talk, and yet no direct question, no direct declaration; but it was decided. She was unable to decide if she were glad or sorry. It had been the decision to spend the whole of their lifetimes in the service of God in one post or another, which Simon had taken when he became a missionary. The exact place, however, and how long they ought to stay in it, were left for the needs of the people they were serving to determine. The island was not considered to be healthy, and they might easily, after this one year, have been transferred somewhere else; but, in this strange elliptical fashion, they knew in these last two days that they were to stay. The service had a grandeur she never knew in it before, as the bishop took it. It was in a very real sense a re-dedication, and she felt uplifted, blessed, in consequence.

The next morning, before the bishop took his leave, he walked a little with Rebecca. They took a bush trail which went directly down to the nearest shore; it was a little secluded bay, where she often went to fish from the rocks. Here they paced, for a while, to and fro together. 'How is it with you, my daughter?' the bishop had said; and she did feel richly blessed indeed, for she felt that in him she had a spiritual father no less dear and important to her than her father in love, Jim Redfearn, or her father in blood, Giffard Boville. She did not complain to the bishop; her heart was lightened, and her spirit high, as they walked together. The things they spoke of were in the main the purposes she

217

was serving in her life on the island.

'What do you miss in your old life?' he asked her once; and she paused before replying, and then said, 'The wind – on the moors, in Yorkshire; the cold wind—' For a space of time she could almost feel it blowing, and the bishop seemed to be sharing it with her, for he had great understanding, the understanding which does not need words. How was it that she felt afterwards that she had unburdened her heart to him, and that he had given her strength to bear her sorrows, and absolution for her sins? For there had been no word spoken between them of any of that. Yet when she stood to wave goodbye to him as the mission boat drew out of sight, her heart was full of peace.

The bishop had left peace behind him; but he had also left a warning of possible dangers to come, for he had given them disquieting news. Away in Fiji, sugar plantations had been started, and labour was needed for them. Traders had begun to tour the islands, inducing men to go as indentured workers, and then shipping them over to Fiji. The indenture had little meaning, for few of these men were able to return to their own islands, when the term of it was over. The effect was as final, as drastic, as though it had openly been a slave trade.

Having found that groups of men torn from their own homes without any understanding of where they were going and why, were not happy, the traders had next started taking women, too, from the islands. They were quite without scruple, and cared nothing for taking wives without husbands, husbands without wives. Word was spreading, in the mysterious way news has among the island populations, and resistance was growing to the traders, so that they were beginning to give up the pretence of persuasion and use force.

This was the news, this the threat, with which the bishop had acquainted the Lloyds. So he left them, truly at peace, but with the worry of this possibility of a threat to their own islanders.

CHAPTER FOURTEEN

The other people in the hotel in Egypt felt a liking for Edward Gilbank and his father. Sir Charles was so bright, so energetic, so little and so fierce when things did not go his way. Edward was kindly, thoughtful for his father, and young and handsome enough to interest the womenfolk. There was something else, though, that intrigued them. In his face there was a shadow, even when he was in a happy company; a ghost of sadness in his eyes, and a hopelessness in the lines of his figure if he happened to be alone and think himself unobserved.

Colonel Harrison had been in the company of the Gilbanks all day, on an excursion to the Pyramids, and had dined with them; now, on returning to the cool, shady drawing-room of the hotel, where the fans were moving slowly, he ordered a bottle of port and glasses and went to their corner.

'Will you join me . . .' he started saying, but realized Sir Charles was already speaking.

'Edward,' said his father in an abrupt manner, 'it's time we were getting home. The sheep will be wanting washing.'

Edward looked at his father in surprise. Sheep had not entered his father's conversation for eighteen months; it was really so long since they had left Yorkshire, without his father worrying about the sheep.

'Sheep, did you say, sir?' said Colonel Harrison, sitting down comfortably between them. 'Have a port with me, won't you both? There's a lot I want to know about sheep.'

'No one who could tell you more about them than my father,' said Edward. 'But why do you want to know? Are you going to settle in England and farm?'

'No.' The colonel settled back in his chair and sipped his port. 'Not England. I might as well tell you, then you can give me the benefit of your advice. I was brought up in and among farming, but it never meant much to me. The army and fighting, that's all I wanted to know about. I wouldn't have thanked you then for telling me about sheep. But a man changes, as he grows older; I've had enough war and fighting, and it's time I retired from the army and made a home for my old age. There's a couple of sons in the army to inherit anything I might manage to build up; one of them has two little sons, just children; so it isn't only for myself that I would be working, if I buy a tract of land in New Zealand and clear it and make a farm.'

'New Zealand?' asked Edward. He knew that Rebecca had gone to the South Pacific, and had spent enough hours gazing at his father's globe to know just how important New Zealand was in that part of the world. His eyes, turned on to Colonel Harrison, looked hungry.

'What has New Zealand to do with getting our sheep washed?' asked Sir Charles fretfully.

'If you're ready for home, father, we'll set off at once.' Edward said pacifically. 'We'll travel back slowly, and arrive in good time for the washing and shearing. You'll be able to see what sort of a hand Joe Sutcliffe's made of looking after them. Thanks, colonel, I will have a glass. Please tell us about New Zealand; what's decided you on settling there? Why not England?'

'It's the climate,' confided the colonel. 'After years in India and Australia I dread the damp and cold. New Zealand is warmer and drier, but not too hot. It's the opportunity, too; once the land is cleared of natives, it's grand farming country, and cheap. Healthy, that's a thing to bear in mind. I've looked round, and more or less settled on a spot. But before I buy, I decided to have one last visit to Europe and see all those things I never have seen – like the Holy Land, I was there for a month, and now the Pyramids, and I'm planning to travel across France slowly and back to England just as summer arrives. Then I really will get down to organizing things; buying stock and supplies and shipping them out.'

'It would be too warm for them,' put in Sir Charles.

'There are some cattle, sheep and pigs out there already, and they are doing quite well.'

'Tell me about the country,' said Edward, and the colonel was ready to stay up all night doing that. He explained the difference between the North Island and the South Island, and discussed the Maoris, their customs, costume and nature. He painted a lurid picture, and Edward, who knew that somewhere in that vast hemisphere his Rebecca was living and working among people very similar to the Maoris – Giffard Boville had had a letter from her, posted from New Zealand, which had taken a year to arrive, and he had written to Edward and told him of it – Edward listened with fear at his heart. Tales of the murder of white people did nothing to reassure him. It was late at night before the talk came round again to farming.

'What I've been wanting, and didn't know how to find it, is a bit of advice. I've been away from farming ways for so long I could make a fool of myself.'

'You're thinking of shipping stock out.'

'And seeds, and maybe one or two experienced men to work on the farm.'

'Why not come home with us?' Sir Charles had a gleam in his bird-like eye. 'We'll show you our methods.'

'They might not suit New Zealand, father.'

'Good farming practice is good practice anywhere.'

'Do you have hills? As I've been saying, New Zealand is a hilly country.'

'Plenty of hills,' replied Edward. 'But our climate is very different.'

The colonel was glowing with enthusiasm. He felt at home with the Gilbanks, and his ideas were burgeoning, shining brightly, taking on new hues as he at last discussed them. As he talked, mountain sides were cleared of forest, farm houses and cottages were built, sheep multiplied into flocks, and their wool was exported to the convict settlements in Australia.

By the end of the evening the holiday acquaintanceship had developed into a friendship; they were almost working partners. Colonel Harrison was to travel back to England with them, and they were to show him their own methods of management. Trips were to be taken to the noted breeders of various types of animal. Interest and excitement for several months were promised by this joint enterprise, and the three men packed their possessions and set sail from Egypt without regret. Edward sent messages ahead that they were returning, and they travelled slowly back across the Continent.

Standing in her drawing-room at the end of the London season, Mrs Giffard Boville looked at her eldest daughter in disgust.

'What have I done,' she wondered, 'to have such a daughter? You have been introduced to all manner of young men, Julia, and have not succeeded in attaching any of them; and now you can only say that you want to go back to Yorkshire! What an ambition!'

'I cannot feel happy anywhere else, mama. Do forgive me. I do appreciate all the trouble you have taken, and that it has been expensive, and I have enjoyed it, but I am homesick; I just long to be back home.'

'Home!' exclaimed Mrs Boville. 'That shooting-box! It is not as though the match with Edward Gilbank has come off; he is somewhere on the Continent, goodness knows where – do you know where they are, Giffard? – and shows no interest. He is best forgotten. To be homesick for Yorkshire!'

'But I am, mama.'

It had looked, in her troublesome teens, as though Julia was taking after her mother, in more than looks. In the time Mrs Boville had been on the Continent, and Rebecca had been at Broxa House, Julia had changed. The owners of rich coal mines had society open to them, but her enjoyment had been flawed. She had been through a growing point in her development, and had grown subtly away from her mother's interests. Then, losing Edward had marked her. She knew she had lost him, as surely as if her father had told her of that fatal conversation. To have bent her proud spirit, to have admitted to tender love, and then to know so surely that she had lost what she had grown to value, and yet not know how, or why. To see her loved one going through loss, and have no comfort required from her; to hear from others that he and his father were leaving the country, and know that they had gone, without a word. How could she blame him? For years she had been haughty and capricious where Edward was concerned; it had dawned on her too late that she loved him. In society she had found no one she liked as well as Edward, and she had often thought of Broxa House, and the happy winter when Rebecca had been with them, the companionship which they had enjoyed. That friendly company was dispersed, scattered . . .

Eliza Ann had been more settled in London than had Julia; the agent, Henry Camm, had been displaced in her thoughts by the excitements of shops and theatres and dances. Now she sat quietly, waiting to see what would happen; she felt that the world was just beginning to open before her, and was disposed to enjoy it.

'They may look like me,' summed up Mrs Boville bitterly, 'but they are pure Boville, both of them.' She included Eliza Ann in her resentful survey of the inhabitants of the room. 'Take Julia back to Yorkshire with you, Giffard; but do not expect me to come with you. Find them husbands among the rural gentry.'

'I will stay with you, mama,' said Eliza Ann.

'It is early to speak of husbands,' put in Giffard. 'Julia is only twenty-two, and Eliza Ann not yet nineteen.' His voice was full of gentle protest.

'Was I more when father married me to you?'

'You were just nineteen, my love.'

'So why should they remain free of all responsibilities? Let them find what life is about. Why should they go on year after year enjoying themselves when at their age I was tied down with babies? You would have been ready enough to have seen either of them marry Edward Gilbank; there would have been no talk then of them being too young.'

'That was different, my dear.'

'That was different! You would think so.'

Giffard sighed. Nothing he could say was right, so he often took the decision to say nothing, and was becoming morose. In looks he was older, now, than his years. His grey, craggy face was more forbidding. It would be a relief to him to go back to his estate, but he was surprised that his wife had given up her matchmaking so quickly. There was the possibility that it bored her, that she could enjoy life more on her own; he inclined to this view. She had a number of friends, women of her own age, and they seemed to be constantly in touch, writing each other little notes, arranging house parties for the weekends, greeting each other with cries of joy.

'She can come back here when she has rusticated for a little while,' went on Mrs Boville. 'I will get up another round of parties for her, when she is in the mood to be grateful. But for now you two had better be off to your precious Yorkshire; I am tired of wasting my time . . . Eliza Ann and I will follow you up in a fortnight or so, with Mrs Palfreyman and her daughters, and we will see what gaiety you can produce to amuse them.'

'Oh, thank you, mama!'

'I can't think why you have become enamoured of the countryside, Julia. At one time London, Paris, Rome, would have been what you wanted. I was never let out of the shire as a girl; I wish I had had your opportunities.'

Julia could not explain. She knew that she had changed, and needed to be alone for a while to understand herself. Since her stay in London, riding had become more of a

224

passion with her and she had a new habit, and a chestnut mare; she felt that if she were to come to terms with life, she needed to be able to think, and riding over the high moorland might give her the chance. Quiet days, in the open air, had suddenly become desirable; she would discover what life was possible for her.

The whole party had brightened, now that they were to split up for a while. Mrs Boville's temper was wonderfully improved, at the prospect of being rid of her family. The evening became quite bearable. If only she were always like this, thought Giffard, looking across at her animated face, her round jaw, her smooth dark hair; she looks now as she used to be, before we grew apart.

In Yorkshire, the rooms which had been shut up were opened to the light and the sun. The front door of Broxa House was propped wide, letting a current of fresh air through to the library. Fresh sand was carted from the river and spread on the garden paths, even the flowers seemed to perk up, prepared to bloom their best, for the family was coming home.

Across the valley the ladders were got out, and the cobwebs swept from the raftered roof of the Great Hall; the pretty little drawing-room had its paintwork washed, and its lustres dusted; the linen covers were taken from the chairs and the beadwork brushed lightly with soft bristles.

In the stables, Bounce realized that something was afoot. He was lying on the floor with the litter of puppies that he had fathered, and they had been rolling all over him, with his complete acquiescence and delight. Now he got to his feet and the tiniest puppy rolled from his back and fell, squealing protests, into the straw. He walked over to the half-open stable door, reared up to put his paws on the top of the lower section, and put his head out into the air.

'Aye, lad,' said the coachman in passing, carrying an armful of harness. 'Aye, lad, thee knows, don't thee? Thy master's on his way home.' He patted the black head, now showing a few grey hairs about the muzzle, and Bounce's

225

eyes gleamed as though he understood every word. Loud and joyously he barked and, dropping from the door, jumped around in the straw of the stable, going over to the grated window at the back, leaping up at the crumbling limewash of the walls, running up to his mate who lay comfortably watching him, nuzzling her face, and then cheerfully knocking over one of the puppies, before going back to the door and rearing up once more to look out. Master was coming home . . .

Rebecca's child, Margaret, was nine months old, and the heavy, humid heat hung over the island like a shroud. Simon hardly seemed to notice it; he was a constant source of wonder to Rebecca. He was still withdrawn from her; still Margaret shared her sleeping mat, and Simon was a few feet away, as distant as the moon. His soul, his innermost feelings and emotions, were as impenetrable as though he were a stranger – only the outer surface was presented, and with this she must be content. His thin, ascetic face, the unruly lock of fair hair, the cool, grey eyes, were the same as they had always been; as they would remain. The heat was bearable to him, the humidity something which could be ignored. The destruction of the Spirit House had given him stature among the people, and his daily prayers and weekly services were well attended. In his work he had sunk the man and become a priest, living and working only for a cause. If he had any thought of life outside the island of Mutu, it did not appear; he sat up late every night working on his translation of the New Testament into the dialect of the island.

Many things which Rebecca had found hard during her first year on the island were now easy. The crops and the cooking took up much less of her time. The language was now familiar, so that she could talk easily with those about her. The daily and weekly routines were second nature. Life seemed, compared with life in England, like some kind of perpetual picnic. There were never any problems of cold to contend with; one could be philosophical about rain, when it was warm rain. If one broke a dish, there was in its place a beautiful shell, or a fresh green leaf. If there was fruit in the bush and Rebecca was not carrying a basket, a new one could be woven in ten minutes by any child from the leaf of a palm tree. There seemed to be such hours of time. Hours in which to watch Margaret, to show her the wonders of her tiny world; the curious flat brown seeds which fell from the vines, and were used as counters in a game the islanders played; the big hairy mango seeds; the strangely shaped seeds of the vutu tree, great green objects like sculpture – little Margaret was not allowed to touch those, for poison was extracted from them.

Yet, in spite of all the beauties and the benefits, Rebecca found the oppressive heat of this summer harder to bear than their first on the island. Then she had been pregnant, but now she was worn down, by heat, by strain – most, by Simon's indifference. She longed for cooler weather, when life would be less effort.

The beauty of the island soaked into Rebecca and her child, the vivid greens and clear blues, the tree ferns and orchid laden forest trees. Yet, though Margaret was flourishing, Rebecca was much thinner. Her ankles still troubled her by swelling, and the mosquitoes tormented her when she went into the areas where they were prevalent. An indolence had crept over her about her appearance. Although her self-respect was still strong, the strain of living without love was telling on her. Simon ate his meals, and as he did not say there was anything wrong with them, she presumed they were to his taste; yet he never expressed any appreciation, not a word. She took care to be neatly dressed, yet his eyes, if anything, avoided her; they did not rest on her with pleasure. If she could have seen her thin cheeks, and the sad pleading in her eyes, she might have understood.

If she concocted something new out of the fabrics in her boxes, and asked his opinion, he would give her a brief glance and say, 'I would tell you if I did not like it.' She hungered for a kindly word, though she received no unkind ones. If only, she thought, she could have a friendly arm laid round her, a loving hand stroking her hair, a cosy hour at sunset, an embrace in the darkness, the weight of his head on her breast. She sat on the matted floor and leaned against his knees as he sat at the table, working on his translation, but he twitched impatiently and asked her not to do it.

The first apprehension they had of any change in their condition was one evening when Simon returned from a long trip to a village on the minor islet of Ota, at the end of Mutu. He had spent some days there, talking to the people and preaching, and felt that he had made good progress; returning to their own village and his home, he was in an unusually talkative mood, and sat telling Rebecca of his experiences. She was glad that he was doing this, and sat with the sleeping Margaret on her knee, listening intently. It seemed to her that he had for once been affected by the sun, for his cheeks were pinker than usual; as he went on talking, the thought of possible ill effects from sun and heat entered her head; by the time an hour had gone by, she was certain that he was ill. There could be no doubt of it by bedtime; he was in a fever which mounted rapidly. It was not, as she had at first thought, heatstroke, or the effect of the sun. Lala and Vivi, on being called, recognized the fever instantly. They shook their heads over the tossing, sweating man, and went off to fetch forest herbs known to be helpful in such cases, and Rebecca was a little reassured by the discovery that they did not think this particular fever would be fatal. It was one well known to them. To her, it was strange, and she did not know what its effects might be; she was thankful that the village custom of looking after one another's babies made it easy for her to keep Margaret out of danger of infection; Lala or Vivi or any one of the other women could take the baby, except for feeding times, and she would be perfectly happy. Simon lay in the tiny light of one candle, complaining incessantly of the pain in his bones. For seven days his fever continued, and she nursed him as best she could. His bones – his bones – and the ache in them, this is what he spoke of, and then there were the delusions, which tormented him, and made that week hard for her to bear.

He did not recognize her for stretches of time, but was kept company by phantasms, people they both had known; now he was back in Cross, after she had left the village, and he spoke deliriously of his future, of Maria Marwood, and his ambitions; then he was visiting Kirkby again, and falling in love with Rebecca; another time, he spoke out in his fever his innermost thoughts . . . how she had ensnared him and how he regretted it . . . how he felt his life as a missionary was a complete waste and he longed to be able to turn back the clock, to be in an English parish, to never have seen her again . . . his sense that he was tied to someone beneath him hurt her more than anything, for she knew in her heart that she was worthy of the love of any man, and that to be married to her did not degrade him.

After a week he stopped being delirious, and gradually the pain in his bones ceased; he sat up and ate normally, and although much thinner and still weak, he was himself again. He obviously had no memory of his delirium, and even smiled at Rebecca and thanked her gently, when she brought him food and looked after him. She was rather serious, and found it difficult to smile. Things he had said had hurt her, and seemed to rise up between them. Repeatedly she told herself that it was all nonsense – people did not mean what they said in a fever, and she should not mind it, should forget it; but she could not.

In a few days time Simon was up and about again, and the fever seemed to have fallen from him as though it had never been. He was as energetic as ever; it had made no difference. Prayers resumed daily, lessons went on, the translation of the Testament proceeded. The next in the sequence of events came a few weeks later.

It was on a morning when a tropical storm on the previous day had brought all village life to a halt. Everyone had crowded shivering into their houses, very little reassured by Simon's calmness, and wondering if their old spirit gods were taking revenge, for the wind crashing through the bush and knocking down trees in its wake fell on the village like a rabid animal and hurled palm leaf thatch and palm trunk ridge poles into the air as though they were straws. The village was lucky to escape with as little damage as it did; stories were told, in the darkness, of whole villages laid waste by such winds, and all possessions blown off into the bush or out to sea.

After their night fear of the vengeance of the spirit gods, the people were very much inclined in the morning, seeing how lucky they had been to escape serious damage, to think on the rebound that Simon's and Rebecca's presence had saved them from the worst of the danger, and to become good Christians in consequence. Ratu Naka, who had found the giving up of his four wives the chief difficulty in being converted, came up to Simon a.id told him that in the height of the storm he had taken a vow to do just that if they were spared.

No sooner had everyone come out of their houses and taken a first survey of the damage, than a messenger from Ratu Vussi's village came trotting in. There was a ship on the other side of the island; a ship of white people.

'The bishop?' asked Simon.

'They say they are from the bishop,' was the cautious reply. 'But we do not believe them. Some men went on board, Mr Lloyd, and they have not come back; and the white men want more to go on board, and women too. They have given the Ratu a gun, like white men have, and last night all had drink of the white men's drink which makes men want to fight.'

'Slavers,' said Simon to Rebecca.

'I thought there were no slavers.'

'You remember the bishop's warning? They call it indentured labour; but it is nothing but slavery. They will be taken to the sugar plantations in Fiji. And women! These vile men care nothing for the sanctity of marriage, they will take women without their husbands, men without their wives. Don't you remember?'

'Is there anything we can do?'

'You must stay here. I will go to speak to them, try to influence them, try to stop the island people going with them. I will point out to these whites who do not deserve the name of Christian the error of their ways.'

'Oh! Simon! They mustn't take the people, it will undo all your work! What idea will they form of white people, if they are taken away and can't get back?'

Simon was ready in a few minutes, and so were the men of the village. The storm damage was forgotten. The women and children could see to that, man's work was afoot. They did not wait to put on their full panoply of war, but they wore their ornaments, carried their spears, blew their horns, and wore wide skirts of palm leaves jutting about them.

They had a journey of about an hour through the bush, picking up the warriors from Ratu Vussi's village as they went, and moving quickly. The day was still young and cool, and silently in single file they trotted through the bush, Simon near the head with Ratu Vussi and Ratu Naka. They were tense, each wondering about the ship of white men. Were they really from the bishop, after all?

Simon soon found that his recent fever had told on him more than he realized. It was a struggle to keep up, and when he saw the chance of a short cut, he took it. This was to wade through the mouth of a river, while the others went up the river bank to a palm tree trunk which lay across it higher up. Simon reckoned that by going straight across he could save his strength, and if it should prove deeper than it looked he was a good swimmer, which none of the natives seemed to be.

He waded in, waving cheerfully to the others and indicating that he would meet up with them again on the other side. It was deeper than he had thought, and by the time he was half-way across and feeling the tug of the tide, Simon was wishing he had not thought of the idea. He stood for a minute in the middle of the water. It came almost up to his chin, and he had a sweeping sense of loneliness and desolation. The scene was completely quiet; not a sound seemed to break the stillness. To his left the grey, muddy waters stretched out to sea, and the strong current of water tugged at him as though it would have taken him too out towards the coral reefs. To his right the river narrowed, and the dense tropical forest pressed in upon it, and seemed to be waiting, and listening. He glanced behind, and the river bank was a long way off. Ahead was a mangrove swamp, and he knew that the land there would be soft and sticky and stinking. Neck-high the water swirled about him, and his feet moved forward unsteadily on the uneven bottom of the riverbed.

His sense of having made a mistake, in throwing everything up to marry Rebecca, was then in the forefront of his mind; what was he doing in this place, this alien place? But Simon had, in spite of his worldliness, trained and practised for a long time in the service of God, and this training asserted itself now. It did not matter that he had made a mistake; he was here, and if nothing else, there was God's work to be done. In the midst of the river he realized that the fate of these people of the island did matter to him. They were his people; they were not to be preyed upon and duped; he would not allow it. The black mood lifted, and he moved his feet forward with confidence, and headed upstream from the mangrove swamp. For the first time for many weeks he felt truly uplifted, really led forward, actually doing something that mattered in the world. He reached the far bank before the band of warriors, and they found him a few minutes later, his clothes already drying out, standing calmly waiting for their approach with a strong air of confidence. They felt a glow of reassurance for secretly they had been afraid. They had never really believed that this new ship was the bishop's, for he never had the drink other white men had, and his gifts were hatchets and fish-hooks. Simon had never doubted for a moment that the talk of the bishop was just a ruse to deceive the people of the island.

When they reached the bay from which the strange ship had been reported they paused, in the bush, and looked down. There was the wide curve of the bay, and offshore a boat, which they could see at a glance was not the bishop's. The mission boat could have been replaced with a new one, Simon supposed, but somehow it did not have the right look. This was an intuition, and Simon was not given to intuitions, but he trusted this one. On the crescent of sand they could see a group of people, black and white together.

It was now that the sense of revelation, which had come so clearly to Simon as he stood neck-high in the water of the river, continued. It was as though it were not one static moment but a continuing, opening experience. Standing with the two chiefs, with George Sulu and Summa behind him, and the rest of the warriors all about, Simon felt that he was nearer to them than he was to the white traders on the shore. He identified with them completely, and knew with his body their sense of fear of the unknown, their mistrust of these strangers. He wished to protect them from the harm which contact with the evils of his own civilization could bring. A few minutes' observation had told them a great deal: some of the natives were obviously the worse for alcohol, which had such a different effect from their own narcotic drink of kava; the white men were pulling some of them towards the small boat which was lying in the water, as though to take them out in it to their ship. Some natives were already sitting in it, quietly waiting.

A sudden rush, Simon thought, would panic the traders into rash action, and they all carried guns. Instead he asked the chiefs to follow him quietly, and only attack if he gave the word. Calmly he led the way down on to the sands of the bay.

The traders looked taken aback at Simon's presence among them.

'Greetings, my friends,' he said. 'I have been told that you bring news from the bishop.' He wondered if they were English, if they would understand him. By their appearance he judged them to be, and he felt ashamed. If they had been Germans or Swedes, at least he would not have had this shame; but he knew that it was largely his own countrymen who were carrying on the near-slave trade, and that they were more likely to be so than any other nationality. He was right.

'Oh,' said a brawny sailor. 'The bishop . . . oh, aye, he is well, thank ye, and sends greetings to ye all . . . we are just inviting these folk to come along with us; there are grand opportunities for them, if we can only persuade them to see it.'

'Opportunities?' said Simon. At his back he could feel the nervousness of his party, their readiness to let fly with their spears and arrows if he lost control of the situation.

The sailor, who seemed to be a spokesman for none of the others joined in though they were all listening, went on, with a little evident nervousness under Simon's bleak eye.

'The settlers in Fiji are starting sugar cane plantations, and need labour. It's a great opportunity for these folk; they can earn money, and come back richer.'

'They don't need money,' replied Simon. 'The island gives them everything they need. Why should they go and work on sugar plantations?'

'Go on, guv'nor, everyone needs money. It'll be a great thing for these blacks.'

'Would you think it a great thing to be torn from your home and family and dumped thousands of miles away to labour hard with no hope of getting back?'

'Oh, we'll bring 'em back, sir, don't you worry about that. What a blessing it is you were here. You can explain to them that we don't mean them no harm.'

'Would you call the press gang harm, if it took you from home?'

'Oh, it ain't the same at all. These blacks don't feel like we do. They're different, see?' And Simon would have thought so once. It was only now that the things he had learned over eighteen months of living on the island were telling.

'They're no different,' he said loudly. 'What you are doing is an evil thing, and I'm ashamed to see my countrymen involved in it. Shame on you. You are no better than slave traders.'

'We're no slavers!' the other men shouted out together. 'Indentured workers, that's what we're taking! There ain't no slavery in that!'

'If you don't agree to leave this island quietly,' said Simon, and he was becoming too incensed to keep the anger out of his tone, 'I'll let these warriors throw you off. Bring all the people back that you have on your ship; none leaves this island if I have anything to do with it.'

'You geroff!' shouted one of the sailors, and Simon thought he seemed the worse for drink. 'Geroff and let us get on with our business. We don't want no holy Joes telling us what to do.' He seized hold of a big islander to whom he had been giving rum until the man was almost insensible, and tried to lead him to the waiting boat.

'Stop!' shouted Simon, and grabbed at the other arm of the native, whom he knew by sight. 'I will not let you do this!' The sailor thrust at Simon, and then raised his arm to strike him, and in a second all the tension which had been building up in the group at Simon's back was released in an explosion of aggression. The warriors rushed forward, brandishing their weapons, and strong hands wrenched Simon, the sailor and the drunken native apart. It seemed to Simon afterwards as though the earth had exploded in a confusion of shouts, rapid movements, blows, gunfire, thuds and shrieks. He himself was twisted sideways and knocked flying, and finished flat on his back looking at the sky, but he scrambled up again, and rushed into the mêlée, crying, 'No! No!'

The invading sailors were first angry, then frightened, at the natives' attack. Being half drunk, they were ready for a fight, and the indentured labour trade was profitable enough for them to refuse to give up without a struggle the spoils of this island, where they had already invested capital in the form of rum, an inferior gun and other gifts, to say nothing of their time. So their first reaction was to fight back, and they were hard, tough men, used enough to brawls. When first one then another of them fell dead, shot through with arrows or pierced with spears, they came a little to their senses and the tales of cannibal feasts came into their heads. Several of the natives also lay dead or wounded, and they knew retribution would follow. They turned tail and fled, jumping into their boat and making as good time as they could with the oars back to their ship in the bay. A shower of arrows followed them, but the natives were in too much of a frenzy to aim accurately or well, and they got off without further loss of life. Simon, standing on the shore and watching them go, saw that one or two arrows did wound them, and wondered if they were tipped with poison, as such arrows often were; and if those wounded knew that they might very well die terribly of lockjaw, which was the most common effect of a non-lethal arrow. His head was ringing and whirling, and it was difficult to have two consecutive thoughts, but as he turned from gazing out to sea he saw that among the dead and dying on the shore was a sailor only wounded in the leg, and several of Simon's own people were obviously about to kill him.

'Don't do that!' he shouted, jumping forward. They paused, holding their positions, still poised to strike, and looked round. 'Spare his life!' Simon spoke again, then realized he was speaking in English, and they were not understanding him. He went over and stood at the man's head. 'You must not kill,' he said in the dialect of the island.

Ratu Vussi looked at him in a puzzled way, and explained, as he might have done to a child, that because warriors' lives had been taken, this sailor's life was forfeit.

'You must be merciful,' Simon said again, and pleaded, explaining that the Christian way was forgiveness. He won, because they would not go against him. He had gained their love and respect during his time on the island, and had come with them to confront the white traders; he could have asked anything and received it, so they gave him the life of the sailor, although to their minds it went against justice.

Simon then set about burying the dead. The islanders had to be carried back to their own villages, to be lamented over and mourned in their traditional manner, but the white sailors – three of them – who lay dead on the shore were Simon's responsibility. He saw the wounded sailor carried to the shade of the trees, and reassured him, then with George Sulu and Summa he set to to dig three graves. The heat of the day had come, but they chose a spot where the earth was in shadow, and worked hard. After his fever of a few weeks previously, and the immersion that morning in the deep waters of the river, the quick march through the bush and the tension of the confrontation, Simon felt sapped, and without strength. The two others were young and strong, and they made up for his weakness. It was not long before Simon was saying the burial service over sailors who had lived lives far from loving their neighbours, and who were to rest for ever on a heathen shore.

Getting the wounded sailor back to safety under Simon's eye, to their own village, was another matter. His wounds made it impossible for him to walk, and the warriors, with their dead to think about, resented too much the fact that he was alive to do anything to help. Summa and George Sulu, and two others of Simon's converts, were willing to help, and together they made a stretcher of branches and woven palm leaves, and began to carry the sailor. Turn and turn about they carried him, on the narrow tracks, past spider webs a yard across with the enormous brilliant spiders stopping spinning to watch, through the hushed aisles of stately trees, through the scented flower-scattered forest, over rushing sparkling streams and the narrow palm trunk bridge of the river Simon had forded earlier in the day, past glimpses of brilliant blue seas and under the

237

powerful brooding presence of the central mountain, until as the sunset flamed in the sky they dragged themselves into the village where Rebecca, who already knew all about it, stood waiting for them.

The sailor, who was the very one who had told Simon to 'geroff', was very frightened. He swore repeatedly about his shipmates, who had left him lying on the shore, and the whole way across the island on his palm leaf stretcher he had grumbled and cried out, making the whole business much more difficult and very unrewarding for Simon, Summa and the others who were helping. He was convinced that he had been saved only to make a cannibal feast, and to be fattened up towards that occasion. Simon did his best to assure him that he was among friends, but it was of no use. Only when he saw Rebecca did he begin to have any confidence in his safety. Then, settled for the night on the floor of their house, he at last relaxed and seemed calmer. The wound in his leg did not seem to be too bad. Simon extracted the arrow-head, with Rebecca holding the man's head on her shoulder, and preventing him from throwing his arms about; they washed and bandaged the wound and hoped that, in a few days, they would know whether or not it had been poisoned, and if lockjaw was going to set in.

The following day he spoke sensibly, and they were all very merry and cheerful together, to raise his spirits. The population of the island as a whole were very far from being either merry or cheerful. Several people had been enticed on board the traders' boat, before Simon's arrival, and their relatives were sure they would never be seen again, and mourned them along with the dead. They loved and trusted Simon and the bishop, and this manifestation of an evil side to the white men was deeply troubling to them. Particularly they found it hard to understand why the sailor was being tended by Simon and Rebecca, and was living with them. It was self-evident that he should be killed in justice to their own dead, and however much Simon talked to them and they agreed, underneath they did not change their minds.

Fate was on the side of the native people. The sailor, after his first apparent recovery from the accident, in a couple of days sickened, and became feverish. Rebecca fetched Lala and Vivi, who were reluctant to collect herbs for this hated stranger, and when she did persuade them to look at him, shook their heads and said that it was a very bad fever and the herbs would not be of any use. Rebecca was surprised when they talked, for it was clear that the fever was not due to his wound – that was doing well; neither was it tetanus. No; from what Lala and Vivi said, she realized that he must have already been sickening with the illness when he came on shore, and that even if his shipmates had taken him with them, he would have become just as ill, on board ship. At last she talked them into doing what they could, and they went off to collect the medicines. Once more baby Margaret was to be looked after by the other women of the village, and Rebecca prepared for the rigours of sick-nursing.

Simon was not happy to see his influence so diminished among the people by their resentment of the sailor, but he untiringly explained to them that they must forgive their enemies, and show mercy to captives. He intervened when Rebecca had completed her preparations to go into isolation to nurse their guest, and insisted on taking her place.

'I won't have my wife exposing herself to the infection,' he said, and now he looked at her, she thought, with a certain affection and kindliness, and she was happy. He did care for her; everything would be all right. Edward vanished from her thoughts, and Simon began to fill her heart and mind. He had changed; she felt that. It was, after all, a long time since she had seen any white man but Simon, and comparing him with the new arrival, the sailor, she was reminded how superior he was to many men she had met. Really, fortune had been good to her! It had spared her from the kind of marriage poor Alice had made; and if she was not to have the happiness Julia would have, as Edward's wife, then it seemed there might be

239

happiness still, of a kind, with Simon. Ever since the day of the strange boat and the fight, he had been subtly changed towards her. It was as though he too were deciding to make the best of life, and of their bargain. It seemed the months of estrangement might pass and be forgotten as though they had never been, and a new understanding take their place.

She did as she was told, and kept away from the sick man. Simon made himself nurse, and Rebecca brought the food to the entrance to the house, and there left it. Summa and George Sulu carried on the school in Simon's place, holding it in the open air. They read the prayers and led the hymn singing, although they were not yet deacons and could not hold a service. The sailor became weaker, and seemed, before Simon's eyes, to waste away. His fever did not abate, and on the fourth day, about noon, he died.

No one could weep for him.

As Simon stood reading the burial service, he began to feel unwell. He remembered his previous fever, and thought he had some slight return of it. Telling Rebecca he would be all right, he returned to the house, cleaned out and burnt all the sleeping mats used by the dead man, and put everything back in order, then held a service, feeling that if he were to endure another week of bone-aching fever his spiritual house must be put in order. Then he took Rebecca in a close embrace, and kissed her, speaking tenderly.

'Keep our child away,' he said. 'Don't risk her health.'

'She'll be well looked after,' answered Rebecca. 'Oh, Simon, are you sure it's like you had before? How do you feel?'

'It's a bit different,' he admitted. 'I'm quite clear-headed at present, just hot and thirsty, yet shivery and cold. My bones aren't aching yet. Don't worry, Becky. I'm strong; and with you to look after me, I'll be all right.'

It was as though all their estrangement were forgotten. He was the old Simon Lloyd again, whom she had hero-worshipped in Cross; everything else might never

240

have been. He stroked her hair gently, and pulled a strand on to her forehead, playing with it lovingly.

'Dear Becky,' he said.

A week later, having borne his fever with fortitude, never becoming deluded even in delirium, and gentle towards her to the last, Simon Lloyd died.

CHAPTER FIFTEEN

Since their return to Yorkshire, Edward and Julia had not yet met. Edward had called on Giffard Boville and introduced Colonel Harrison to him; but it was on a day when Julia had gone with a friend to visit the shops of the industrial town farther down the valley. Mrs Moore had called for her in the trap she drove herself, and they had set out for the day. Giffard, conscious as Edward had been of the proximity – or relative proximity – of New Zealand to the Melanesian islands, welcomed Colonel Harrison, and listened as avidly to him as Edward had done. He had returned the visit, and entered into the discussions, and given Colonel Harrison his advice, still without Julia's presence. They were bound to meet, even though it had not taken place at once. At any moment Julia was half-expecting to come across Edward, in Kirkby, on the moors, or ensconced in her drawing-room; and she was looking forward half fearfully to doing so.

He, on the other hand, never thought of her at all. The friendship with Colonel Harrison had grown, and they liked each other a good deal; enough for the colonel to suggest that if Edward wished to give up the pursuit of farming in these bleak northern parts, and come to New Zealand with him, he would put him in the way of buying a very promising tract of country, and introduce him to the rest of the English community. It was tempting. Sir Charles's eye looked bright, and he looked in contrast almost disappointed when Edward laughed and said that it was out of the question.

'Don't think about me, Edward!' said the old man. 'I'm

past the age when I could have come with you; but if you want to go, don't let me hold you back.' He felt that it would be a vicarious adventure, and that in Edward he would take part in it. Edward smiled and said nothing. Once more, on seeing his home moors and valleys, he was feeling his loss of Rebecca acutely. His love of them seemed to intensify his love of her.

The district had been preparing for the annual sheep washing. The lambs were now growing large and independent, their mothers were becoming impatient with them, and fretted, in the increasingly hot weather, by their thick woolly coats. Clean wool fetched more than dirty wool, so before shearing they were to be washed. The shepherds and their dogs gathered the flocks down from the high moorland where they led a wild free life, finding their food among the heather, and brought them together into large protesting masses, all converging on the upland stream which had for generations been used for the same purpose. It could not have been more beautiful. Locked away from the world by rocky, near impassable moorland, the stream hurtled down into a natural amphitheatre, where it spread out into deep pools before going more lingeringly on its way, down past a solitary high scribbling mill and down to join a greater river, a couple of miles or so farther on. The main mass of the sheep were held back, and in a thin trickle, they were brought down to the pool, where every year, with shouts and commotion, they had to go into the water.

Julia had been taking a good many lonely rides on the moor; and she could see no reason why on the sheep washing day she should not ride to the sheep washing pool and watch the fun. She could not be accused, even by her own conscience, of throwing herself in the way of Edward, because she had seen the sheep washing every year in her childhood. Even in recent years it had been the occasion of many outings and picnics, in company with many of the neighbours, not only the Gilbanks. The Moores of Huntingtower, cousins of her friend Mrs

Moore, of the independent mind and the horse and trap, and the Hutchinsons of Bradshaw, were only two of the families who had been in the habit of making sheep washing the excuse for a jaunt. The children had loved it, watching the protesting sheep plunging into the water, pushed under by long sticks, chivvied by the sheepdogs, only to scramble out a bit lower down, streaming with water, looking half their previous size, miserably staggering up the bank and standing looking woebegone in groups about the field, complaining to each other of their treatment.

When she rode up on to the bend of the rough track which gave her the first glimpse down into the valley, Julia was taken back in time to the years when it had been an eagerly anticipated treat of her childhood. Several of the neighbouring families had come over; two or three horses and traps or wagonettes stood on the margins of the track, and children were running to and fro over the heather, the girls catching their skirts on bushes of it and showing pantaloons and petticoats as they untangled themselves. Julia rode slowly down towards the washing pool, recognizing first one and then another of her neighbours. Her father was there himself, talking to Colonel Harrison. Sir Charles was leaning on a rock next to Hutchinson of Bradshaw, and Moore of Huntingtower was talking to her friend Mrs Moore. The shepherd who, on Rebecca's first arrival in Kirkby, had told her where Giffard Boville's house was, was there with his two dogs, Dawn and Peggy; and there were many other faces Julia had known all her life.

Edward, looking up from the sparkling water and bobbing grey woolly backs, saw Julia sitting quietly on her horse, gazing round her at the scene. Her cheeks were pinker than usual in the crisp summer air of the moor, and she sat alert and energetic. Her shining deep black hair was drawn back simply into a knot at the back of her head, and her face, short rather than long, with its rounded, babyish forehead, little straight nose, large eyes and small endearing chin, was immensely attractive. He straightened his back, and went over towards her, reaching her just a yard or so behind Moore of Huntingtower, who was already holding up his arms to help her alight. Julia glanced quickly at Edward's face, then dropped her eyes again. She found she was trembling, and did not know where to look.

'Let me take charge of your horse, Miss Boville,' said Moore, somehow managing to get the reins in his left hand and Julia's arm tucked under his right elbow. 'Come down and see what's going on. My cousin Betsy is here.'

'We met only last week,' replied Julia, all womanly dependence on the strength of his arm and the efficacy of his help, and acknowledging only with the briefest of smiles Edward's greeting. Edward took a position on her other side, and the three of them, with the horse, walked down to meet and talk with the other people standing about.

There was a sense of openness and freedom, on the height of the moor. The wind was enough to move the exhilarating air, in its vast vault of heaven, so pale as to be white rather than blue, with the cries of the sheep, and the short, sharp pantings of the silent-footed dogs isolated by spaces of singing air from the cry of the curlews above the heather.

'Every year,' remarked Moore, who was usually rather a silent man, 'every year for most of our lives, I suppose, we three have met here at sheep washing time.'

Julia agreed, with some surprise. She could not help being glad that she had insisted on coming home. The scene before her moved her, and no doubt it was as Frederick Moore had said: years before, the three of them had been among the children running about freely, long before Frederick had become known as 'of Huntingtower' – it had been his father in those days who had been Moore of Huntingtower. There was more than their youth binding the three of them into fellowship: shared life; shared ancestry, for all the old hill families were distantly related one to another – how could it be otherwise in an isolated mountain region which had been for centuries considered inaccessible? Going along with a hand on the arm of both men, she was profoundly stirred by the love of her region and everything concerning it, and was more a Boville than she had ever been. Edward looked down at her. If he had not been attracted to the Boville girls, he would never have thought of marriage with one of them; and for an instant he was about to cover Julia's hand, resting so confidingly on his arm, with his own. Then he drew back sharply, so that Julia thought he had stumbled on a stone; and exclaimed to himself, 'No! Not while she lives!'

'What? What did you say, Mr Gilbank?' asked Julia, looking up into his face. He gave her a ghastly kind of grin, and said with an effort, 'I said that you must meet Colonel Harrison; he is staying with us. He is planning to settle in New Zealand, and I am going back with him.'

It had not been decided; he had not really been thinking seriously of it; but now he knew that he was going to go, and cursed himself for a fool. What would it benefit him, even if he did see Rebecca? Would the sight of her married happiness and her useful life make his misery more bearable? 'I am going back with him,' he repeated, and did not notice the colour had paled in Julia's cheeks. If Rebecca had been by his side, he would have known the least flutter of an eyelash, the least stir of her hair.

'Did you say Betsy was coming over next week?' Julia had turned her face to Frederick Moore. 'I will come with her, if you wish me to.'

'Yes!' he answered eagerly. 'It is years since you were at Huntingtower.'

'Some four years, it must be,' she answered. 'But when I was out riding the day before yesterday, I paused at the head of your valley, and looked over; I was in two minds about coming down.'

'Why didn't you?' The young man pressed her hand with his.

Ahead of them, Edward could see Giffard Boville and Sir Charles together, leaning on a great grey outcrop of rock and looking towards them with a gleam of hope in their faces. Not wishing to have to counter that hope, he dropped Julia's hand from his arm, and walked over to the edge of the stream, calling out, 'Come over here, Miss Boville, and you, Moore; stop bothering about other things; you have come to watch sheep being washed, and they are going on without you.' The clear brown water swirled round the stone on which he stood balanced at the edge of the pool, and a dog, climbing out after an excited run into the water, shook itself all over him.

The Maoris felt that their dear mother the Queen Victoria could not know how some of her white subjects were behaving in the country Her Majesty called New Zealand. There were some of her white subjects who would steal and kill, and take tribal lands; they thought on the whole it would be better if they – her Maori children – had a king of their own – under her supreme sovereignty of course – and were not governed by the white people who obviously did not know how to do it properly. They would be guided by the Good Book she had sent them, and render her their homage as ever . . .

'The damned savages are rebelling,' said Colonel Harrison. 'But you needn't let it worry you, Gilbank; they'll soon be put down. Nothing to it. What do you think of that valley we looked at yesterday? Eh?'

'Very nice,' said Edward abstractedly. He did not take to New Zealand; he had not realized until going there how much of a home-bird he was. A year and a half away in Europe had, it seemed, been enough for him, and he had felt uneasy all the many weeks on the boat, and the month he had been staying with Colonel Harrison. It was all just too different to home, and the sheep washing day, with the gathering of old neighbours, recurred to him at times in bright colours. If only Rebecca and he . . . One night on the boat, he had let slip something which told Colonel Harrison enough for him to guess that Edward had not come only to see if he could make a life for himself in a

247

new country. Edward had quickly covered up his mistake, but there was unspoken between them the knowledge that Edward had a reason for his journey which was undivulged. He knew what the colonel would have said, if he had known everything. 'Hankering after a married woman', he would have called it. All the same, Edward made enquiries. He learned about the annual journey of the bishop to the islands, and that he was away now, and would be returning shortly; then Edward thought, he might at least hear the latest news of the Lloyds. He did not want to meet them, he had suddenly decided. No, he couldn't meet them. It was unlikely from what he had heard that they could come back with the bishop. He could ask after them – for the latest news; he would go to the bishop himself, if he discovered that the Lloyds were still on the island of Mutu. Telling Colonel Harrison enough to make it seem natural that he would want to ask after these friends of his before leaving to go home, he asked to be told when the bishop returned, and in due course a Maori appeared to say that he had. Colonel Harrison was becoming preoccupied with the king movement among the Maori tribes, and set off to see if he could be of any help to the government, at the same time as Edward left for the coast.

Edward had been sitting in the shade of a clump of trees for some time, watching the activities in the bay. The mission ship had arrived the day before, and so far he had contacted no one from it. He could see it lying at anchor, and also watch the clipper, which had for a week been gathering up cargo and passengers for its return journey to England. There was enough bustle to interest the eye. Edward had half a mind to go to the captain of the clipper, book his passage and return to England without seeing Rebecca at all. The entire hopelessness of his quest had almost overcome him. He had begun to wonder what inner conviction it was which had so buoyed him up, what will-o'-the-wisp had led him on, for the last two years. He might as well have given up first as last. At a time when he had justification for optimism – when he might, by inquiry, have at least had recent news of Rebecca, and, if she and Simon Lloyd had come back with the bishop, even seen and spoken to her – he was caught in a despairing mood which kept him seated under the shade of the trees, watching the harbour, and taking no part in the scene.

As he sat and watched, a woman with a child walked along the beach, and approached the captain of the clipper. He saw her idly, and without much attention. She was draped in black; thin black skirts fluttered behind her, and a thin shawl of black was draped over her head and fell on to her shoulders. The tiny child at her side was also in black, and what caught his eye in the end was the mass of golden curls the child had, gleaming in contrast to its black garments, as it clung to the hand of its mother. Edward liked children, as he liked colts and puppies and all young things, and his eyes dwelt on the plump little figure so topped with golden curls. He thought of the long sea voyage, and the sad heart he would have on it, and how much easier it would be with a little child on board. He imagined himself holding it firmly, as it reached out its tiny hands with joy to the leaping waves; telling it a story, when the long day drew to a close; playing games with it, to while away the time. The long seaboard weeks would be enlivened if he made them on the same clipper as this widow with her child; if she was seasick, he would be useful. He decided that it was only the dread of the voyage and its lack of occupation which had kept him so long in New Zealand, once he had known it could never be his home.

Getting up from the ground, Edward walked down towards the water's edge. There were plenty of people about, sailors, white settlers from the nearby village and Maoris, some busy, some loitering. He went nearer to the place where the woman in black was talking to the captain, her child looking for shells in the sand near her feet. He could see now that the child was a small girl, between one and two years old. The mother had her back to him, and as he came nearer, and she put up her hand to adjust her shawl, he looked at her with more attention. She had a tall, graceful figure, but was very thin; her arm and hand were almost emaciated. Edward found his eyes fixed on the pale flesh, the arm poised so unselfconsciously against the black stuff of her clothing; the thought that he had been denying as he grew closer – that this might be Rebecca – now became a positive identification, although he had never seen her so wasted. She turned, and he caught sight of a projecting cheek bone; he moved forward and spoke, and she looked fully at him.

'Mrs Lloyd,' he said.

She looked at him half fearfully and, in that first second, almost unrecognizing. He was the last person she had expected to see under that tropical sun. The Edward of her dreams, and this man speaking to her on the beach, did not at first seem to be connected. Then she spoke.

'Edward . . .' Her eyes had not changed, and he stood transfixed, bathed in that rich blue gaze, no longer sensible of standing on earth but only knowing that this was Rebecca, and that she was Rebecca still. With an effort, she went on, 'Mr Gilbank, I should say . . . what are you doing here?' And then: 'Where is Julia?'

'Come,' he said, 'we must talk.' He reached out his hand to her and, like an automaton, she gave him hers, and allowed herself to be led along the beach away from the scatter of people, with baby Margaret, crowing with delight, toddling after her.

Her first thought, in the maze of emotion which was incoherent, was that his hair had become so grey as to be almost white, and that his face was thinner. In all the surging emotion which she felt, it was this surface thing which occupied her, which her mind seized on as a point to cling to. While he, if he could be said to be thinking, might be going through the shock of realization of her thinness and of the signs of recent illness.

They were walking together, along the beach, where the

250

sea, with all its murmuring warmth, lay on their right hand, and the bush, with its violet shadows and brilliant emerald green foliage, lay on their left. Ahead the curve of the bay was progressively more empty as they left behind the ships and the little settlement. They walked slowly, still hand in hand, and the little child kept up easily, stopping now and then to search for a pebble or pick up a shell, then running after them and catching hold of Rebecca's skirts.

'You are a widow, then?' He hardly needed to ask.

'Yes, six months since.' It was as if the memory of the reason for her flight from him, so long before, would not let her rest, for then she asked again, 'Where is Julia?'

'The last time I saw Miss Boville,' he answered, 'she was hanging on the arm of Frederick Moore of Huntingtower, and arranging to visit Huntingtower with Betsy Moore during the following week.'

'Oh,' she said, and did not pour out aloud the urgently following words, though they trembled on her lips to be spoken. 'You did not marry her then?' she almost said.

The point was somehow silently settled between them, that they were both free of obligations to other people, and further explanation seemed unnecessary. She could not have said quite how it was so clearly settled, except that Edward's eyes had met hers, and they both knew that division between them was over. They strayed to some rocks in the shade at the edge of the beach, and sat down.

'I came over thinking of settling in New Zealand,' he said tentatively. There had been a long silence between them, as they sat there with their hands clasped, alternately glancing at each other, then at little Margaret, then ahead at the sea, then back again at one another. 'But I don't like the fighting that's taking place; it looks to me like growing into a war.'

'How can they!' she cried passionately. 'We've tried so hard to bring them out of their heathen darkness; how can the others – the soldiers and the traders – do this to them? Teach them our different ways of savagery? I've been hearing of the trouble. On Sundays, while the Maoris, as the missionaries have taught them, stop the fighting and spend the day in prayer, our soldiers have gone on attacking! The poor natives cannot understand how they can so go against our teaching. How can we explain it to them? Sometimes I think we have brought them nothing but trouble.' She trembled, and he realized how wrought-up she was.

'It must have been difficult for you, after your husband died,' he said gently, trying to take her mind away from the Maori fighting to her own concerns.

'Yes.' Then, after a pause, 'It wasn't really; except that it is difficult for the natives to accept a white woman among them, particularly on her own. Women to them are such an inferior race. It was easier when Simon was there in many ways. They were kind, but uneasy. They gave me all their sympathy and support, but in their hierarchy there was no place for me. I could not take Simon's place as a priest, and if I spent my time with the women, as I had done before, I was associating myself with the lowly ones, yet my skin being white I was obviously one of the demi-gods.' She smiled at him. 'It was difficult. But as soon as the bishop arrived in his ship, and they knew I was going away, it was quite different. The young chief from the island of Ota walked to our village through the bush to bring me a farewell present of a white parrot; he appeared at the edge of our clearing with it on his arm, young and earnest and sorry that I was going; and when we at last went on board, the whole of the population, I do believe, was on the beach, most of them waist deep in the edge of the sea, as though they could not bear to let us go. I was loaded with presents. We stayed at anchor all night, and in the moonlight I could see them all sleeping on the warm sand, and hear them singing. The bishop asked me if I would like to go back on shore, for that last night, but I did not think I could go through all those farewells again; it was bad enough hearing their voices across the waves, in the long dreamlike island songs.'

'And in the morning?' asked Edward.

'In the morning they were still there; but we drew away from the coral reef, away from the island. For a while we went alongside it, and could watch the shining shores and their fringes of waving palms, and the places where the mountains sweep down to the sea without a beach – deep, deep green, so bright under the sun! Then we turned and left it, and gradually it fell away to the stern, and the bright green became grey, until the whole island was only a grey cloud on the horizon, and our world was one of satin blue water and cloudless sky, with, it seemed, nothing in the world but ourselves.'

'Did you have a good voyage here?' asked Edward. He was content to sit and listen to her, and hold her hands, and look into her eyes. He wanted to kiss her, but the time for that would come; the time for everything would come, now that they were together, and at last there was no misunderstanding between them: no Julia, no Simon. He reached his hand down to little Margaret, and drew her within their magic circle, and for a minute Rebecca's eyes lingered on her child, and she smiled lovingly at her, and stroked her hair.

'What a pretty shell, little one,' she said, and her voice had the soft caress of the island mothers. The child laughed and patted her mother's face with a fat little hand, then broke away impatiently from the restraint of their arms, and sat playing on the ground in front of them. They watched her for a while, then Edward, tightening his hold on Rebecca's hand, and gently stroking her fingers, asked again, 'How was your voyage here?'

'It was a strange one . . . I had been so long on the island, even the few white men on the boat seemed as foreign to me as they must always do to the natives, and the way they organized their day, their whole way of thinking – I was surprised how much I had grown away from them, how much I had become an islander. The littlest things struck me as extraordinary, which once had been quite familiar. It is really since Simon died that I have become so much part of the islands; before that he was always militating against it, and reminding me of our own ways. Alone, quite alone, and mourning . . . it was easy to dream of England, but not so easy to keep up English ways. The ways of the natives are those that are right for the country. Why eat from a plate when there is a leaf, or a sea shell, or the polished shell of a coconut?'

Every now and then in her talk Rebecca paused to glance at Edward, then to look down at their clasped hands, or over to her child; and her voice was gentle, dreamy, as though the islands themselves had grown into it. Edward stroked her fingers still, and once put up his hand and caressed her hair.

'The voyage, you asked me about? We had left the islands behind, and I was beginning to notice all those little things which, as I said, I had forgotten. We went on for days, in perfect weather; there was no cloud, only haze. How sick I had been on the voyage out! But coming back there was no such problem. The sea looked so calm. Yet it seethes with life. It is easy to forget that, on board, when you can only see the surface of it. But we were trailing a fishing line behind us.'

'Did you catch much?'

'We caught a lot of small fish, six inches to a foot long. Then one day we caught something big. The sea behind was turbulent with struggle. The men swarmed down into our dinghy and tried to haul in the creature, by the fishing line. It seems incredible that below that satin surface there should be such vigorous life! They heaved it into the boat, and it lay there, flapping helplessly. It was vivid yellow, grey fins with blue spots, and a hammer head, and about four feet long. They pulled it up on to the deck, and it thrashed about, trying to get back into the water. How it longed to get back into the water! But it was killed, by one of the crew, and the blood washed from the deck.' She turned her head away, and Edward was silent in sympathy, seeing with her that captive life sadly ended. 'And then it was cooked, and we ate it,' said Rebecca tonelessly.

'And the bones were thrown back to the sea, and we washed our hands, and the sea was as blue, the sun as hot, as though the fish had never been. It was wild, strange and beautiful.'

'And life goes on,' finished Edward for her.

'So it does.'

Edward put his arm round her shoulders, and drew her closer to him. Gradually the strangeness of being together was disappearing. He was used to her thinness, and the threads of grey in her hair, but knew that he would never be used to Rebecca herself, and to the fact that she belonged to him, and he to her. To look at her would always be a new blessing, however long it might be they would have together.

'What were you talking to the captain about?' he asked.

'I was arranging a passage to England.'

'That's strange.'

'Why?'

'Just that the first time I saw you, you were arranging for a journey. Do you remember the day we met – on the train going from Lincolnshire to Kirkby?'

'How could I do anything but remember?'

'Did you know that I had been standing and watching you? Father was in front of you at the ticket office; he loved all those little arrangements. I stood back and waited for him, and you were behind him; I believe I loved you from that moment. You were calm, yet hesitant; frightened, yet brave. And beautiful,' he added as an afterthought.

'I was thin, and in mourning; as I am now,' she said. 'Oh, Edward, did you really love me?' She turned her face up towards him, and he kissed her gently on her temple.

'Always. From that first moment, and always afterwards. How could you expect me to marry Julia, once I had seen you?'

She was silent.

'And now you think nothing of arranging to travel across the world.'

255

'You were so kind,' she said reminiscing. 'On that journey, you were so kind, although I had taken your seat. You helped me off the train when we reached Kirkby.'

He tightened his arm round her in reply.

'Did you say you had come out here to settle? It is so strange, meeting you here!'

'What do you want to do, Rebecca? Would you like me to buy some land here, and make a life for us? If we go home, you might have prejudice to face; Mrs Boville will not be pleased.'

The child had strayed a little away from them and tumbled; thinking she would cry, Rebecca rose, ready to go to her. Edward got up too, and they stood side by side. Little Margaret was not hurt, and did not cry; she turned herself right way up again, unconcernedly, and Rebecca's mind returned to what Edward had said. She half turned towards him, and then they were in each other's arms, and he was kissing her hair, her cheeks, her overflowing eyes.

'Oh, Edward,' she said, 'Take me home . . .'